HOW TO TRAIN YOUR
DRAGON

DRAGONVINE

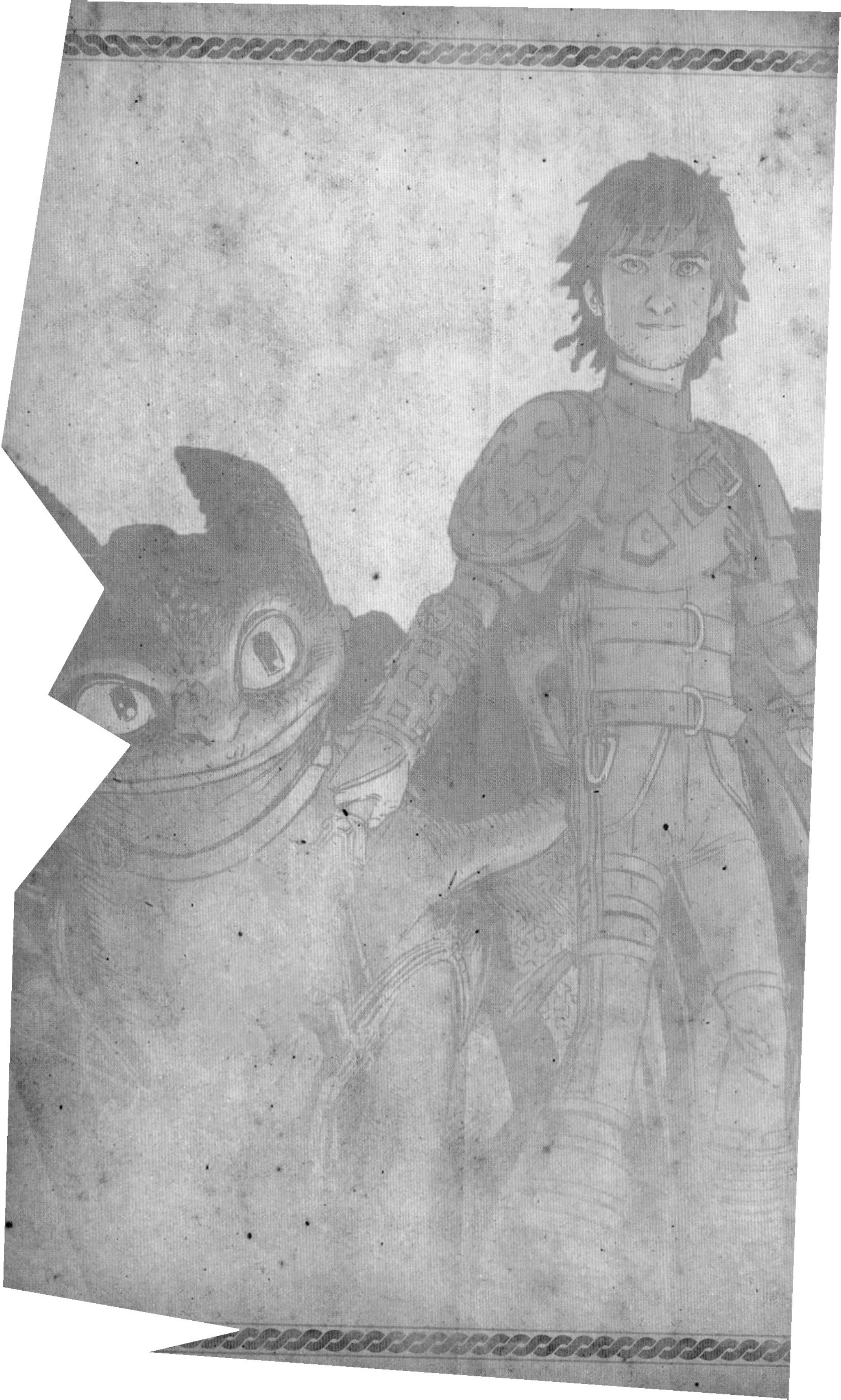

DREAMWORKS

HOW TO TRAIN YOUR
DRAGON

DRAGONVINE

SCRIPT BY
DEAN DEBLOIS &
RICHARD HAMILTON

BASED ON THE BOOK SERIES BY
CRESSIDA COWELL

ART, PAGES 7–16 BY
DOUG WHEATLEY

ART, PAGES 17–86 BY
FRANCISCO DE LA FUENTE

COLORING BY
WES DZIOBA

LETTERING BY
NATE PIEKOS OF BLAMBOT®
AND **MICHAEL HEISLER**

COVER ART BY
LUCAS MARANGON

DARK HORSE BOOKS

PRESIDENT AND PUBLISHER
Mike Richardson

EDITOR
Randy Stradley

ASSISTANT EDITOR
Kevin Burkhalter

COLLECTION DESIGNER
David Nestelle

DIGITAL ART TECHNICIAN
Christina McKenzie

Special thanks to Bonnie Arnold, Elizabeth C. Camp, Corinne Combs, Lawrence "Shifty" Hamashima, Kate Spencer Lachance, Barbara Layman, Megan Startz, Mike Sund, John Tanzer, Joe Vance, and Pierre-Olivier Vincent (POV) at DreamWorks Animation.

How To Train Your Dragon: Dragonvine

Published by Dark Horse Books
A division of Dark Horse Comics LLC
10956 SE Main Street
Milwaukie, OR 97222

DarkHorse.com

To find a comics shop in your area,
visit comicshoplocator.com

First edition: August 2018
ISBN 978-1-61655-953-3

3 5 7 9 10 8 6 4
Printed in China

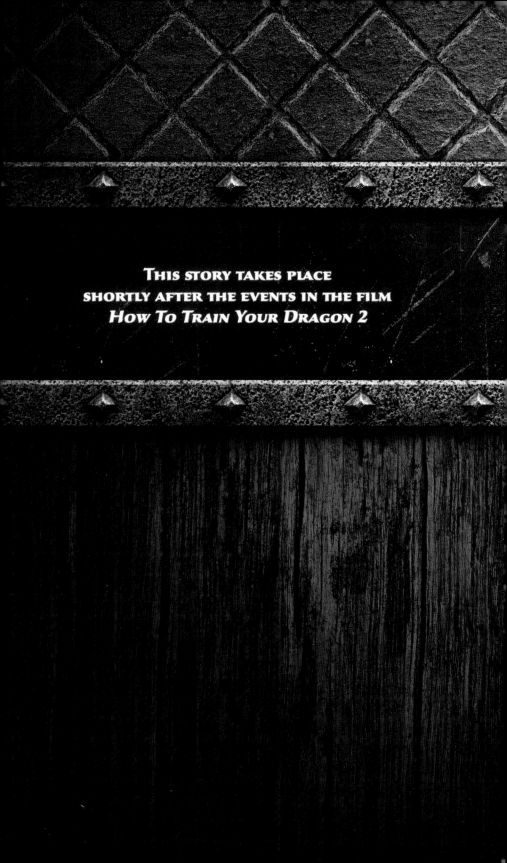

THIS STORY TAKES PLACE
SHORTLY AFTER THE EVENTS IN THE FILM
HOW TO TRAIN YOUR DRAGON 2

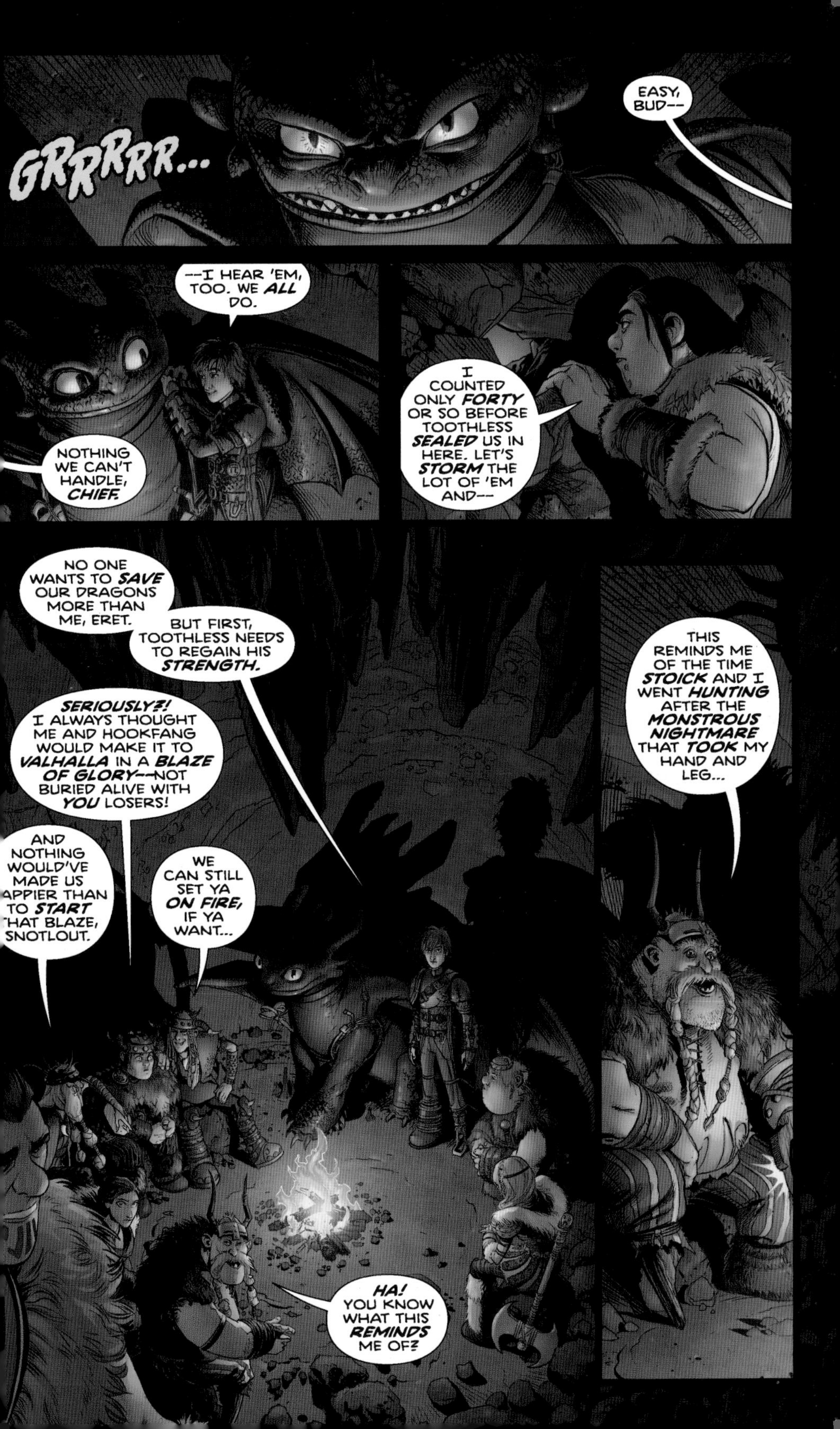
GRRRRR...
EASY, BUD--
--I HEAR 'EM, TOO. WE ALL DO.
NOTHING WE CAN'T HANDLE, CHIEF.
I COUNTED ONLY FORTY OR SO BEFORE TOOTHLESS SEALED US IN HERE. LET'S STORM THE LOT OF 'EM AND--
NO ONE WANTS TO SAVE OUR DRAGONS MORE THAN ME, ERET.
BUT FIRST, TOOTHLESS NEEDS TO REGAIN HIS STRENGTH.
SERIOUSLY?! I ALWAYS THOUGHT ME AND HOOKFANG WOULD MAKE IT TO VALHALLA IN A BLAZE OF GLORY--NOT BURIED ALIVE WITH YOU LOSERS!
AND NOTHING WOULD'VE MADE US APPIER THAN TO START THAT BLAZE, SNOTLOUT.
WE CAN STILL SET YA ON FIRE, IF YA WANT...
HA! YOU KNOW WHAT THIS REMINDS ME OF?
THIS REMINDS ME OF THE TIME STOICK AND I WENT HUNTING AFTER THE MONSTROUS NIGHTMARE THAT TOOK MY HAND AND LEG...

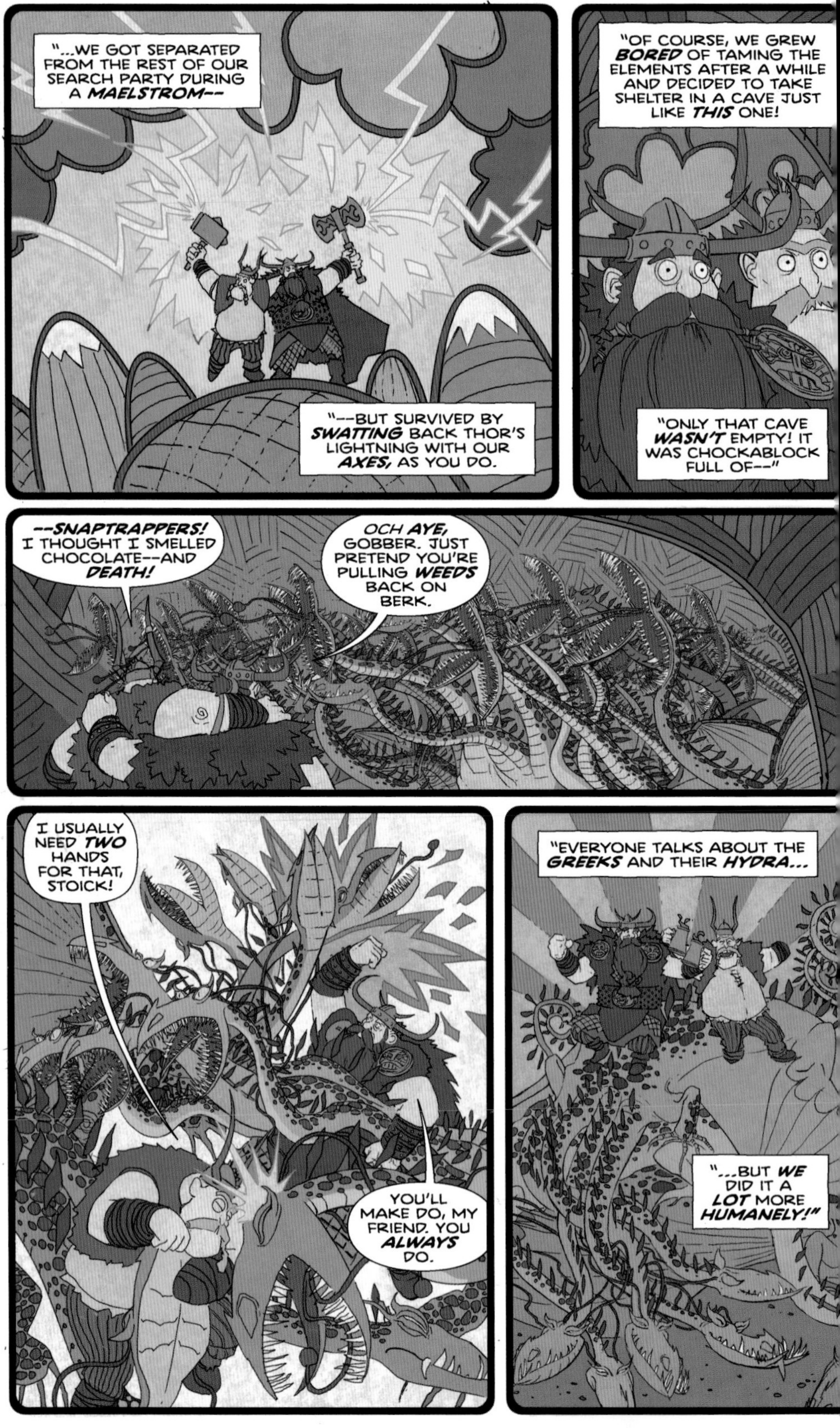
"...WE GOT SEPARATED FROM THE REST OF OUR SEARCH PARTY DURING A *MAELSTROM*--
"--BUT SURVIVED BY *SWATTING* BACK THOR'S LIGHTNING WITH OUR *AXES,* AS YOU DO.
"OF COURSE, WE GREW *BORED* OF TAMING THE ELEMENTS AFTER A WHILE AND DECIDED TO TAKE SHELTER IN A CAVE JUST LIKE *THIS* ONE!
"ONLY THAT CAVE *WASN'T* EMPTY! IT WAS CHOCKABLOCK FULL OF--"
--*SNAPTRAPPERS!* I THOUGHT I SMELLED CHOCOLATE--AND *DEATH!*
OCH AYE, GOBBER. JUST PRETEND YOU'RE PULLING *WEEDS* BACK ON BERK.
I USUALLY NEED *TWO* HANDS FOR THAT, STOICK!
YOU'LL MAKE DO, MY FRIEND. YOU *ALWAYS* DO.
"EVERYONE TALKS ABOUT THE *GREEKS* AND THEIR *HYDRA...*
"...BUT *WE* DID IT A *LOT* MORE *HUMANELY!*"

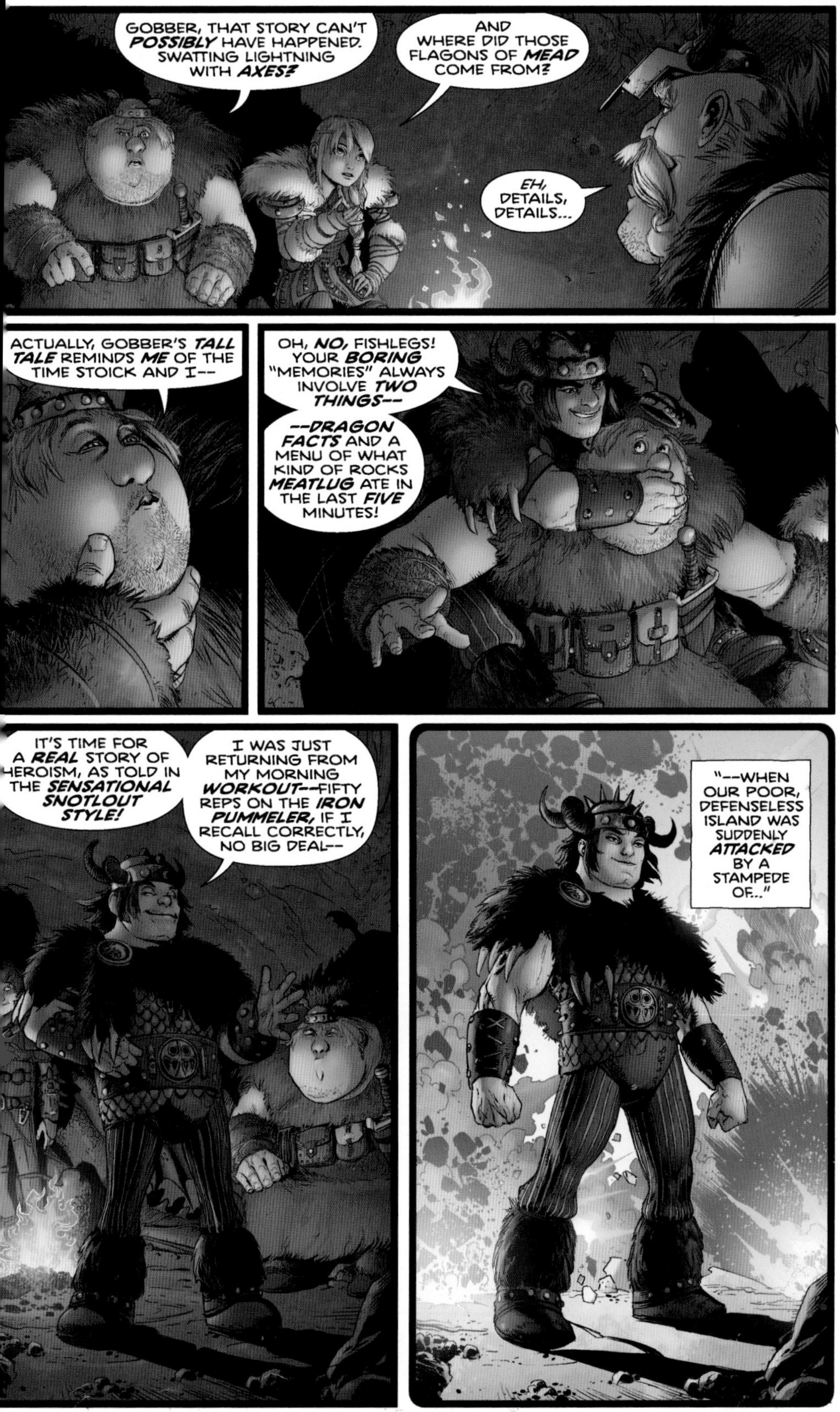
GOBBER, THAT STORY CAN'T POSSIBLY HAVE HAPPENED. SWATTING LIGHTNING WITH AXES?
AND WHERE DID THOSE FLAGONS OF MEAD COME FROM?
EH, DETAILS, DETAILS...
ACTUALLY, GOBBER'S TALL TALE REMINDS ME OF THE TIME STOICK AND I--
OH, NO, FISHLEGS! YOUR BORING "MEMORIES" ALWAYS INVOLVE TWO THINGS--
--DRAGON FACTS AND A MENU OF WHAT KIND OF ROCKS MEATLUG ATE IN THE LAST FIVE MINUTES!
IT'S TIME FOR A REAL STORY OF HEROISM, AS TOLD IN THE SENSATIONAL SNOTLOUT STYLE!
I WAS JUST RETURNING FROM MY MORNING WORKOUT--FIFTY REPS ON THE IRON PUMMELER, IF I RECALL CORRECTLY, NO BIG DEAL--
"--WHEN OUR POOR, DEFENSELESS ISLAND WAS SUDDENLY ATTACKED BY A STAMPEDE OF..."

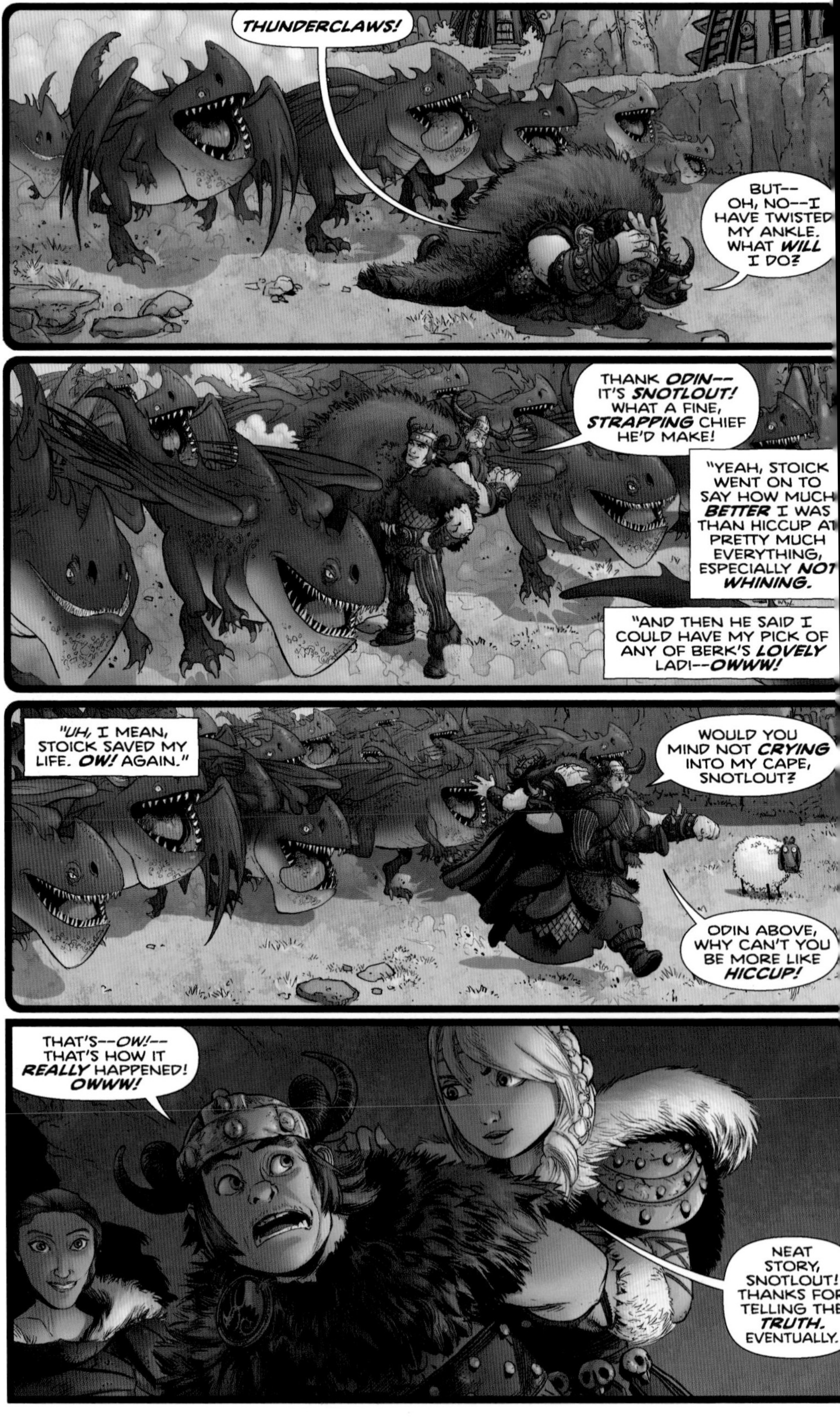
THUNDERCLAWS!
BUT-- OH, NO--I HAVE TWISTED MY ANKLE. WHAT *WILL* I DO?
THANK *ODIN--* IT'S *SNOTLOUT!* WHAT A FINE, *STRAPPING* CHIEF HE'D MAKE!
"YEAH, STOICK WENT ON TO SAY HOW MUCH *BETTER* I WAS THAN HICCUP AT PRETTY MUCH EVERYTHING, ESPECIALLY *NOT WHINING.*
"AND THEN HE SAID I COULD HAVE MY PICK OF ANY OF BERK'S *LOVELY* LADI--*OWWW!*
"*UH,* I MEAN, STOICK SAVED MY LIFE. *OW!* AGAIN."
WOULD YOU MIND NOT *CRYING* INTO MY CAPE, SNOTLOUT?
ODIN ABOVE, WHY CAN'T YOU BE MORE LIKE *HICCUP!*
THAT'S--*OW!*-- THAT'S HOW IT *REALLY* HAPPENED! *OWWW!*
NEAT STORY, SNOTLOUT! THANKS FOR TELLING THE *TRUTH.* EVENTUALLY.

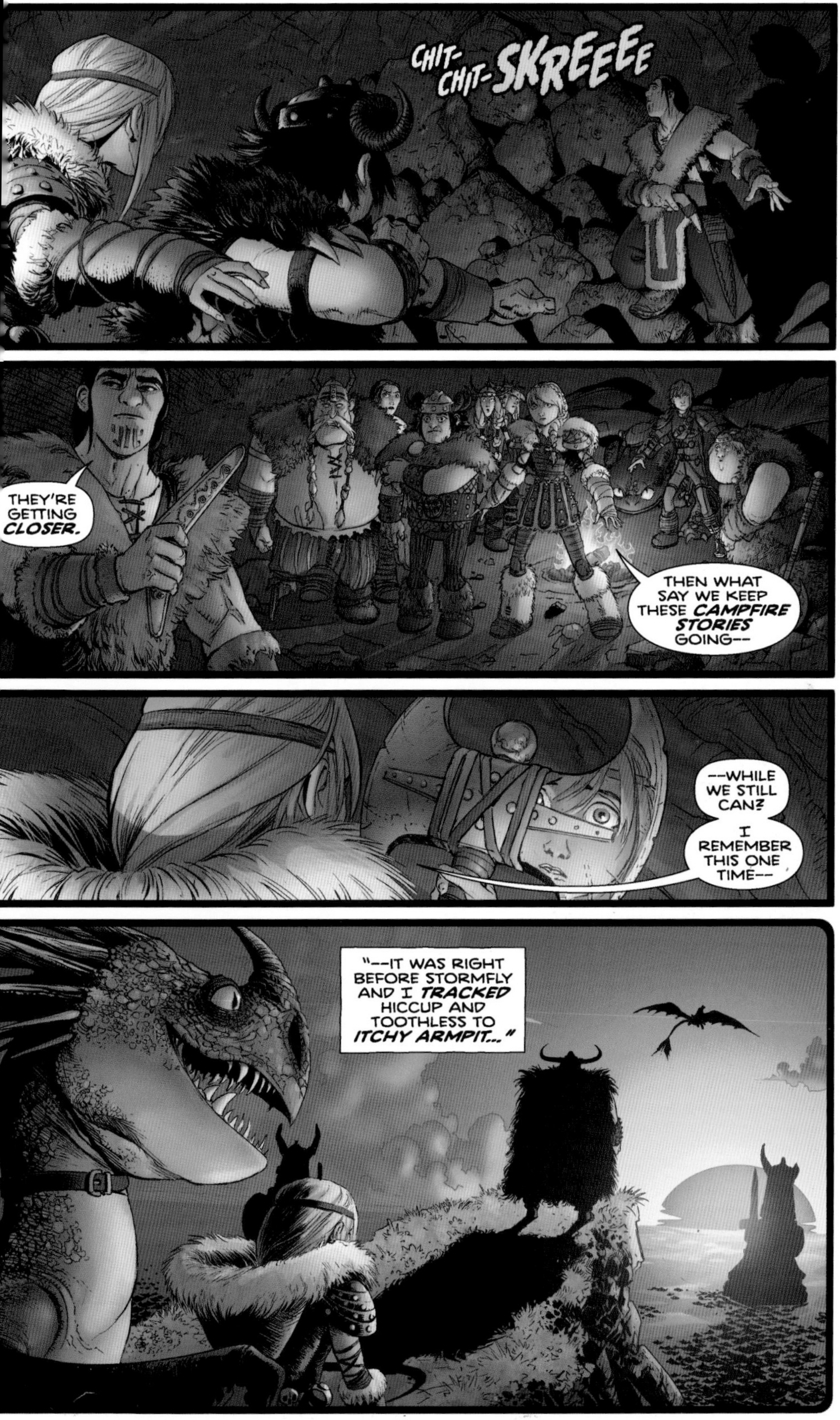
CHIT-CHIT-SKREEEE
THEY'RE GETTING CLOSER.
THEN WHAT SAY WE KEEP THESE CAMPFIRE STORIES GOING--
--WHILE WE STILL CAN?
I REMEMBER THIS ONE TIME--
"--IT WAS RIGHT BEFORE STORMFLY AND I TRACKED HICCUP AND TOOTHLESS TO ITCHY ARMPIT..."

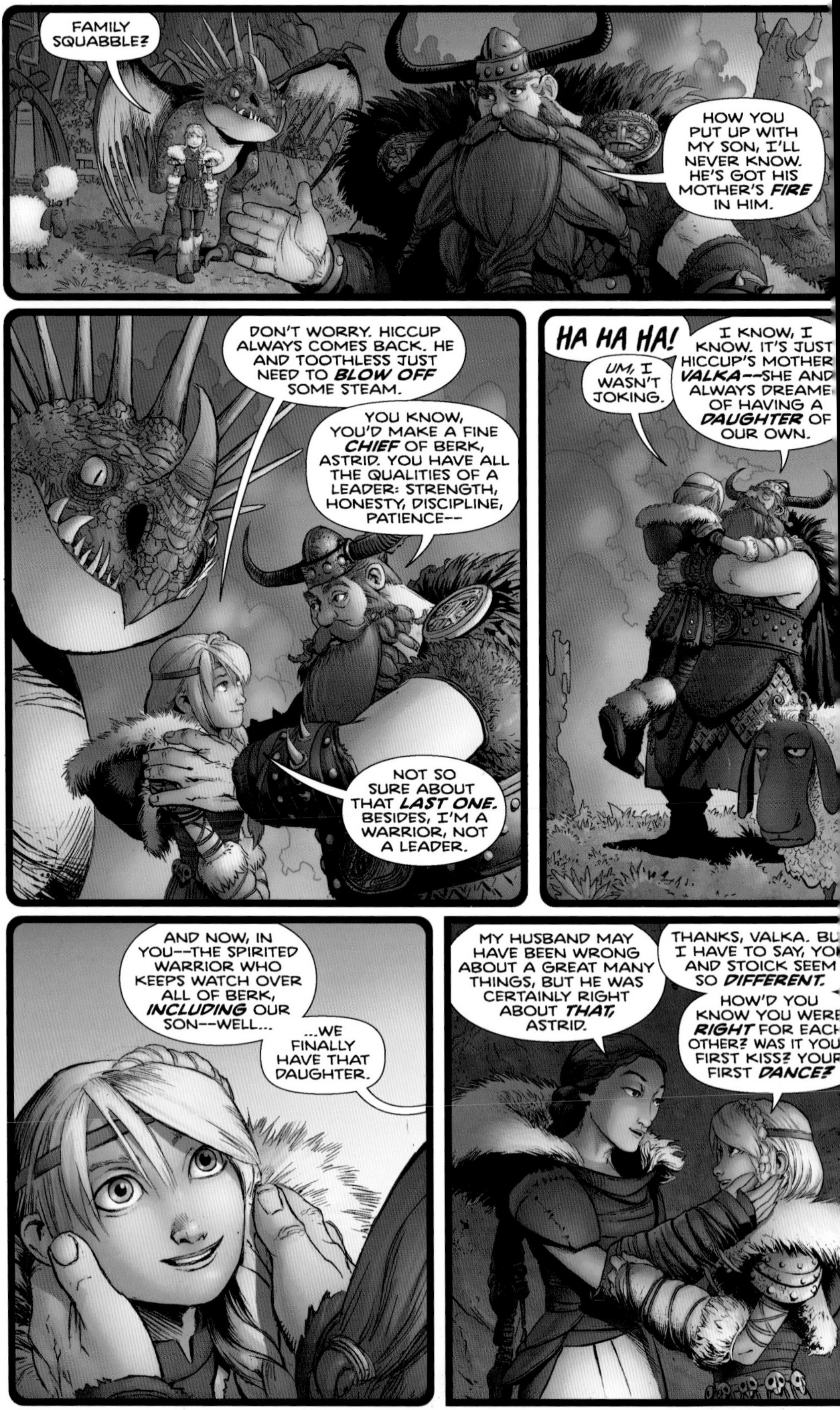
FAMILY SQUABBLE?
HOW YOU PUT UP WITH MY SON, I'LL NEVER KNOW. HE'S GOT HIS MOTHER'S *FIRE* IN HIM.
DON'T WORRY. HICCUP ALWAYS COMES BACK. HE AND TOOTHLESS JUST NEED TO *BLOW OFF* SOME STEAM.
YOU KNOW, YOU'D MAKE A FINE *CHIEF* OF BERK, ASTRID. YOU HAVE ALL THE QUALITIES OF A LEADER: STRENGTH, HONESTY, DISCIPLINE, PATIENCE--
NOT SO SURE ABOUT THAT *LAST ONE.* BESIDES, I'M A WARRIOR, NOT A LEADER.
HA HA HA!
UM, I WASN'T JOKING.
I KNOW, I KNOW. IT'S JUST HICCUP'S MOTHER *VALKA*--SHE AND ALWAYS DREAME OF HAVING A *DAUGHTER* OF OUR OWN.
AND NOW, IN YOU--THE SPIRITED WARRIOR WHO KEEPS WATCH OVER ALL OF BERK, *INCLUDING* OUR SON--WELL...
...WE FINALLY HAVE THAT DAUGHTER.
MY HUSBAND MAY HAVE BEEN WRONG ABOUT A GREAT MANY THINGS, BUT HE WAS CERTAINLY RIGHT ABOUT *THAT,* ASTRID.
THANKS, VALKA. BU I HAVE TO SAY, YO AND STOICK SEEM SO *DIFFERENT.*
HOW'D YOU KNOW YOU WERE *RIGHT* FOR EACH OTHER? WAS IT YOU FIRST KISS? YOUR FIRST *DANCE?*

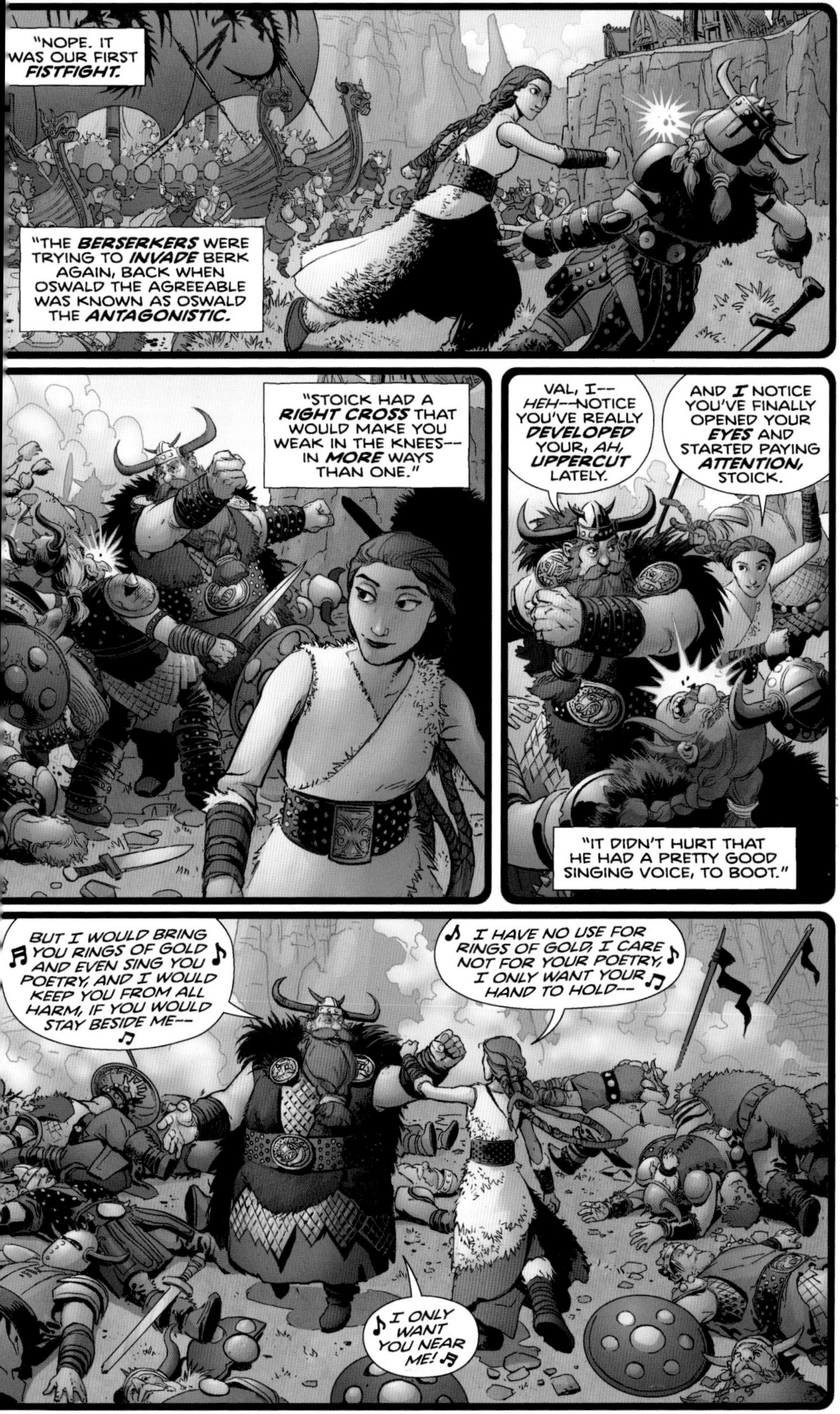
"NOPE. IT WAS OUR FIRST FISTFIGHT.
"THE BERSERKERS WERE TRYING TO INVADE BERK AGAIN, BACK WHEN OSWALD THE AGREEABLE WAS KNOWN AS OSWALD THE ANTAGONISTIC.
"STOICK HAD A RIGHT CROSS THAT WOULD MAKE YOU WEAK IN THE KNEES-- IN MORE WAYS THAN ONE."
VAL, I-- HEH--NOTICE YOU'VE REALLY DEVELOPED YOUR, AH, UPPERCUT LATELY.
AND I NOTICE YOU'VE FINALLY OPENED YOUR EYES AND STARTED PAYING ATTENTION, STOICK.
"IT DIDN'T HURT THAT HE HAD A PRETTY GOOD SINGING VOICE, TO BOOT."
♫ BUT I WOULD BRING YOU RINGS OF GOLD ♪ AND EVEN SING YOU POETRY, AND I WOULD KEEP YOU FROM ALL HARM, IF YOU WOULD STAY BESIDE ME-- ♫
♪ I HAVE NO USE FOR RINGS OF GOLD, I CARE NOT FOR YOUR POETRY, ♪ I ONLY WANT YOUR HAND TO HOLD-- ♫
♪ I ONLY WANT YOU NEAR ME! ♫

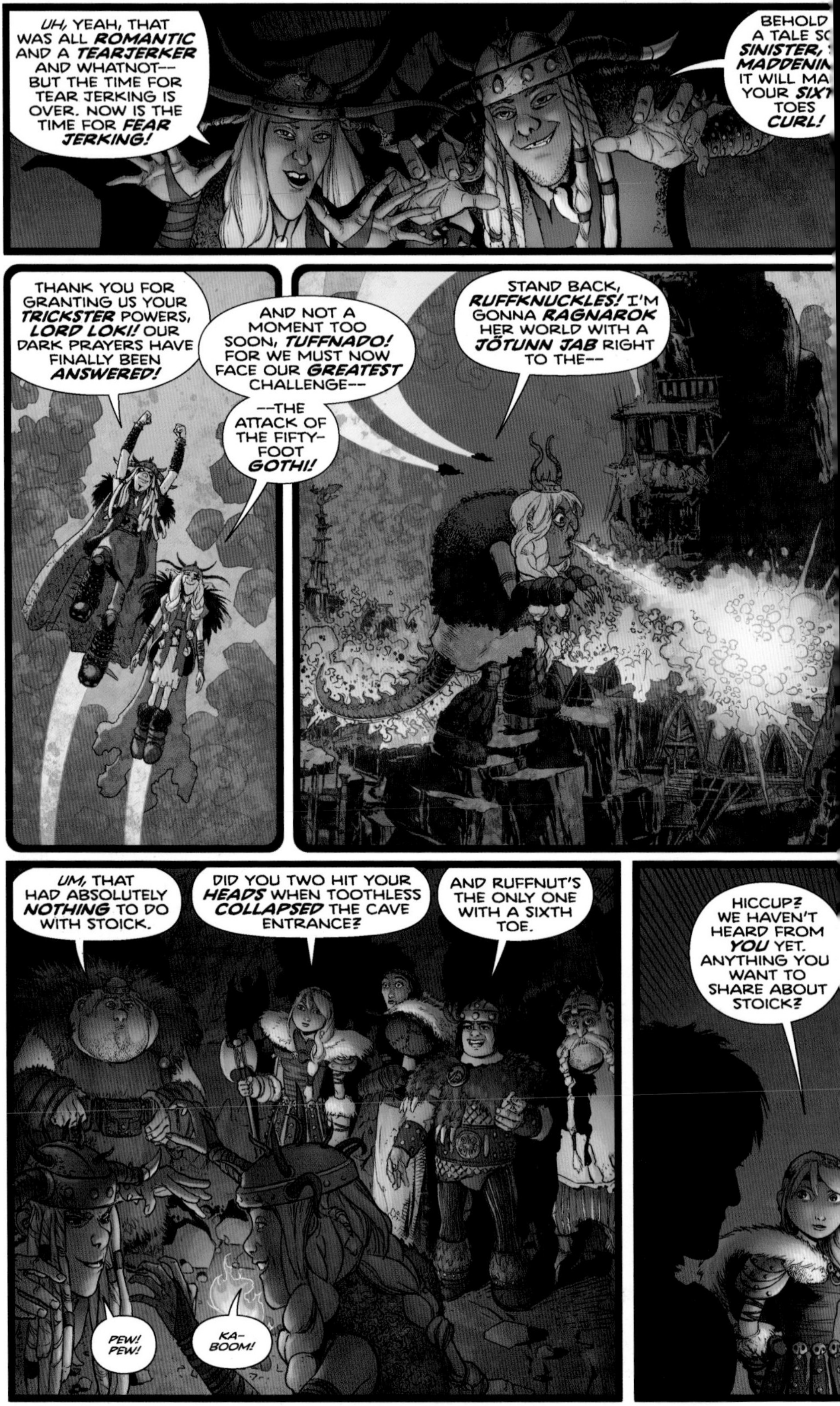
UH, YEAH, THAT WAS ALL ROMANTIC AND A TEARJERKER AND WHATNOT-- BUT THE TIME FOR TEAR JERKING IS OVER. NOW IS THE TIME FOR FEAR JERKING!
BEHOLD A TALE S SINISTER, MADDENIN IT WILL MA YOUR SIXT TOES CURL!
THANK YOU FOR GRANTING US YOUR TRICKSTER POWERS, LORD LOKI! OUR DARK PRAYERS HAVE FINALLY BEEN ANSWERED!
AND NOT A MOMENT TOO SOON, TUFFNADO! FOR WE MUST NOW FACE OUR GREATEST CHALLENGE--
--THE ATTACK OF THE FIFTY-FOOT GOTHI!
STAND BACK, RUFFKNUCKLES! I'M GONNA RAGNAROK HER WORLD WITH A JÖTUNN JAB RIGHT TO THE--
UM, THAT HAD ABSOLUTELY NOTHING TO DO WITH STOICK.
DID YOU TWO HIT YOUR HEADS WHEN TOOTHLESS COLLAPSED THE CAVE ENTRANCE?
AND RUFFNUT'S THE ONLY ONE WITH A SIXTH TOE.
PEW! PEW!
KA-BOOM!
HICCUP? WE HAVEN'T HEARD FROM YOU YET. ANYTHING YOU WANT TO SHARE ABOUT STOICK?

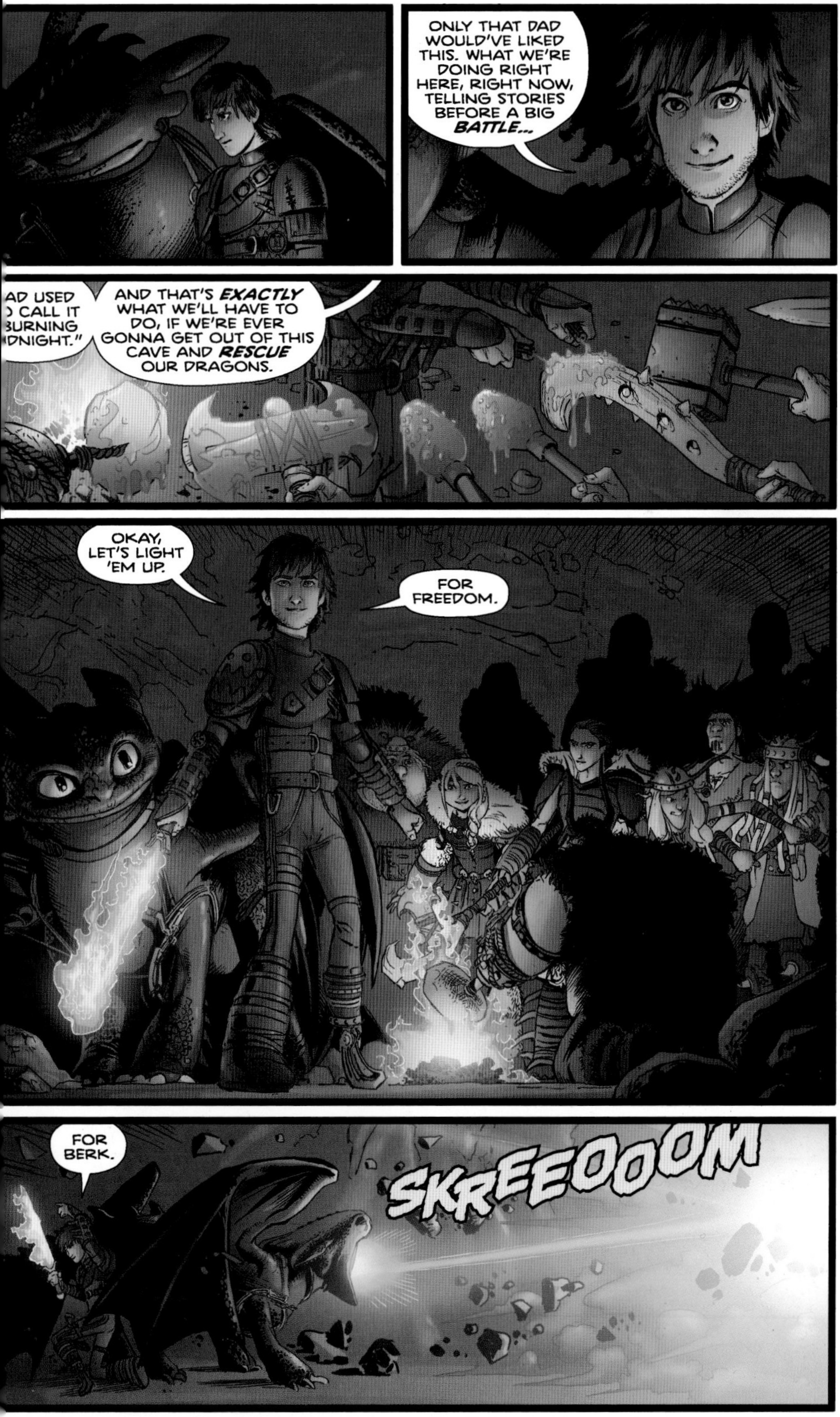
ONLY THAT DAD WOULD'VE LIKED THIS. WHAT WE'RE DOING RIGHT HERE, RIGHT NOW, TELLING STORIES BEFORE A BIG BATTLE...
AD USED CALL IT BURNING DNIGHT."
AND THAT'S EXACTLY WHAT WE'LL HAVE TO DO, IF WE'RE EVER GONNA GET OUT OF THIS CAVE AND RESCUE OUR DRAGONS.
OKAY, LET'S LIGHT 'EM UP.
FOR FREEDOM.
FOR BERK.
SKREEEOOOM

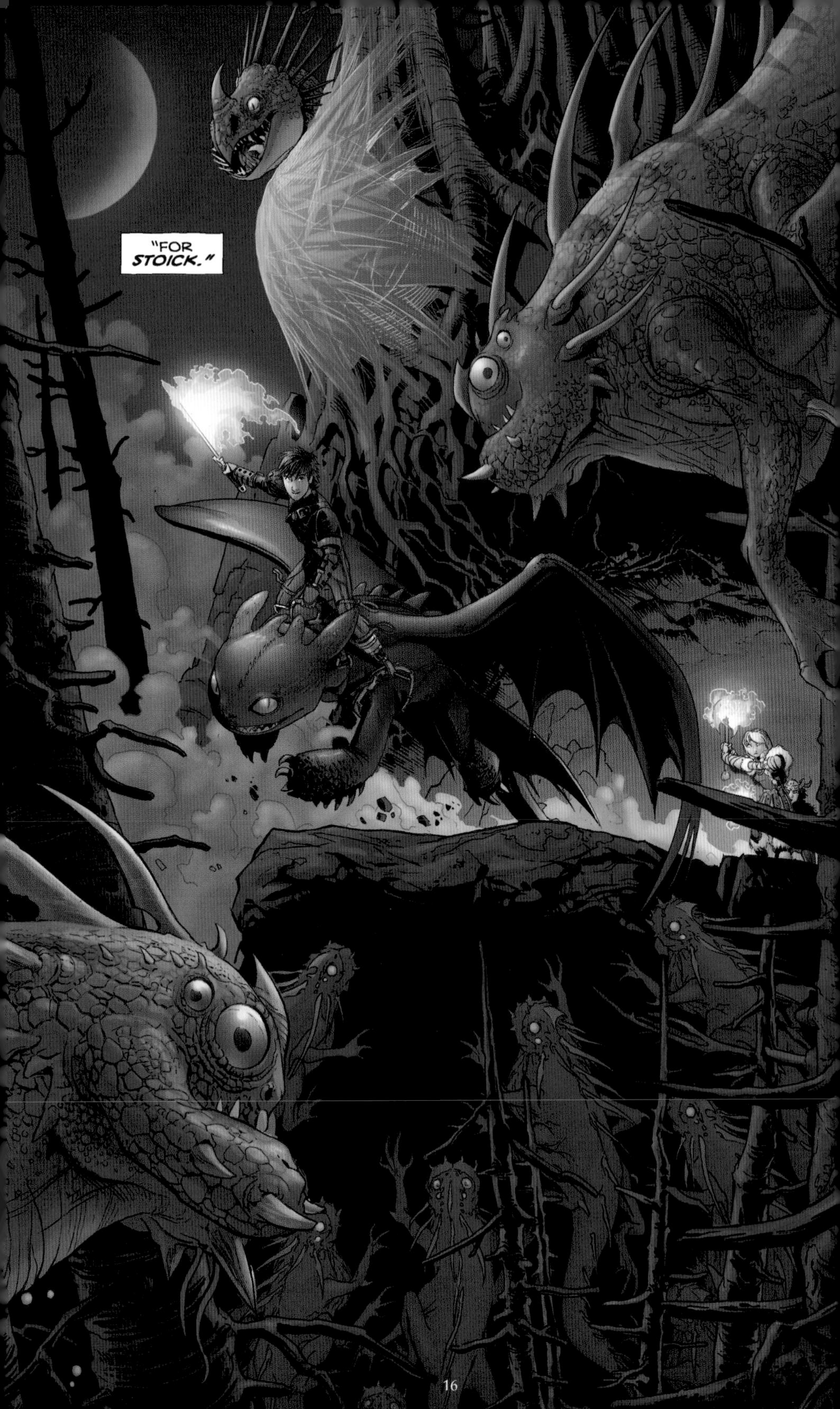
"FOR STOICK."

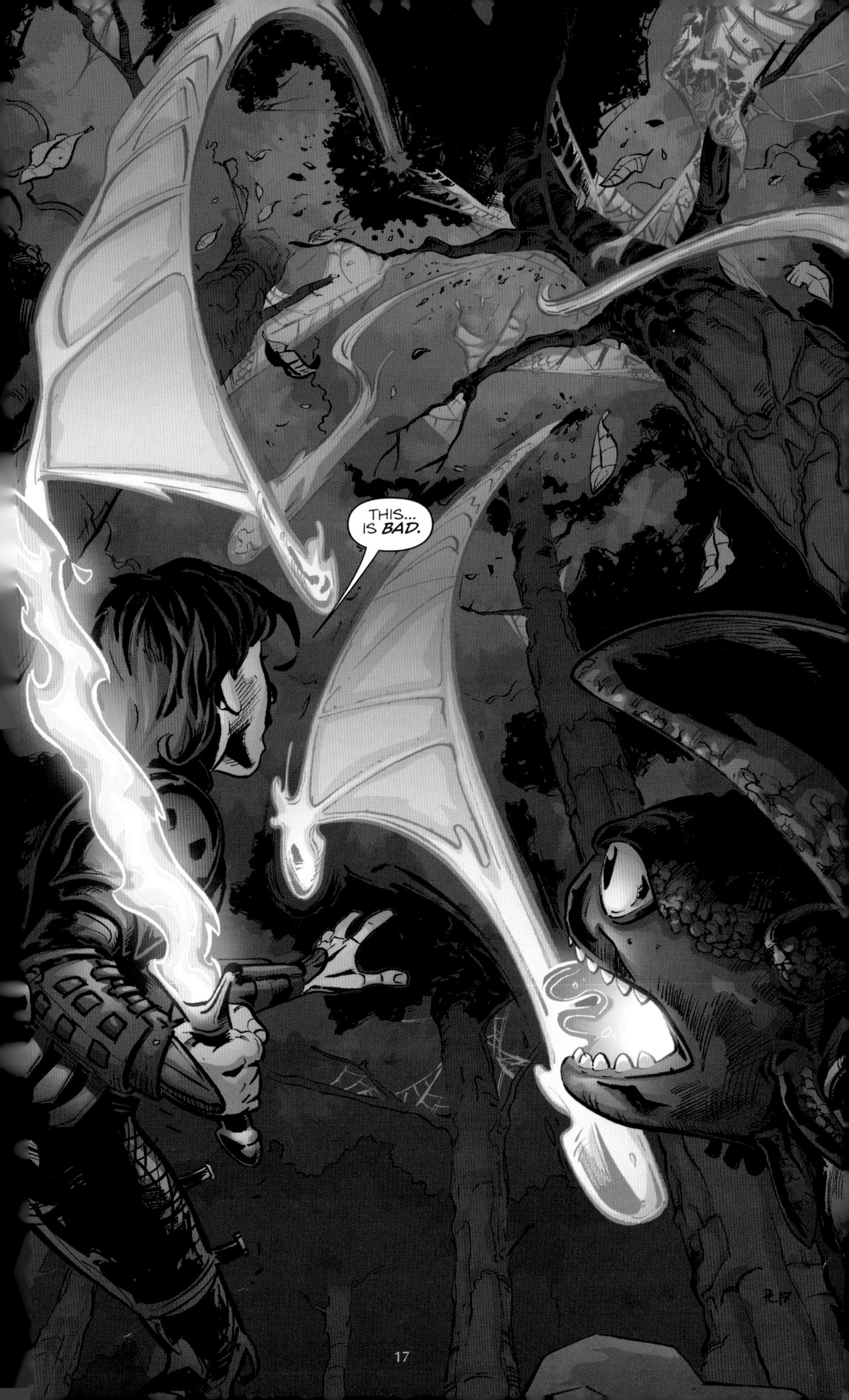
THIS... IS **BAD.**

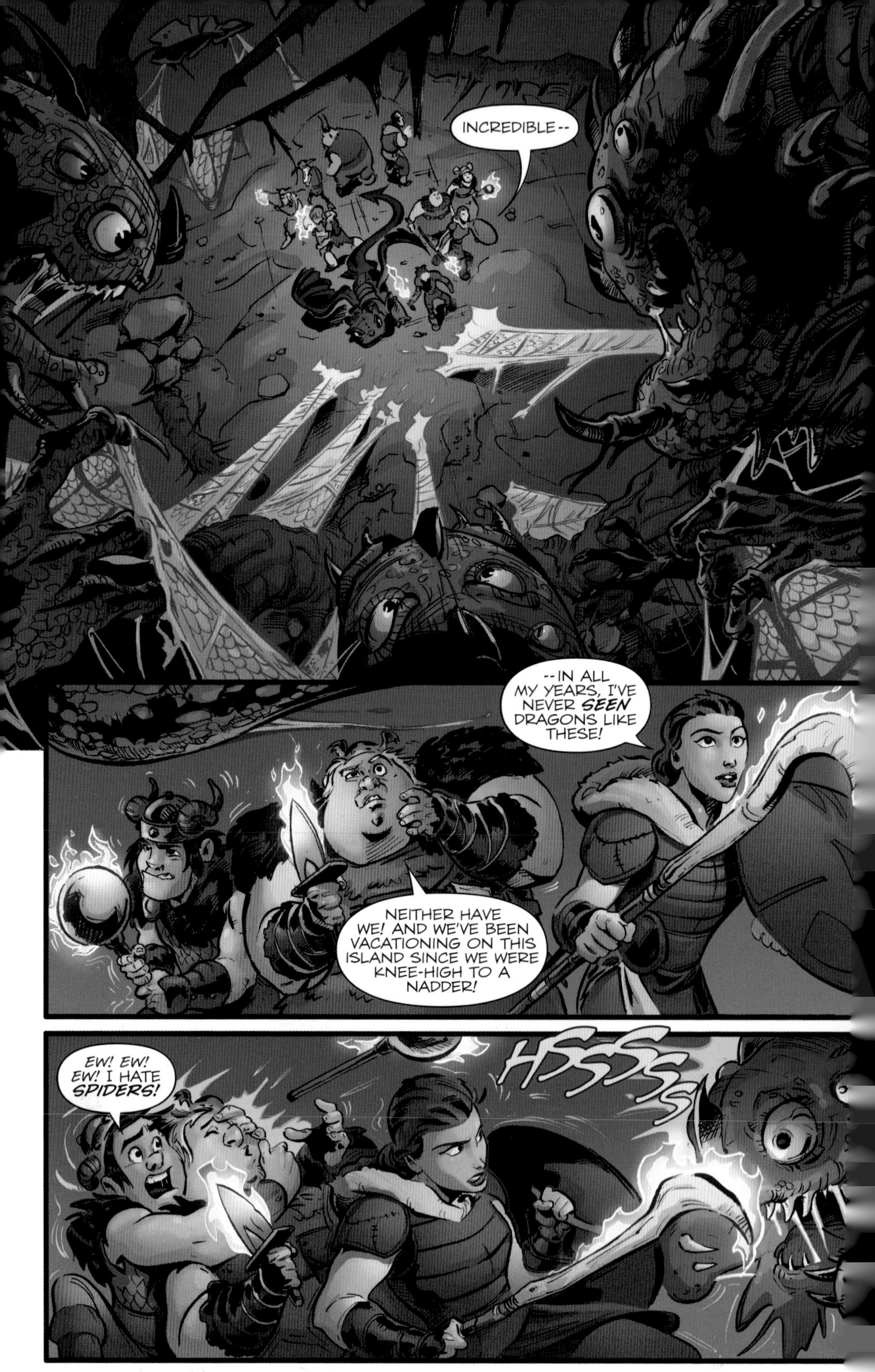
INCREDIBLE--
--IN ALL MY YEARS, I'VE NEVER SEEN DRAGONS LIKE THESE!
NEITHER HAVE WE! AND WE'VE BEEN VACATIONING ON THIS ISLAND SINCE WE WERE KNEE-HIGH TO A NADDER!
EW! EW! EW! I HATE SPIDERS!
HSSSSS

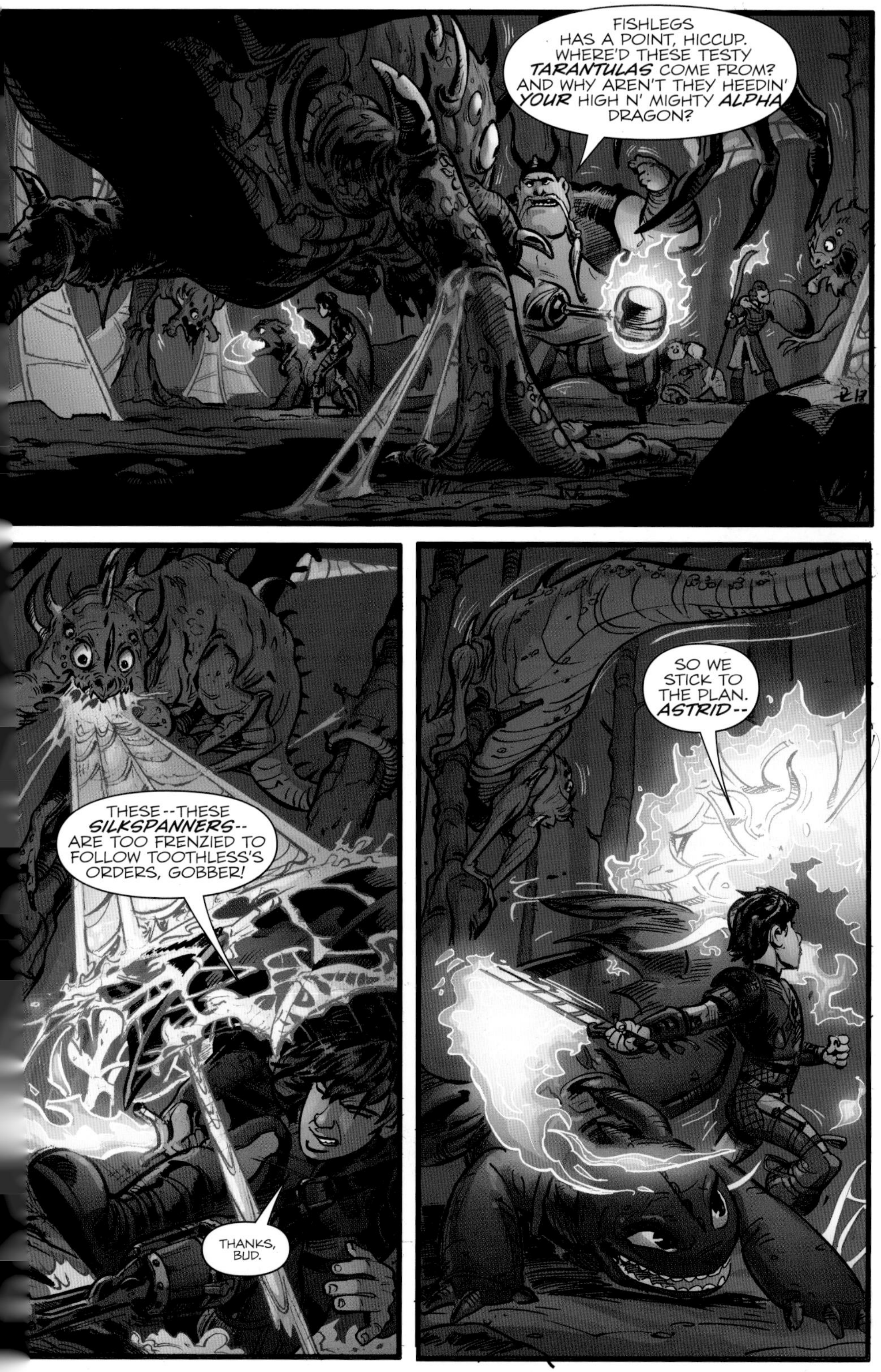
FISHLEGS HAS A POINT, HICCUP. WHERE'D THESE TESTY TARANTULAS COME FROM? AND WHY AREN'T THEY HEEDIN' YOUR HIGH N' MIGHTY ALPHA DRAGON?
THESE--THESE SILKSPANNERS--ARE TOO FRENZIED TO FOLLOW TOOTHLESS'S ORDERS, GOBBER!
THANKS, BUD.
SO WE STICK TO THE PLAN. ASTRID--

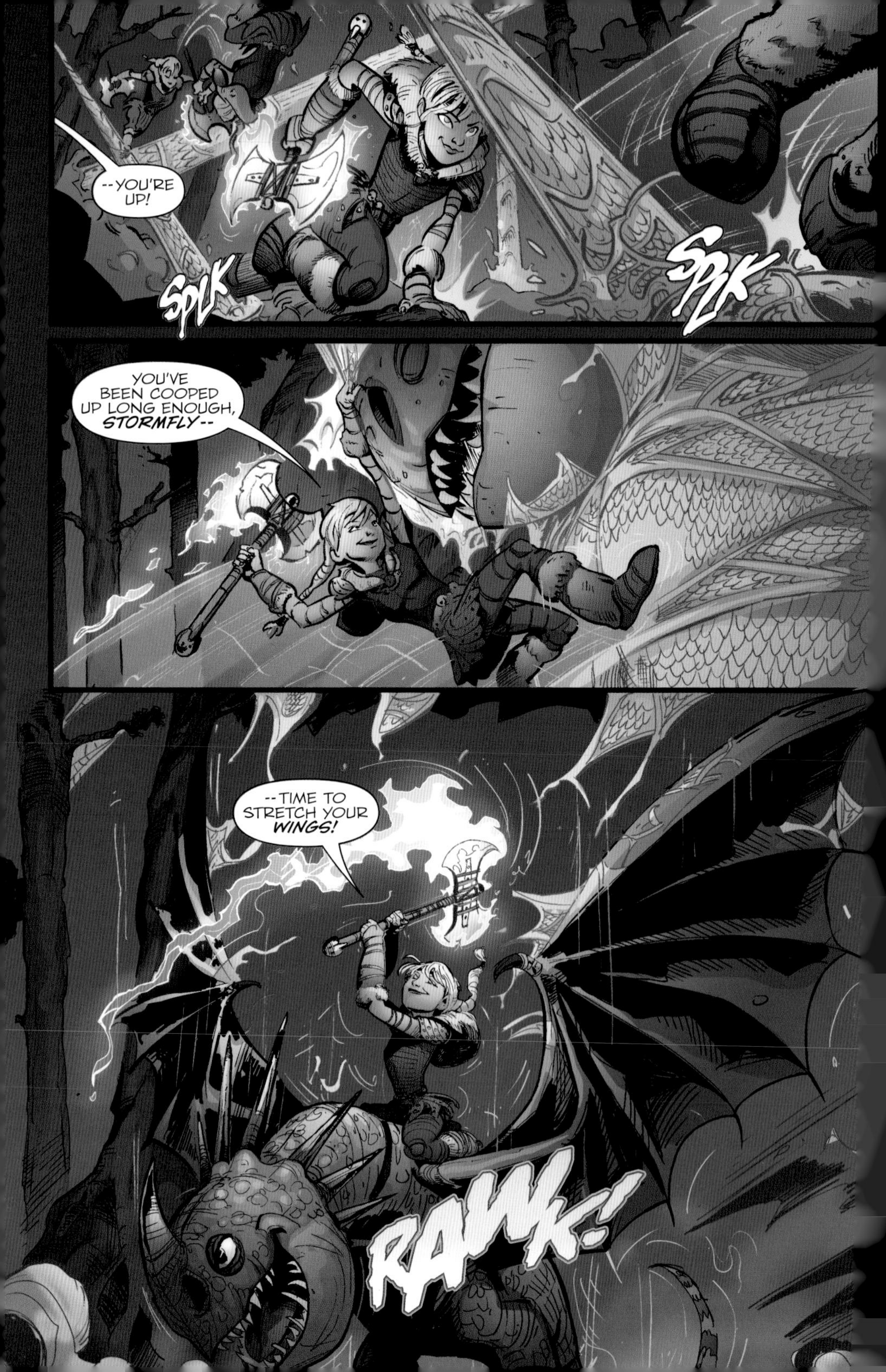

--YOU'RE UP!
SPLK
SPLK
YOU'VE BEEN COOPED UP LONG ENOUGH, STORMFLY--
--TIME TO STRETCH YOUR WINGS!
RAWK!

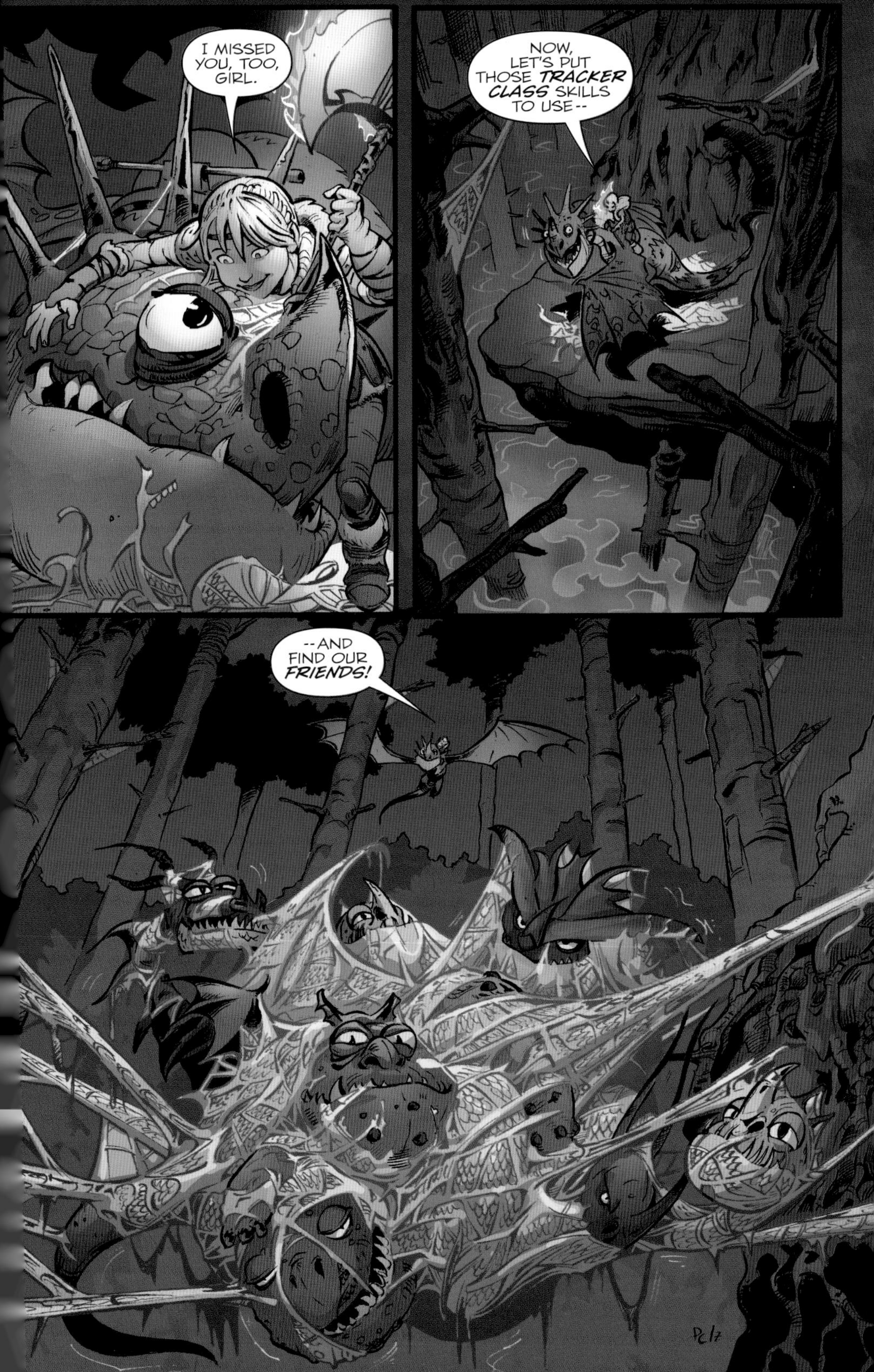
I MISSED YOU, TOO, GIRL.
NOW, LET'S PUT THOSE TRACKER CLASS SKILLS TO USE--
--AND FIND OUR FRIENDS!

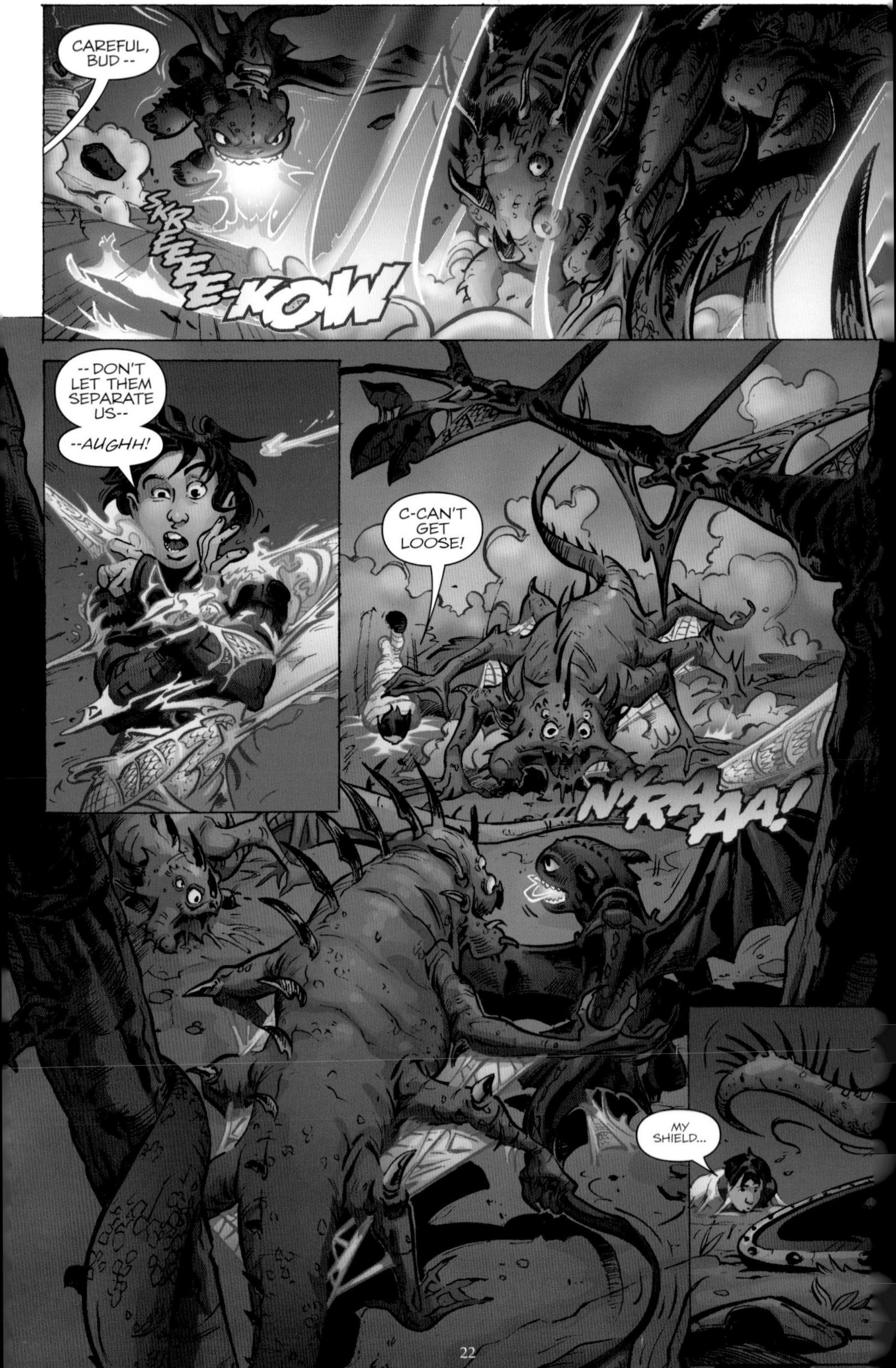
CAREFUL, BUD --
SKREEEE-KOW
-- DON'T LET THEM SEPARATE US--
--AUGHH!
C-CAN'T GET LOOSE!
N'RAAA!
MY SHIELD...

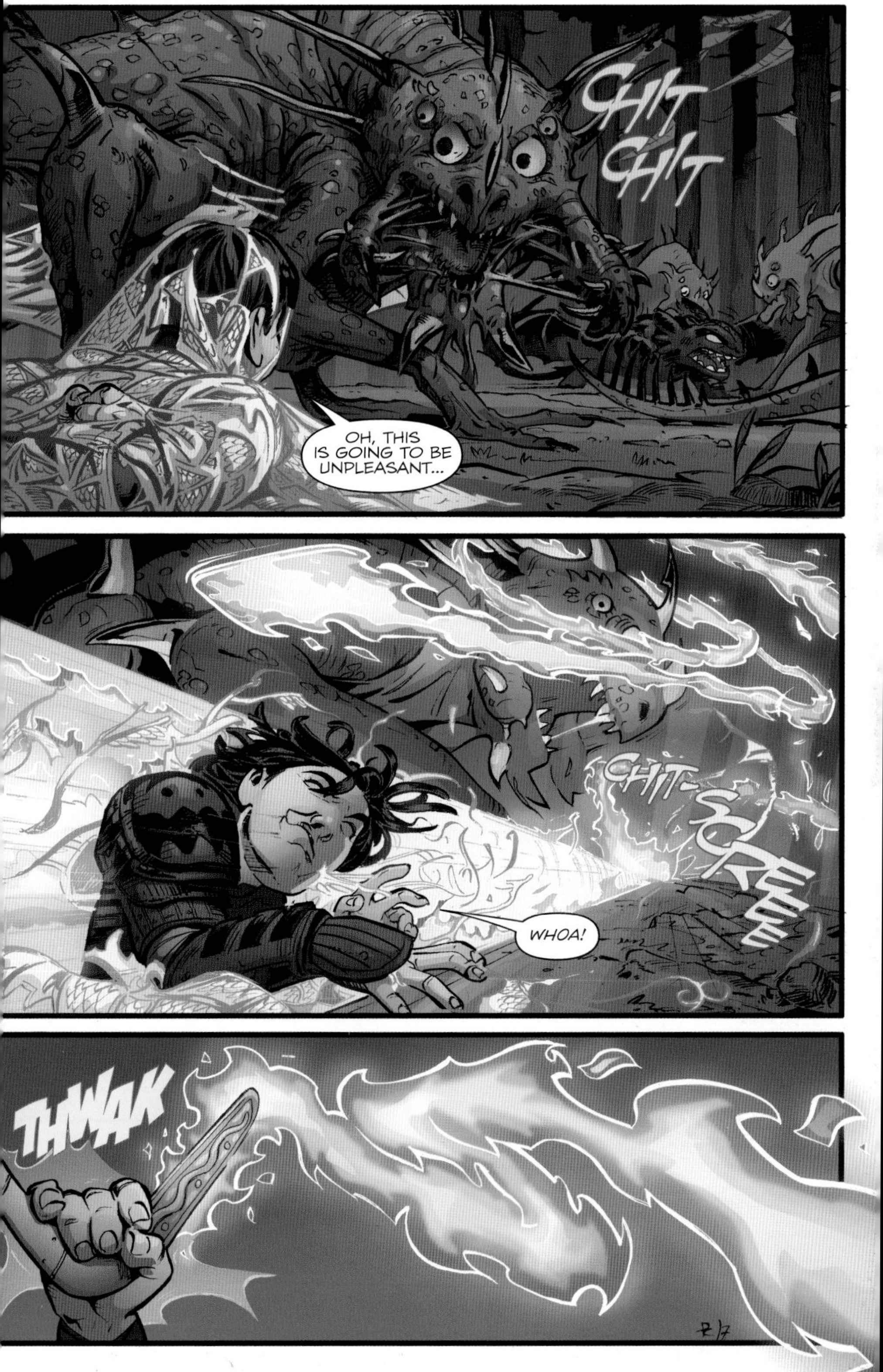
CHIT CHIT
OH, THIS IS GOING TO BE UNPLEASANT...
CHIT-SCREEE
WHOA!
THWAK

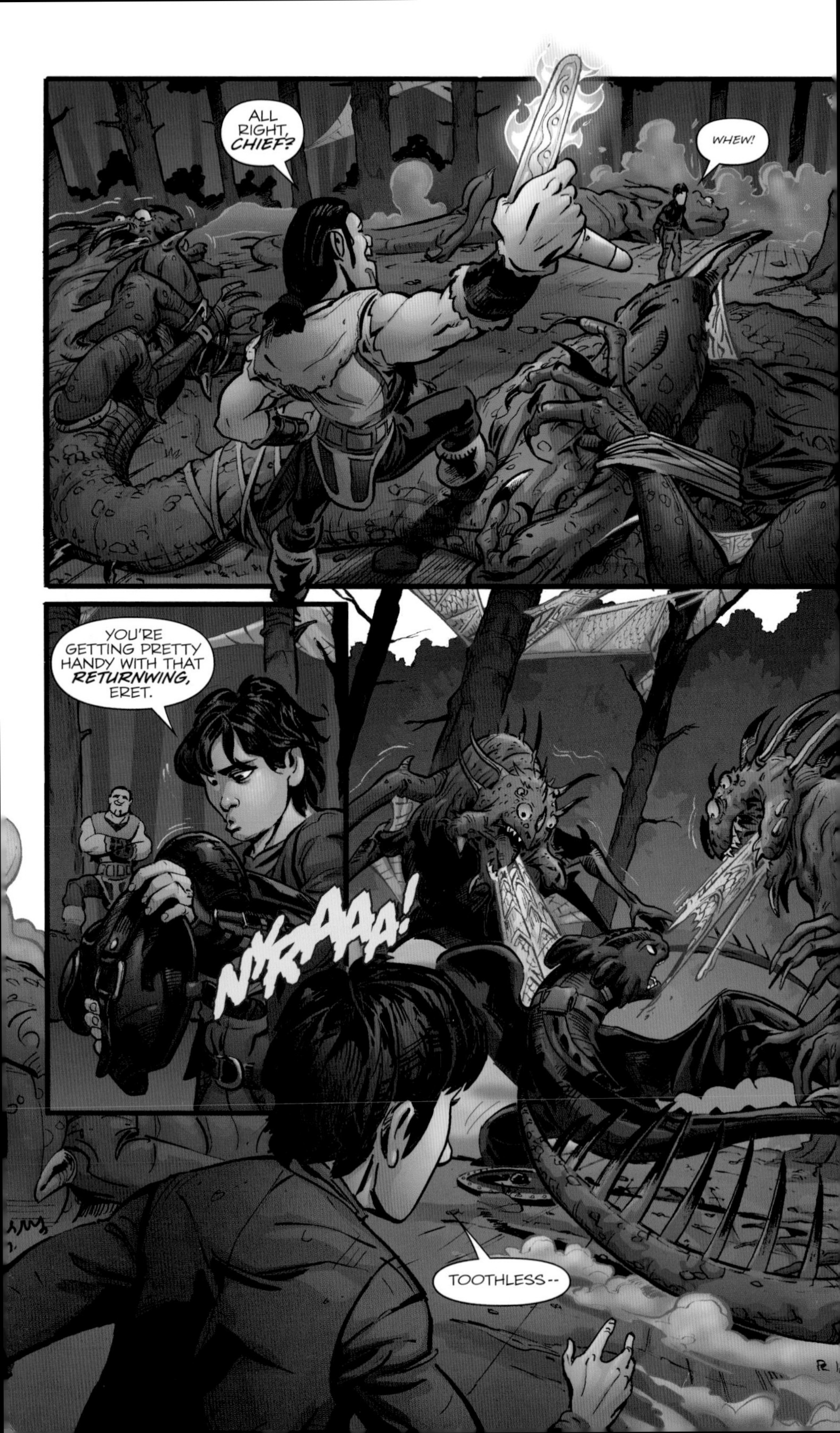
ALL RIGHT, CHIEF?
WHEW!
YOU'RE GETTING PRETTY HANDY WITH THAT RETURNWING, ERET.
NYRAAA!
TOOTHLESS--

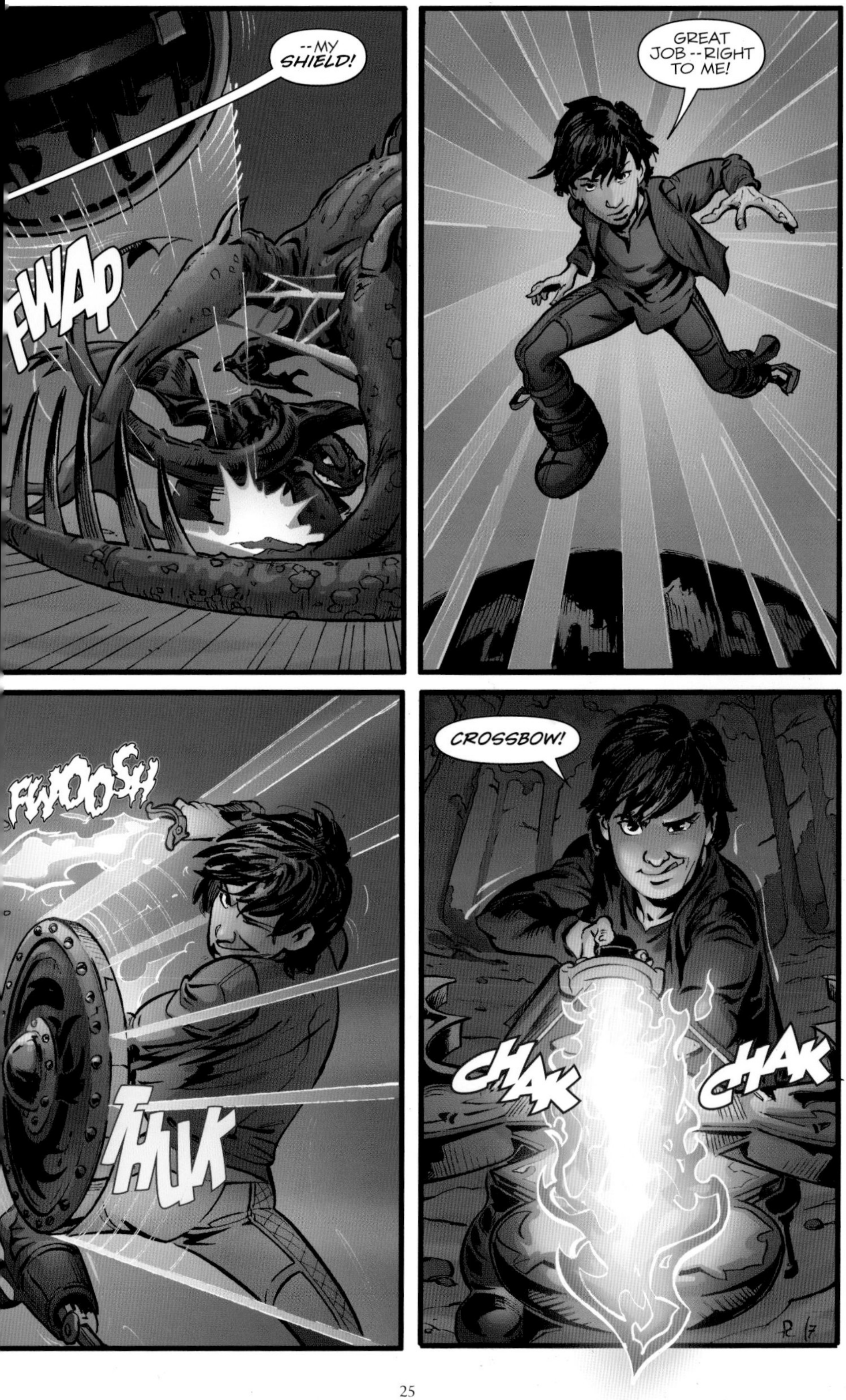
--MY SHIELD!
FWAP
GREAT JOB--RIGHT TO ME!
FWOOSH
THUK
CROSSBOW!
CHAK
CHAK

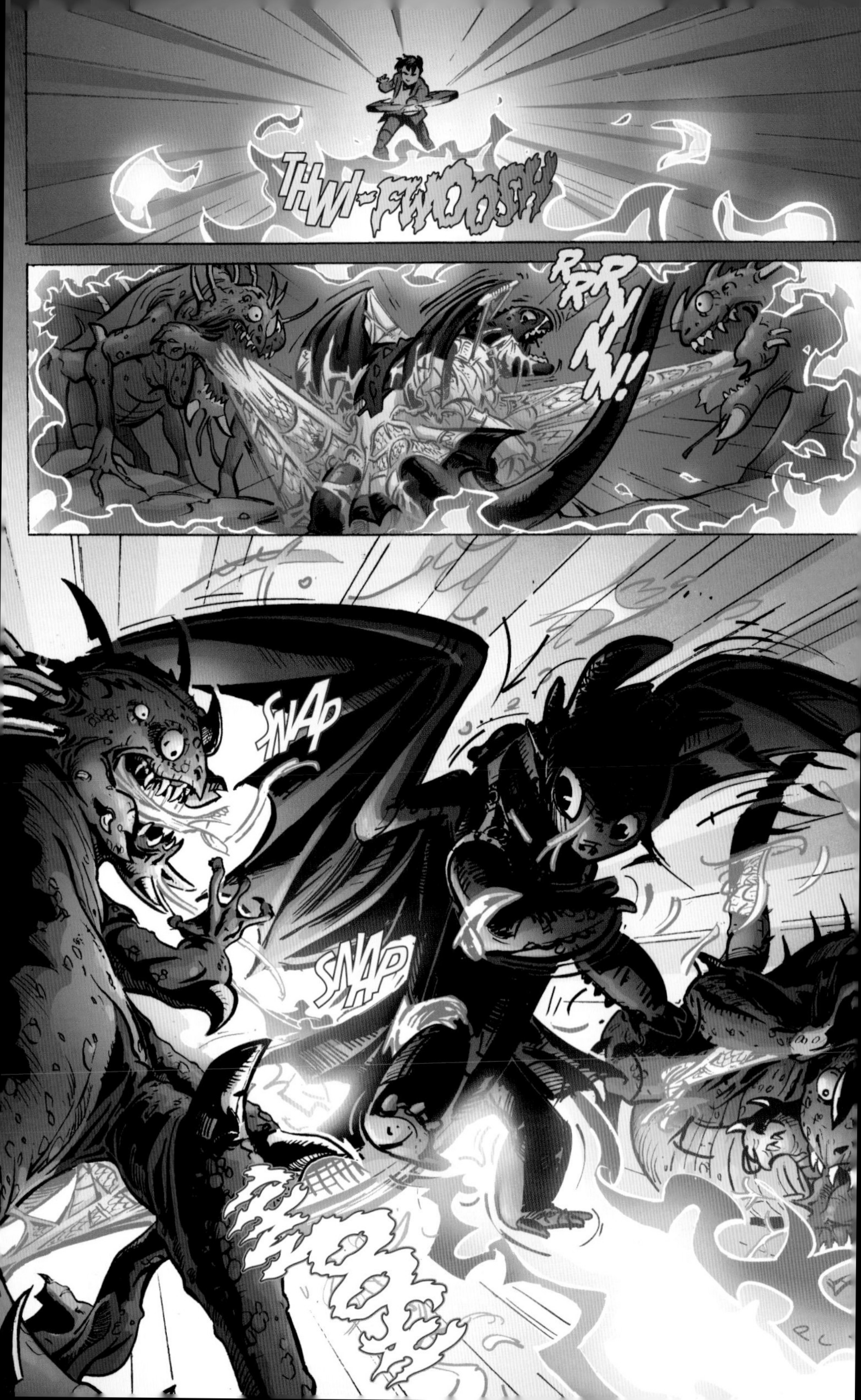
THWI-FWOOSH
RRNN!
SNAP
SNAP

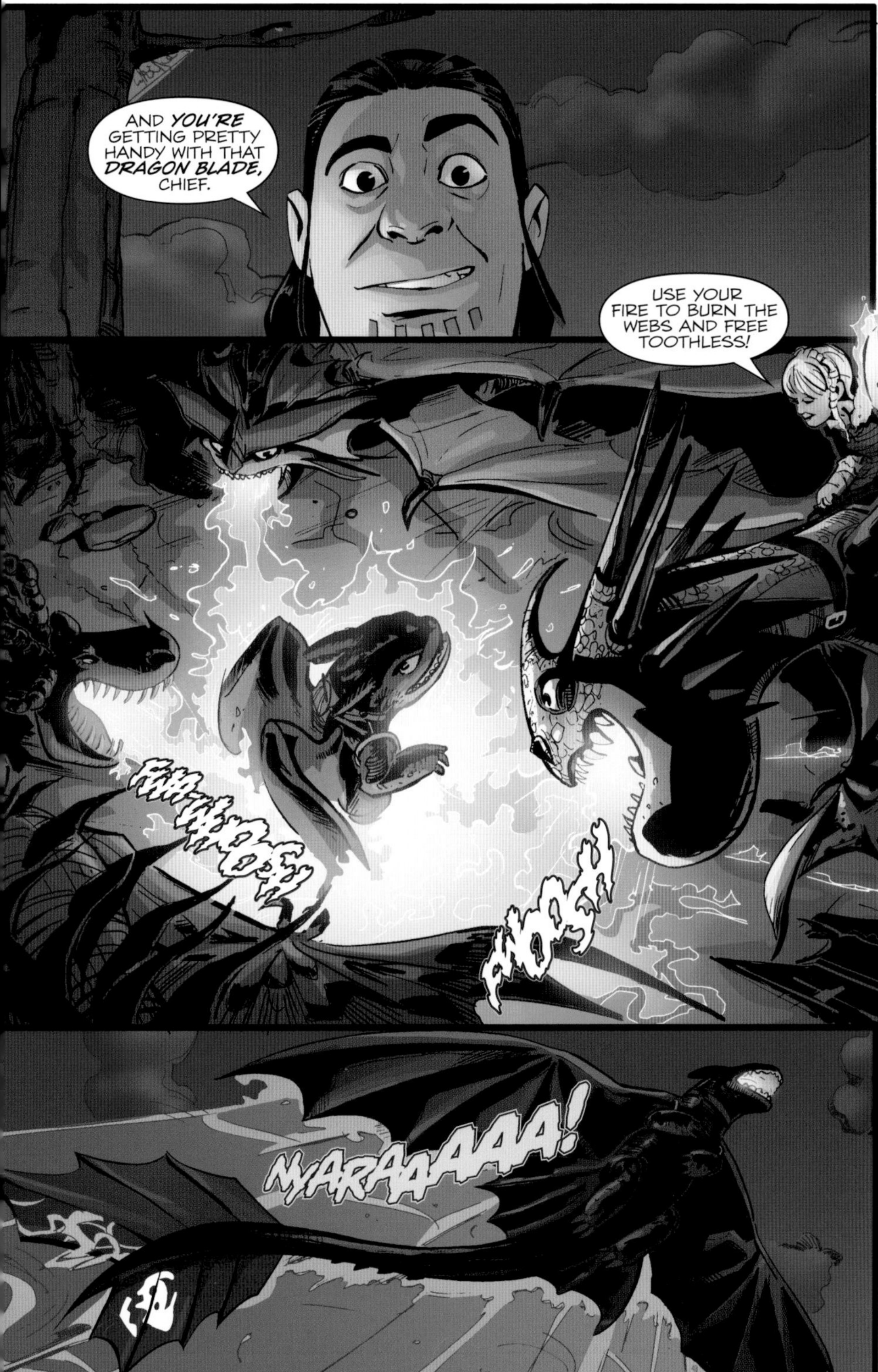

AND YOU'RE GETTING PRETTY HANDY WITH THAT DRAGON BLADE, CHIEF.
USE YOUR FIRE TO BURN THE WEBS AND FREE TOOTHLESS!
FWA-WOOSH!
FWOOSH!
NYARAAAAAA!

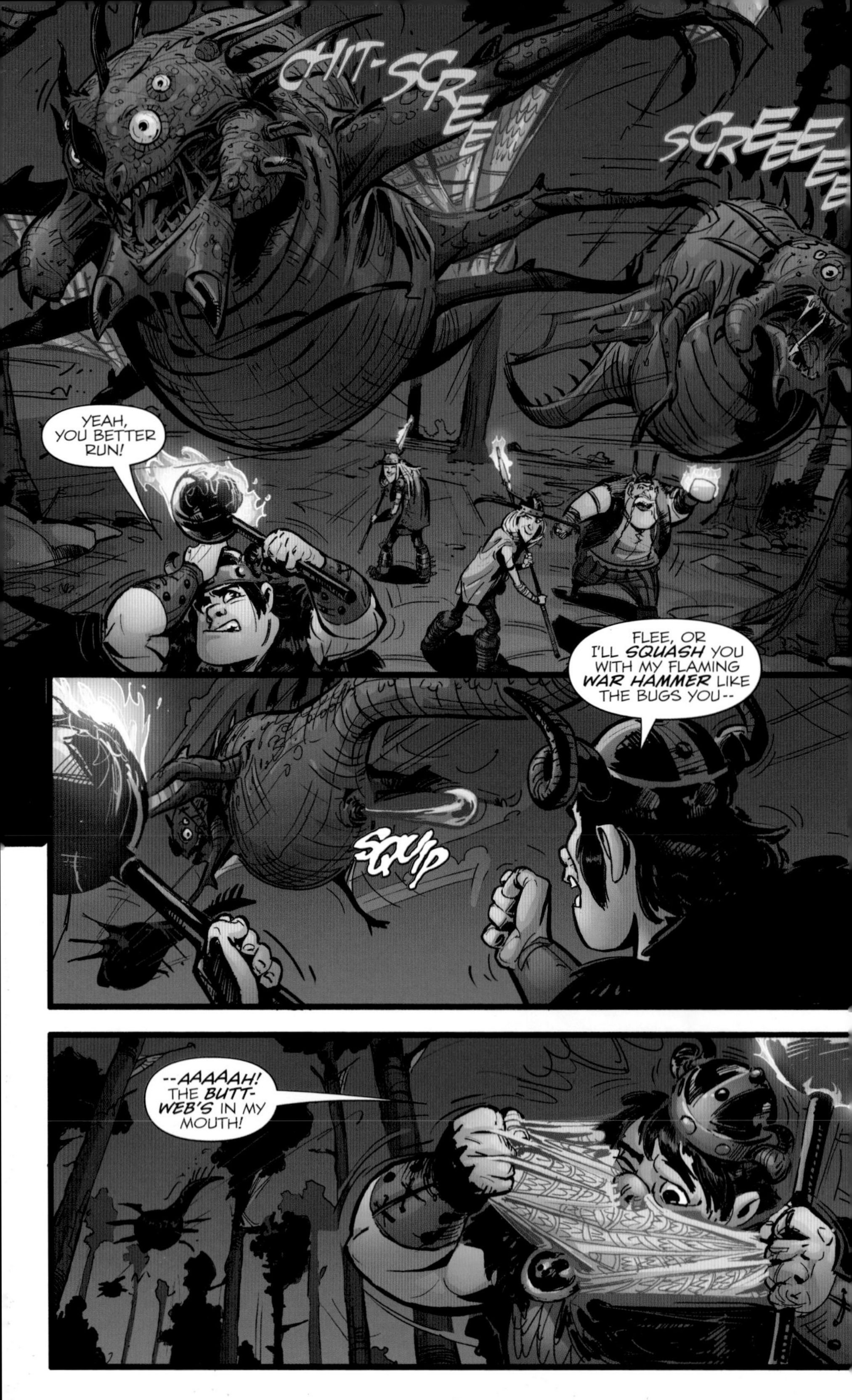
CHIT-SCREE
SCREEEEEE
YEAH, YOU BETTER RUN!
FLEE, OR I'LL SQUASH YOU WITH MY FLAMING WAR HAMMER LIKE THE BUGS YOU--
SQUIP
--AAAAAH! THE BUTT-WEB'S IN MY MOUTH!

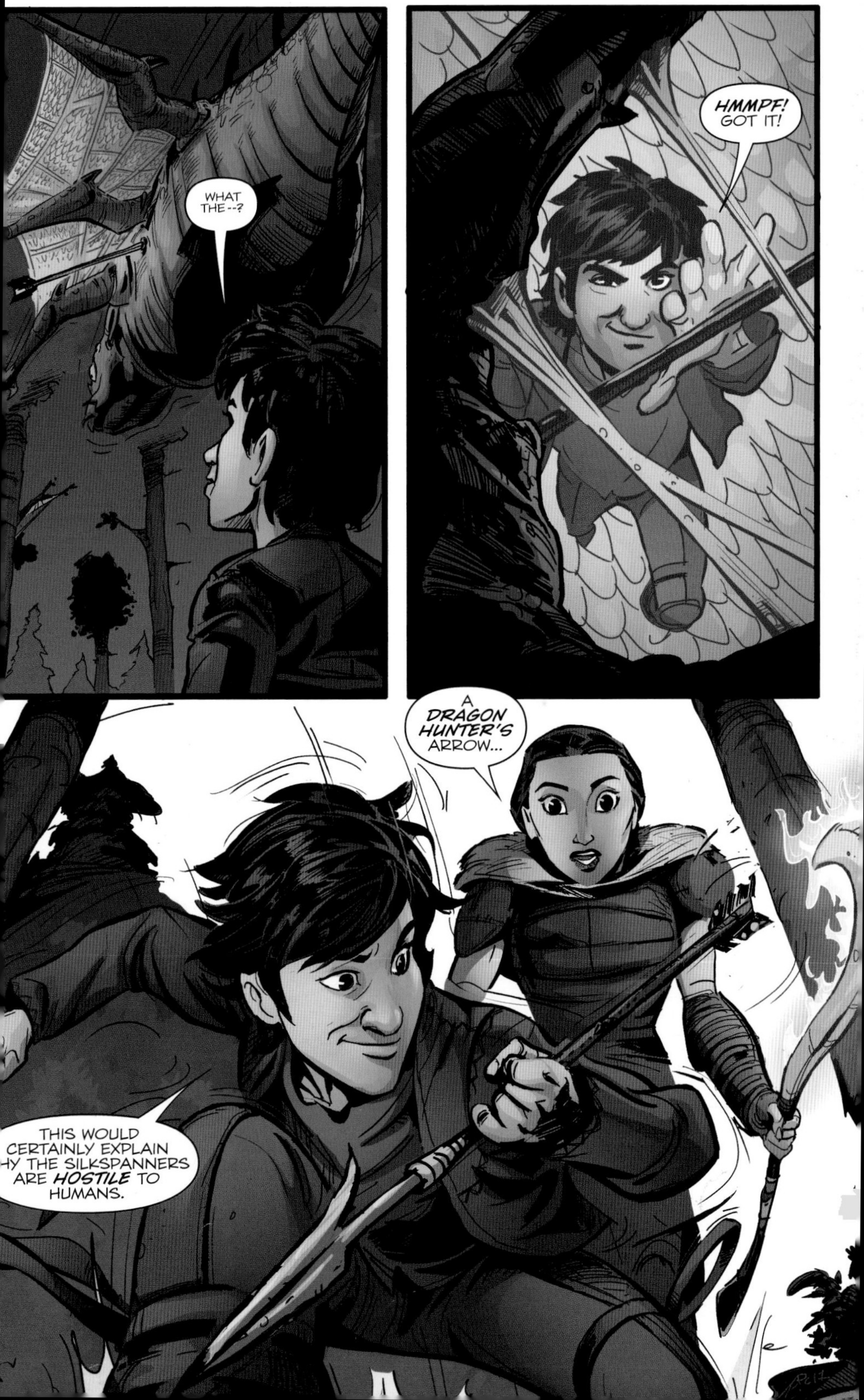
WHAT THE--?
HMMPF! GOT IT!
A DRAGON HUNTER'S ARROW...
THIS WOULD CERTAINLY EXPLAIN HY THE SILKSPANNERS ARE HOSTILE TO HUMANS.

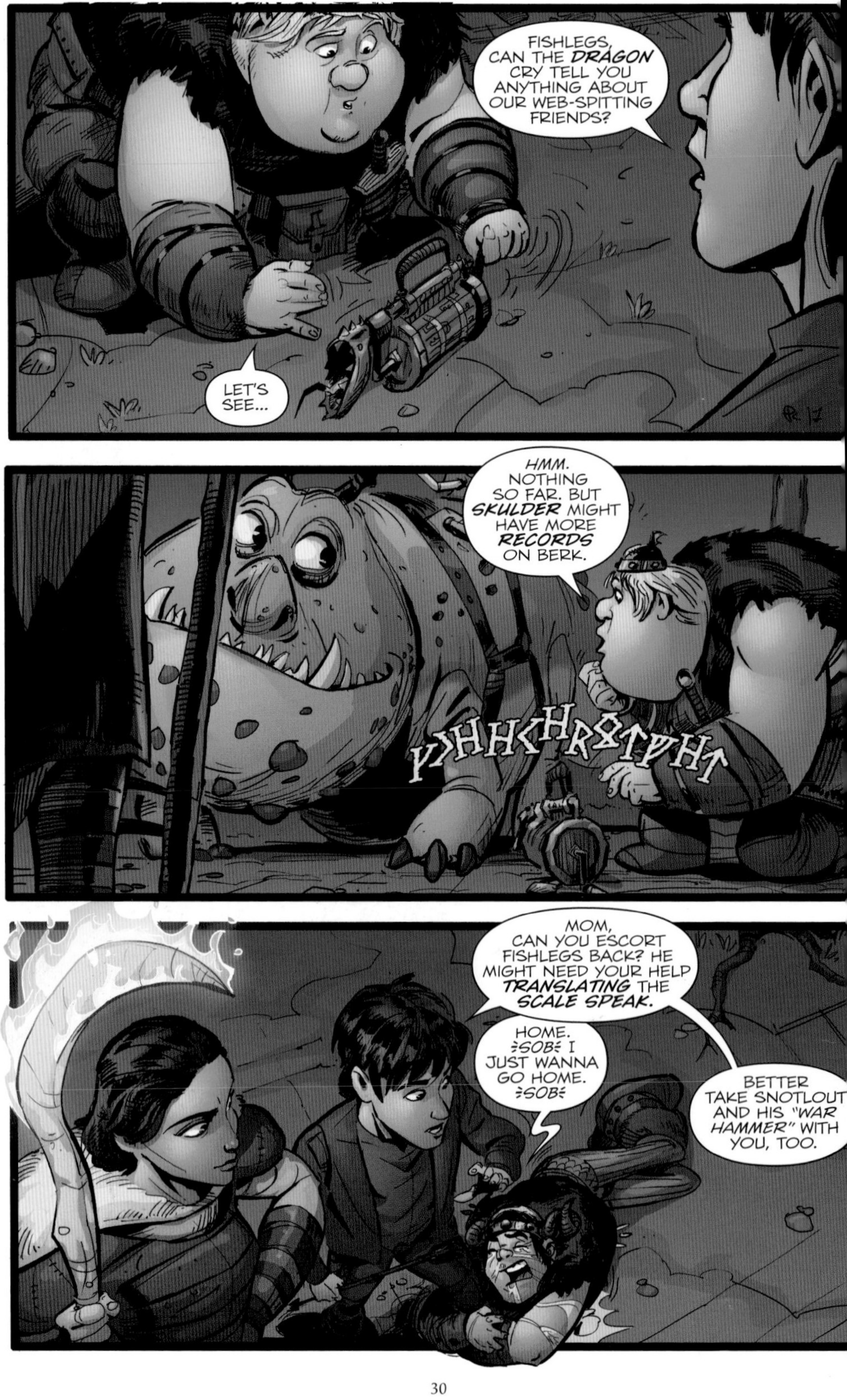
FISHLEGS, CAN THE DRAGON CRY TELL YOU ANYTHING ABOUT OUR WEB-SPITTING FRIENDS?
LET'S SEE...
HMM. NOTHING SO FAR. BUT SKULDER MIGHT HAVE MORE RECORDS ON BERK.
MOM, CAN YOU ESCORT FISHLEGS BACK? HE MIGHT NEED YOUR HELP TRANSLATING THE SCALE SPEAK.
HOME. SOB I JUST WANNA GO HOME. SOB
BETTER TAKE SNOTLOUT AND HIS "WAR HAMMER" WITH YOU, TOO.

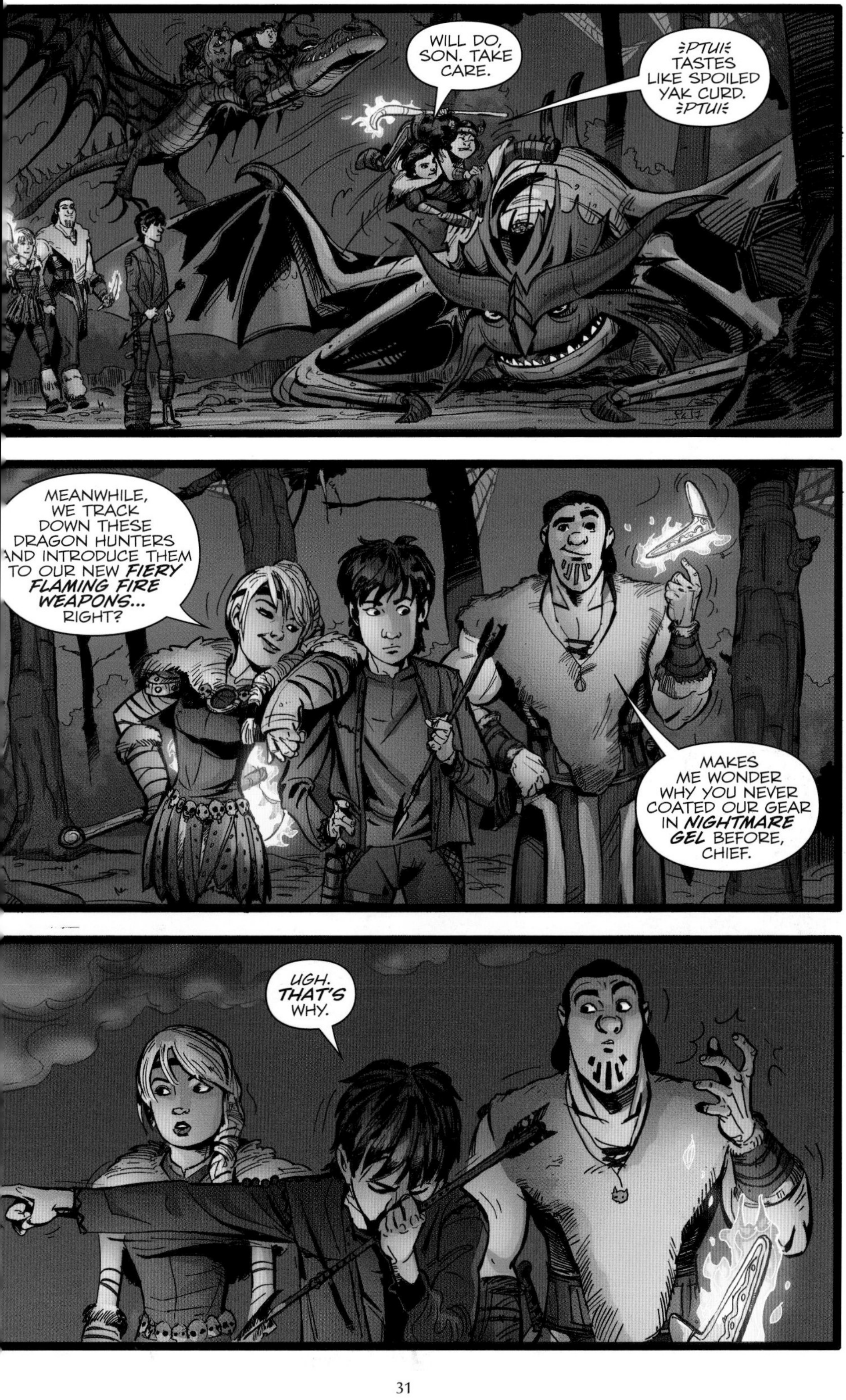
WILL DO, SON. TAKE CARE.
≷PTUI≶ TASTES LIKE SPOILED YAK CURD. ≷PTUI≶
MEANWHILE, WE TRACK DOWN THESE DRAGON HUNTERS AND INTRODUCE THEM TO OUR NEW *FIERY FLAMING FIRE WEAPONS...* RIGHT?
MAKES ME WONDER WHY YOU NEVER COATED OUR GEAR IN *NIGHTMARE GEL* BEFORE, CHIEF.
UGH. *THAT'S* WHY.

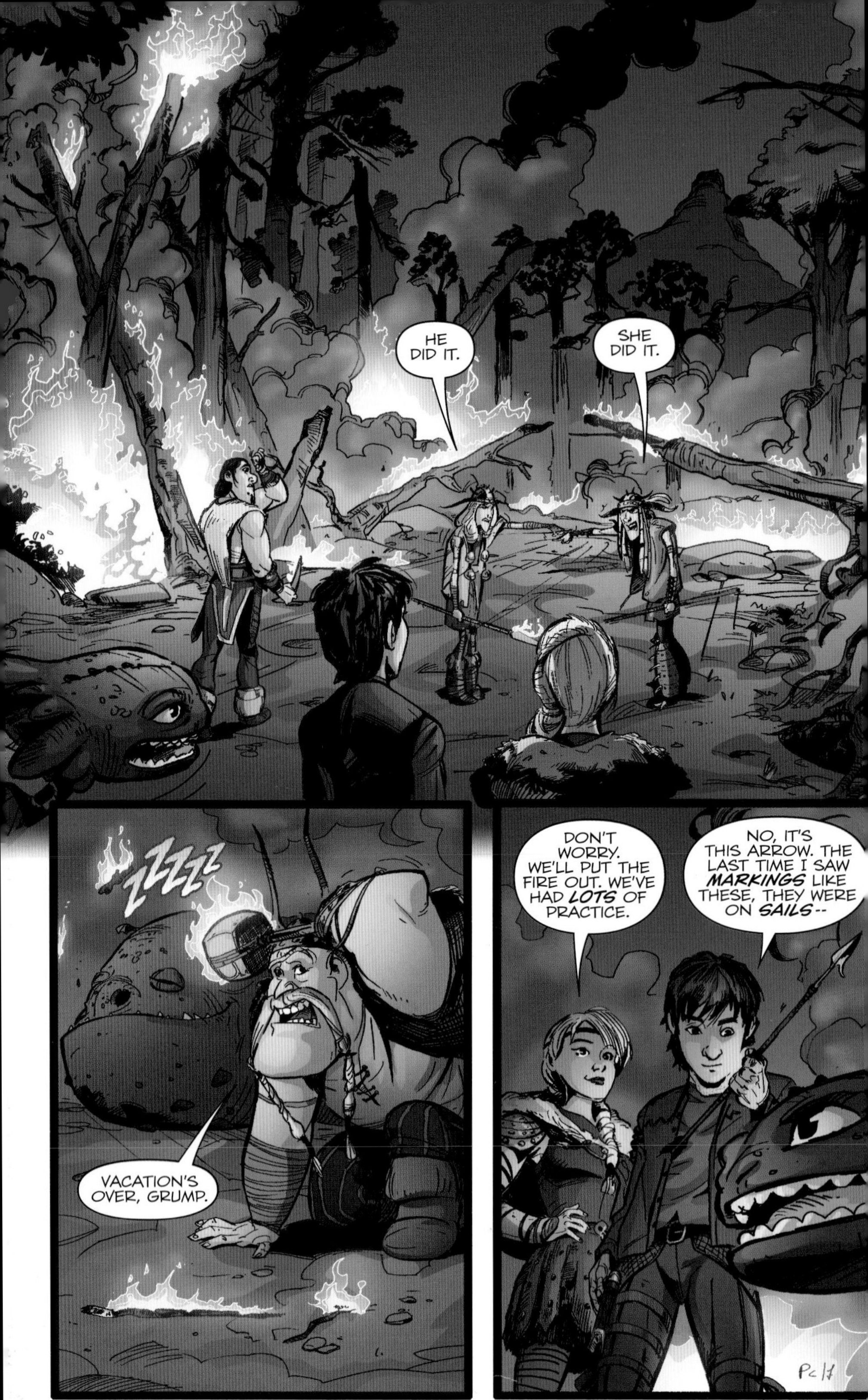
HE DID IT.
SHE DID IT.
ZZZZZ
VACATION'S OVER, GRUMP.
DON'T WORRY. WE'LL PUT THE FIRE OUT. WE'VE HAD *LOTS* OF PRACTICE.
NO, IT'S THIS ARROW. THE LAST TIME I SAW *MARKINGS* LIKE THESE, THEY WERE ON *SAILS*--

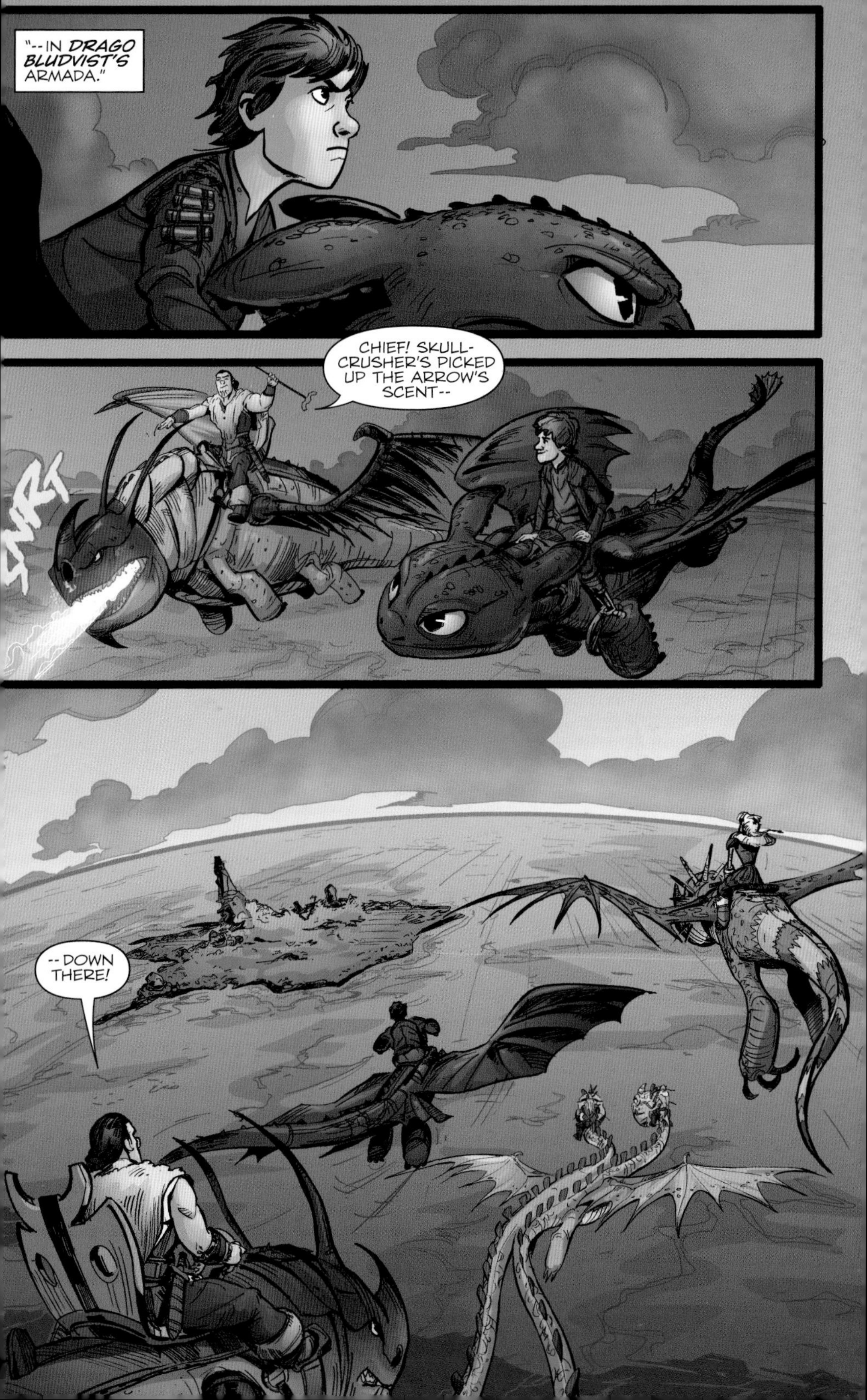
"--IN DRAGO BLUDVIST'S ARMADA."
CHIEF! SKULL-CRUSHER'S PICKED UP THE ARROW'S SCENT--
SNRT
--DOWN THERE!

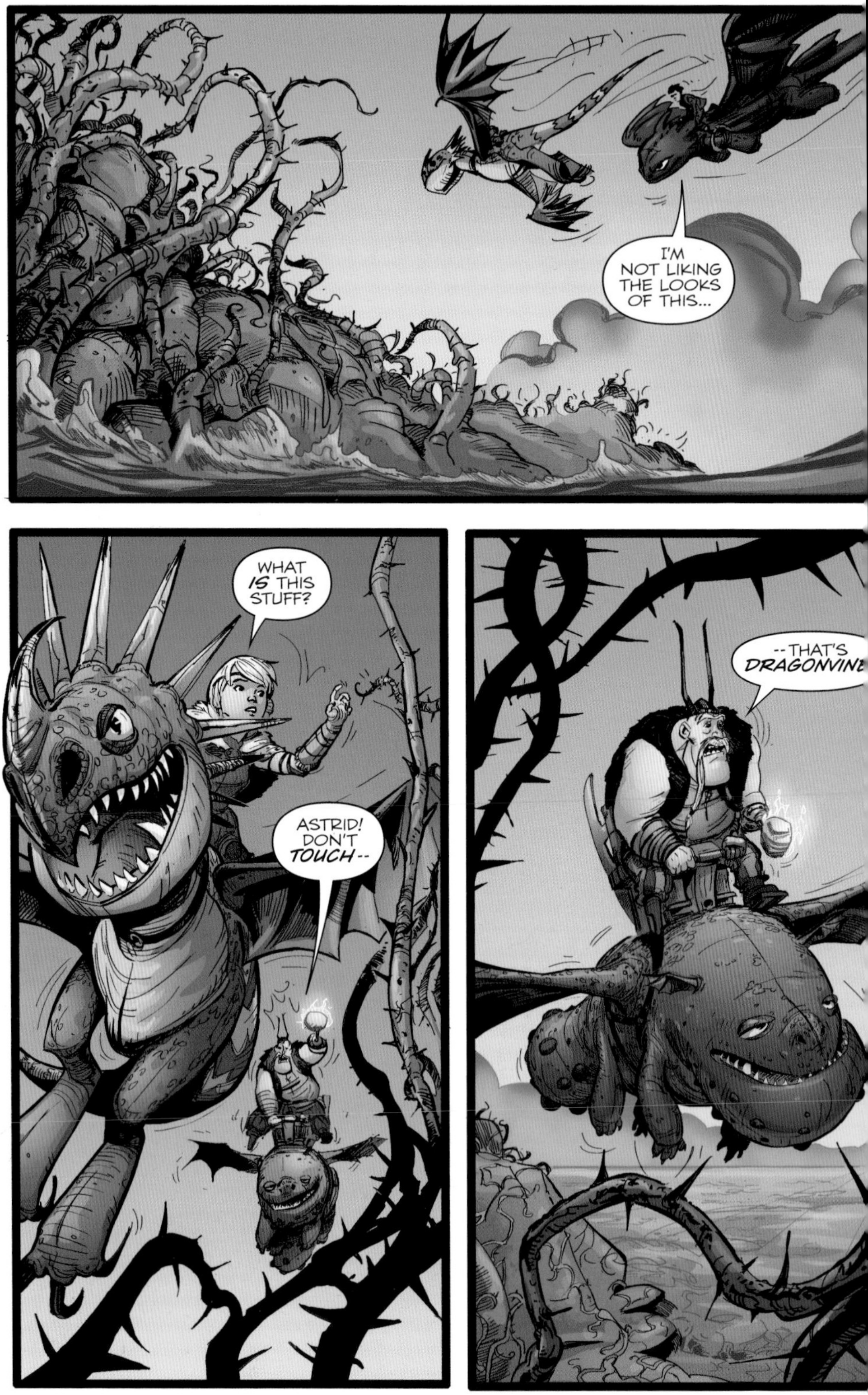
I'M NOT LIKING THE LOOKS OF THIS...
WHAT *IS* THIS STUFF?
ASTRID! DON'T *TOUCH*--
--THAT'S *DRAGONVINE*

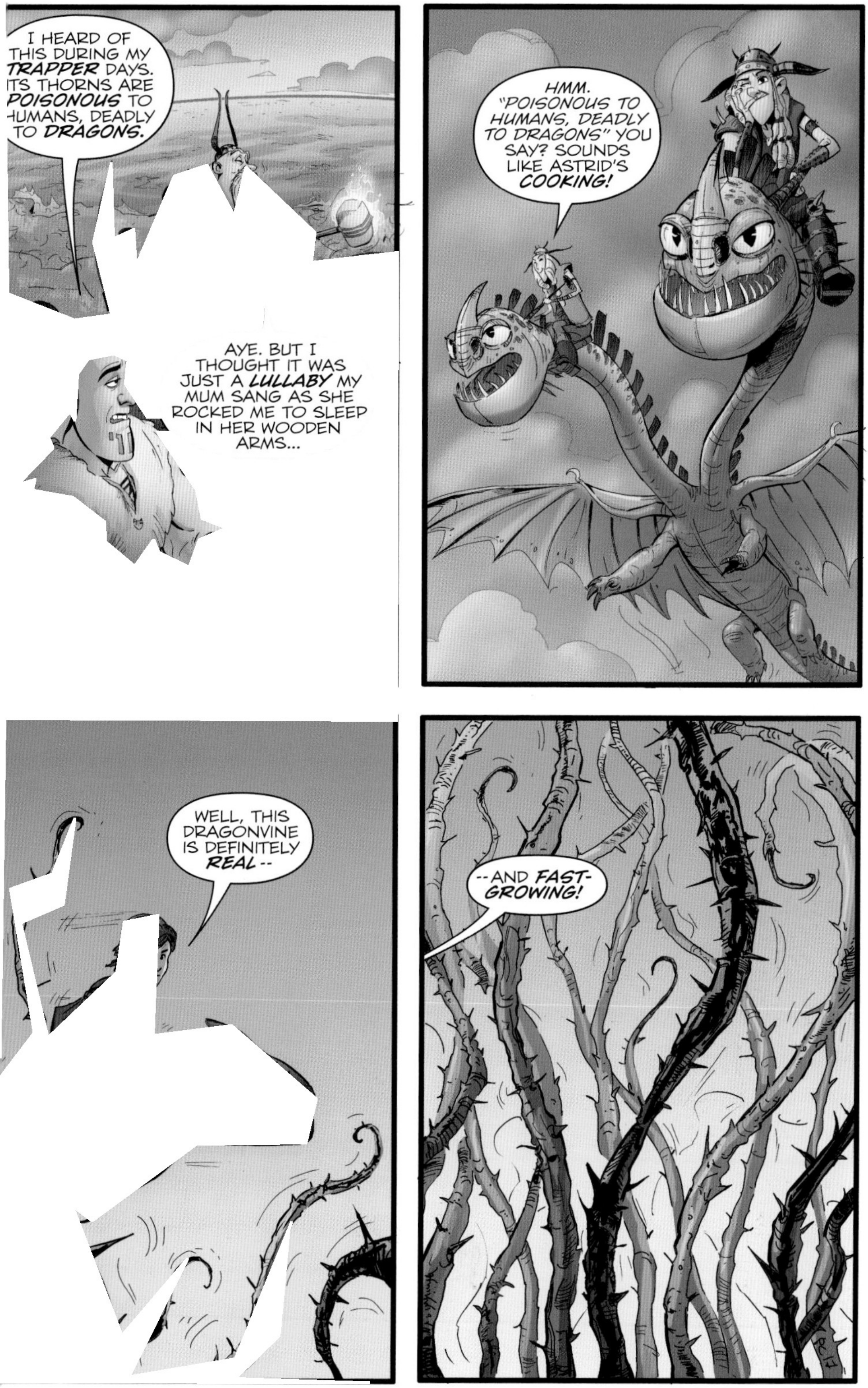
I HEARD OF THIS DURING MY TRAPPER DAYS. ITS THORNS ARE POISONOUS TO HUMANS, DEADLY TO DRAGONS.
AYE. BUT I THOUGHT IT WAS JUST A LULLABY MY MUM SANG AS SHE ROCKED ME TO SLEEP IN HER WOODEN ARMS...
HMM. "POISONOUS TO HUMANS, DEADLY TO DRAGONS" YOU SAY? SOUNDS LIKE ASTRID'S COOKING!
WELL, THIS DRAGONVINE IS DEFINITELY REAL --
--AND FAST-GROWING!

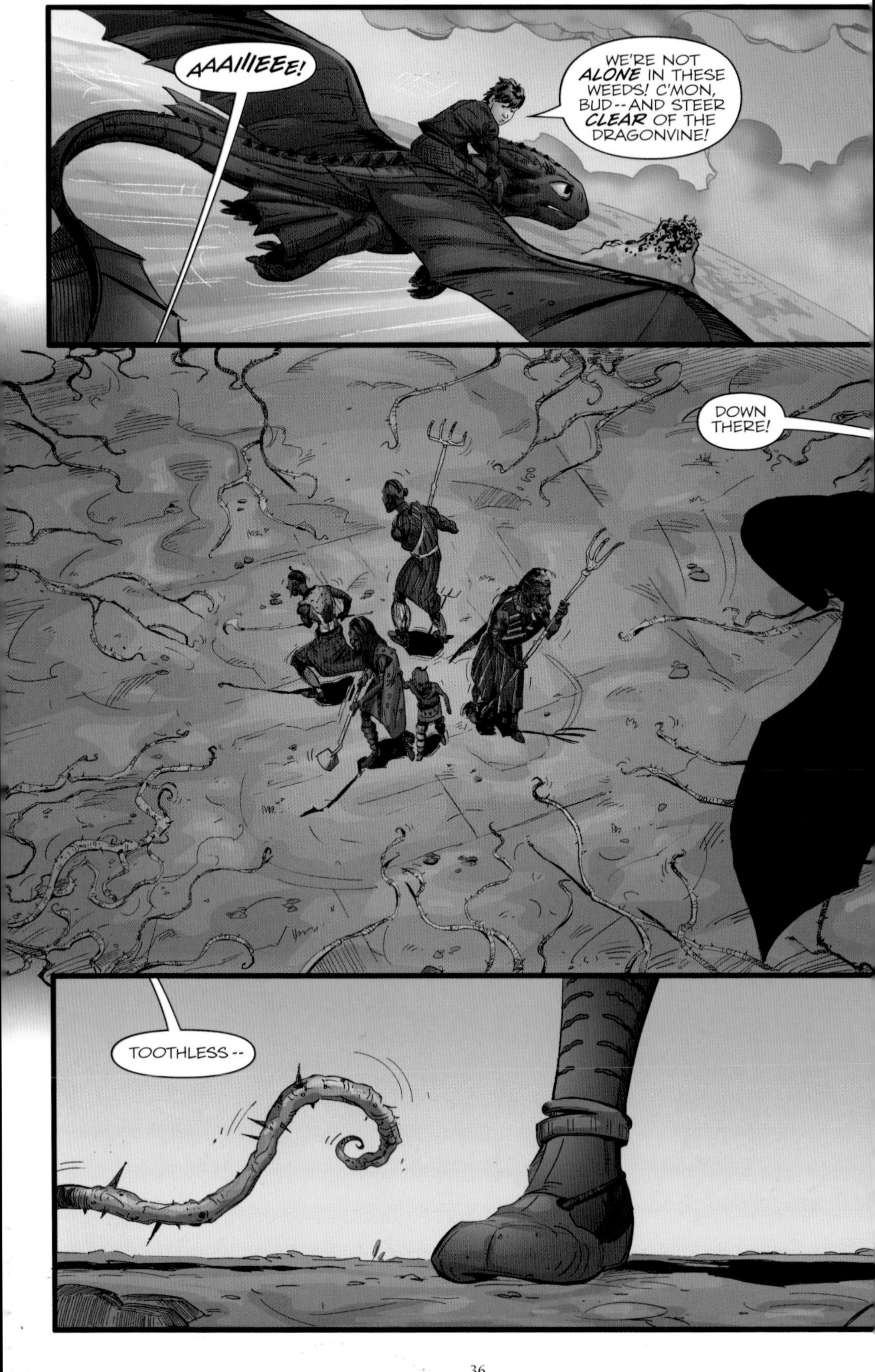
AAAIIIEEE!
WE'RE NOT ALONE IN THESE WEEDS! C'MON, BUD--AND STEER CLEAR OF THE DRAGONVINE!
DOWN THERE!
TOOTHLESS--

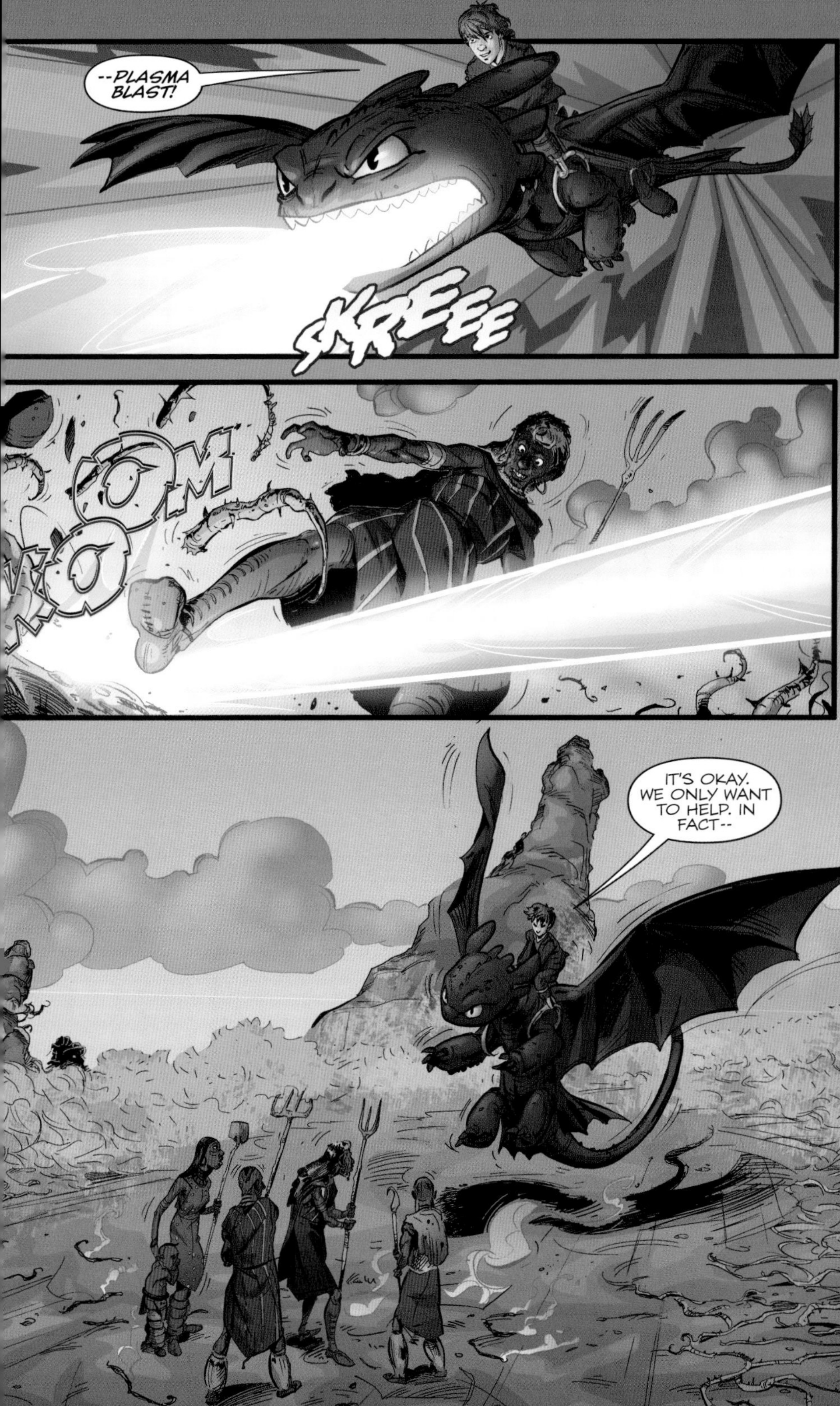
--PLASMA BLAST!
SKREEE
KA-BOOM
IT'S OKAY. WE ONLY WANT TO HELP. IN FACT--

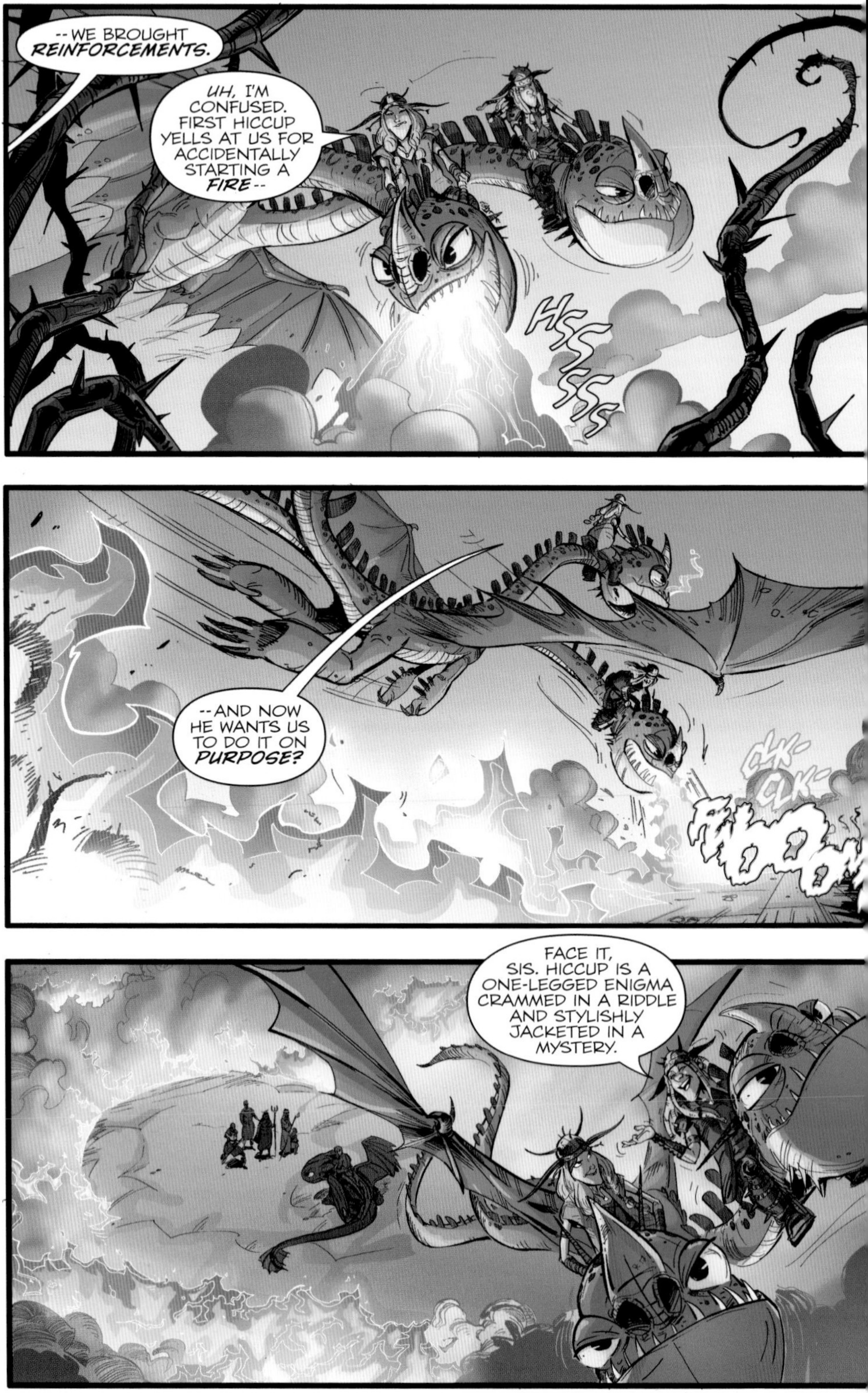
--WE BROUGHT *REINFORCEMENTS.*
UH, I'M CONFUSED. FIRST HICCUP YELLS AT US FOR ACCIDENTALLY STARTING A *FIRE*--
--AND NOW HE WANTS US TO DO IT ON *PURPOSE?*
FACE IT, SIS. HICCUP IS A ONE-LEGGED ENIGMA CRAMMED IN A RIDDLE AND STYLISHLY JACKETED IN A MYSTERY.

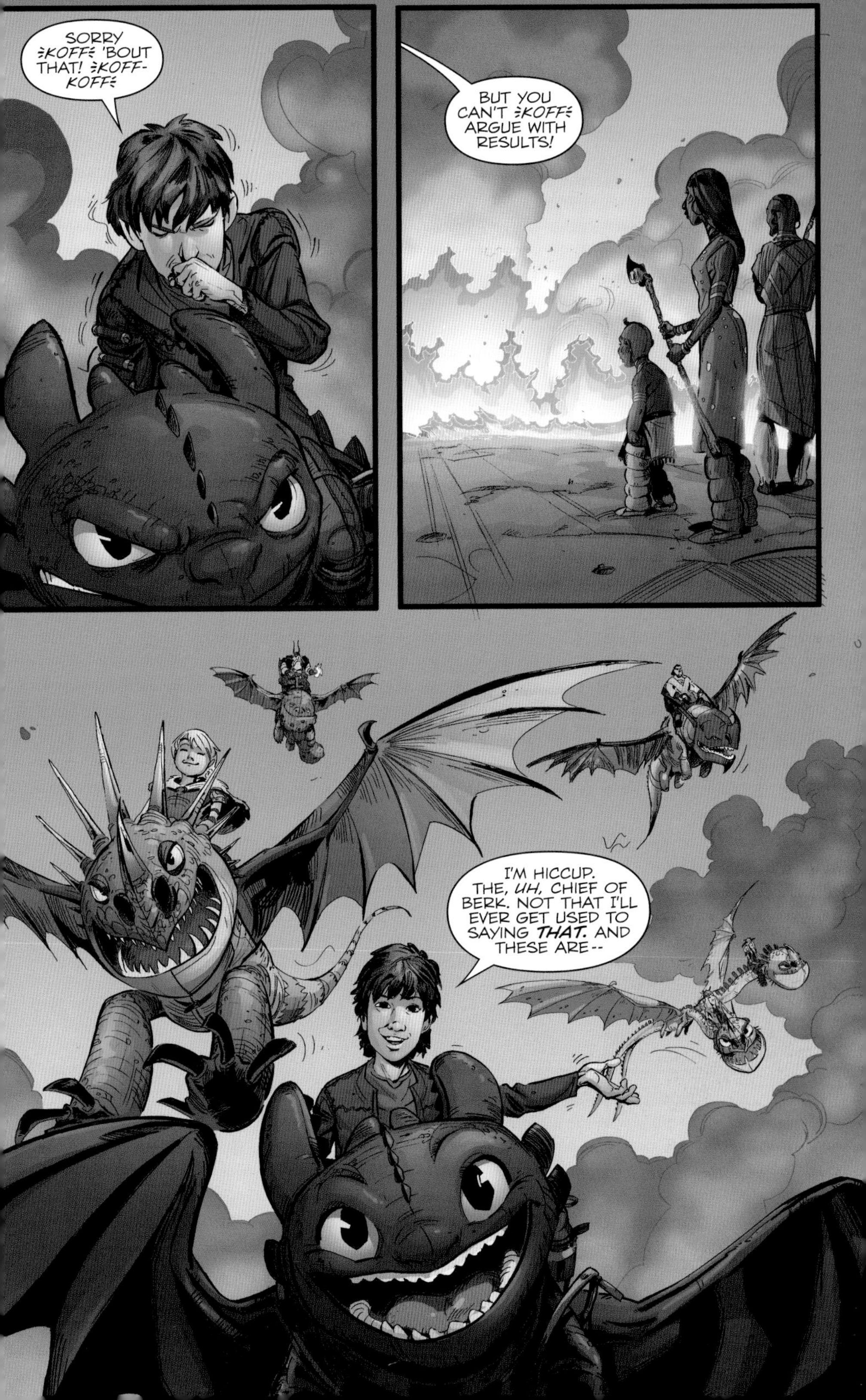
SORRY ⁼KOFF⁼ 'BOUT THAT! ⁼KOFF-KOFF⁼
BUT YOU CAN'T ⁼KOFF⁼ ARGUE WITH RESULTS!
I'M HICCUP. THE, *UH*, CHIEF OF BERK. NOT THAT I'LL EVER GET USED TO SAYING ***THAT.*** AND THESE ARE--

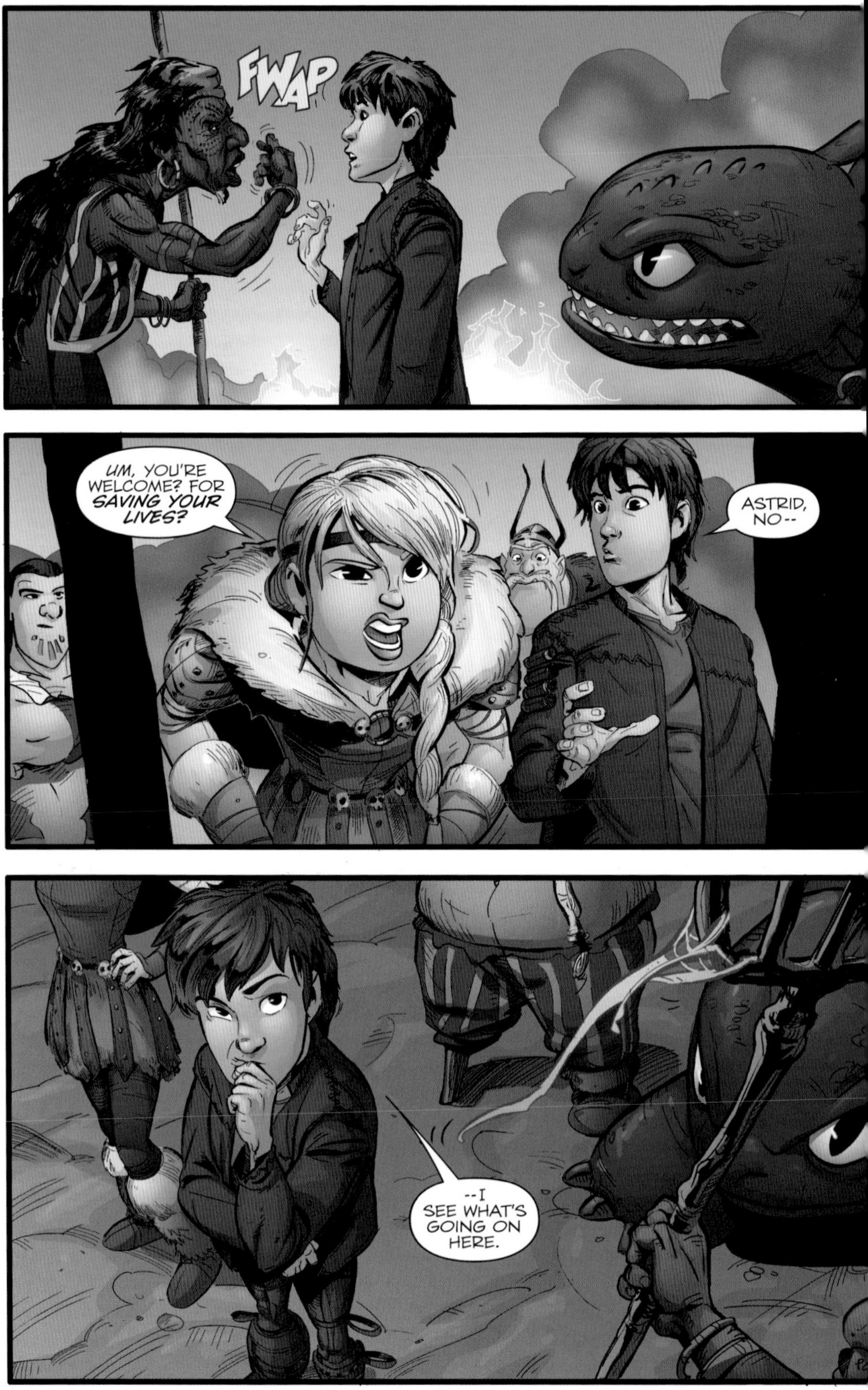
FWAP
UM, YOU'RE WELCOME? FOR SAVING YOUR LIVES?
ASTRID, NO--
--I SEE WHAT'S GOING ON HERE.

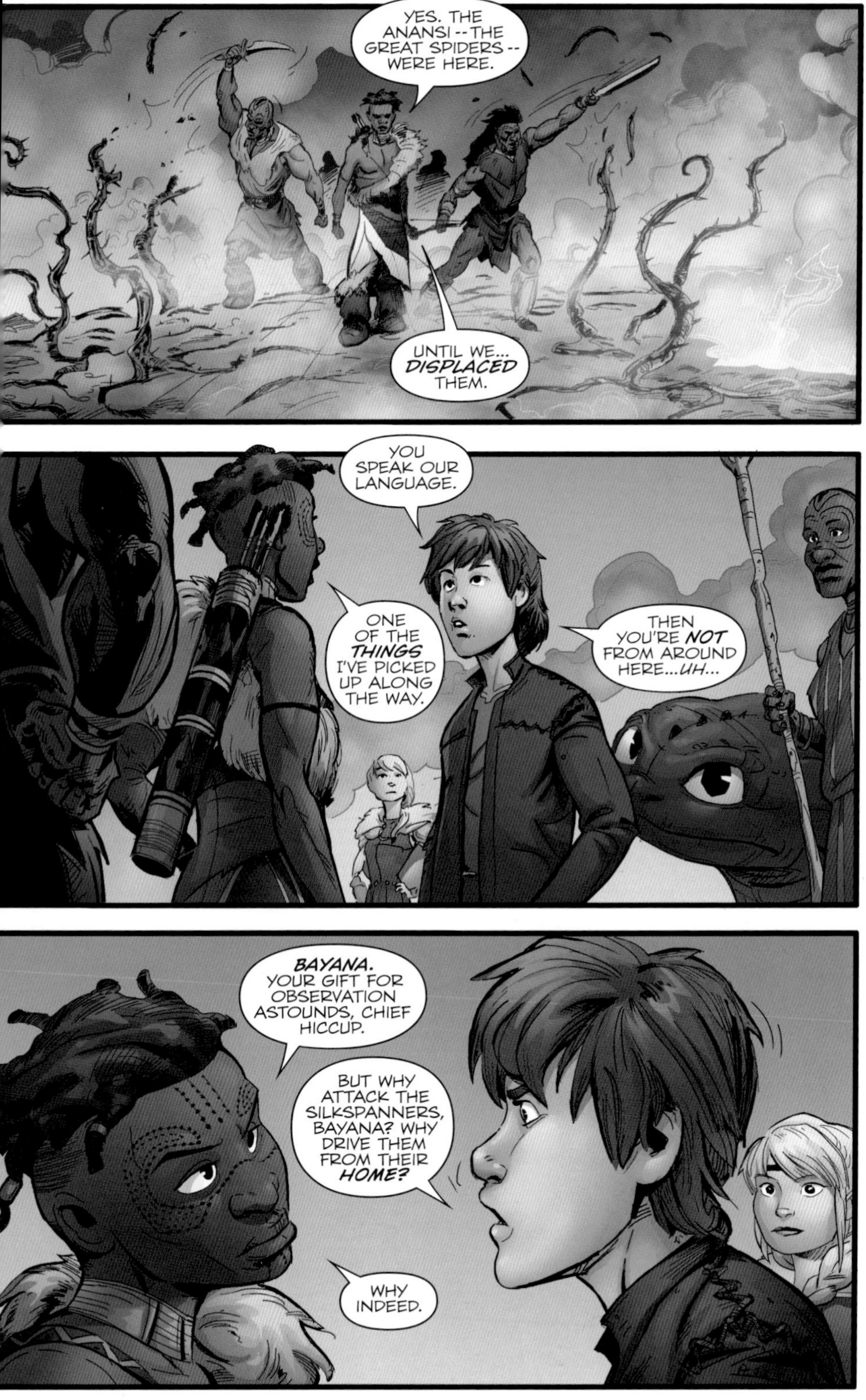
YES. THE ANANSI -- THE GREAT SPIDERS -- WERE HERE.
UNTIL WE... *DISPLACED* THEM.
YOU SPEAK OUR LANGUAGE.
ONE OF THE *THINGS* I'VE PICKED UP ALONG THE WAY.
THEN YOU'RE *NOT* FROM AROUND HERE...*UH*...
BAYANA. YOUR GIFT FOR OBSERVATION ASTOUNDS, CHIEF HICCUP.
BUT WHY ATTACK THE SILKSPANNERS, BAYANA? WHY DRIVE THEM FROM THEIR *HOME?*
WHY INDEED.

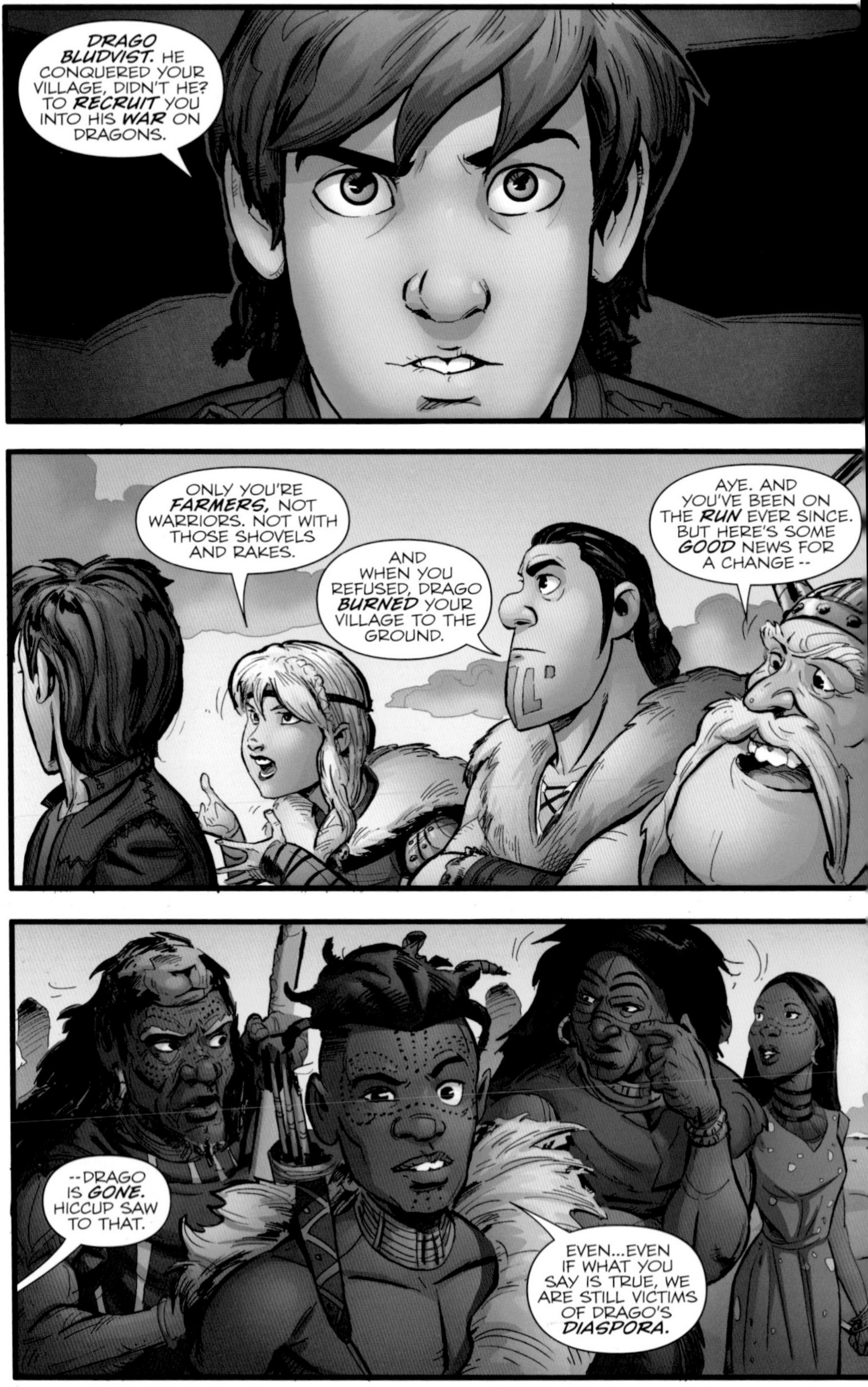
DRAGO BLUDVIST. HE CONQUERED YOUR VILLAGE, DIDN'T HE? TO RECRUIT YOU INTO HIS WAR ON DRAGONS.
ONLY YOU'RE FARMERS, NOT WARRIORS. NOT WITH THOSE SHOVELS AND RAKES.
AND WHEN YOU REFUSED, DRAGO BURNED YOUR VILLAGE TO THE GROUND.
AYE. AND YOU'VE BEEN ON THE RUN EVER SINCE. BUT HERE'S SOME GOOD NEWS FOR A CHANGE --
--DRAGO IS GONE. HICCUP SAW TO THAT.
EVEN...EVEN IF WHAT YOU SAY IS TRUE, WE ARE STILL VICTIMS OF DRAGO'S DIASPORA.

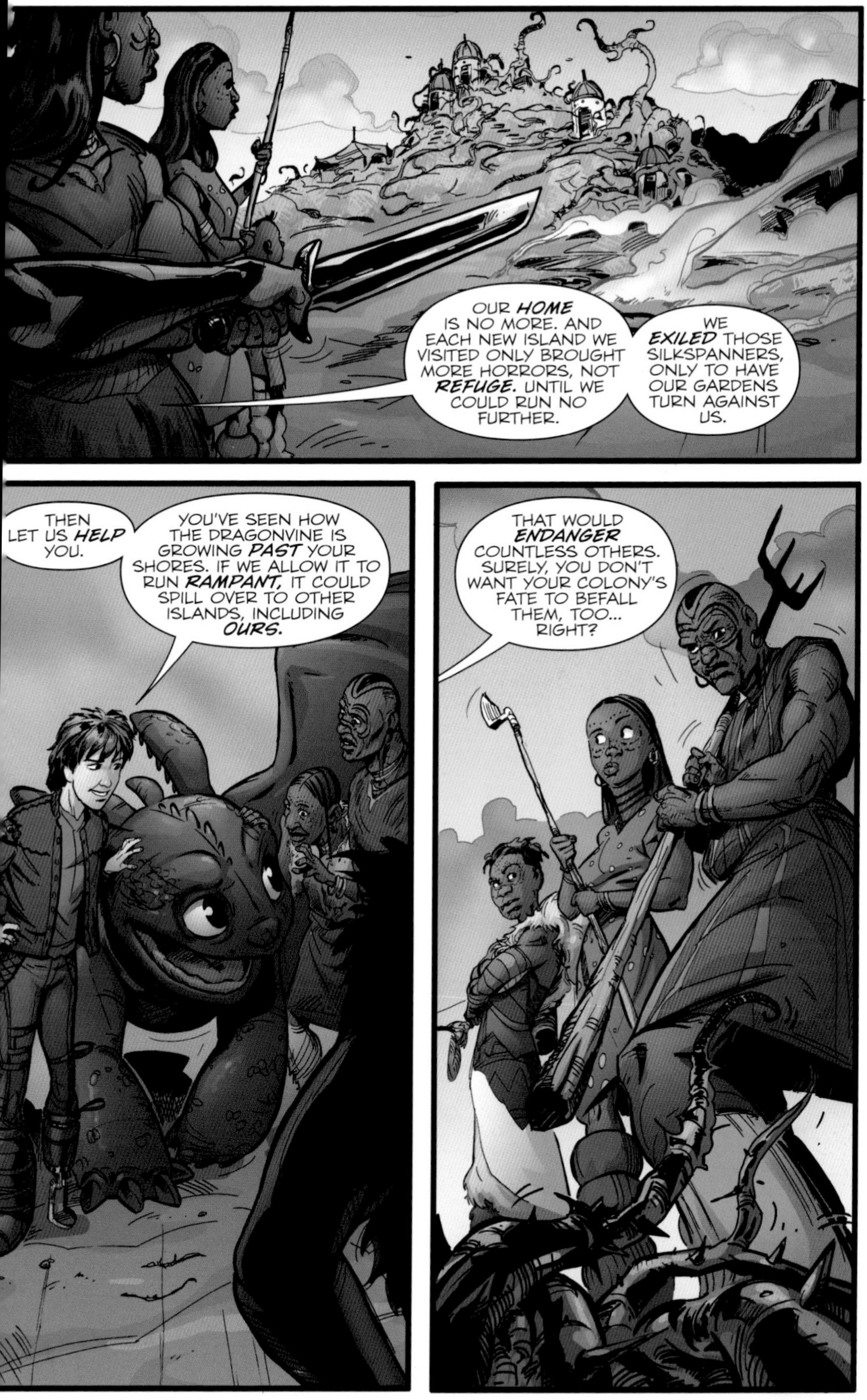
OUR HOME IS NO MORE. AND EACH NEW ISLAND WE VISITED ONLY BROUGHT MORE HORRORS, NOT REFUGE. UNTIL WE COULD RUN NO FURTHER.
WE EXILED THOSE SILKSPANNERS, ONLY TO HAVE OUR GARDENS TURN AGAINST US.
THEN LET US HELP YOU.
YOU'VE SEEN HOW THE DRAGONVINE IS GROWING PAST YOUR SHORES. IF WE ALLOW IT TO RUN RAMPANT, IT COULD SPILL OVER TO OTHER ISLANDS, INCLUDING OURS.
THAT WOULD ENDANGER COUNTLESS OTHERS. SURELY, YOU DON'T WANT YOUR COLONY'S FATE TO BEFALL THEM, TOO... RIGHT?

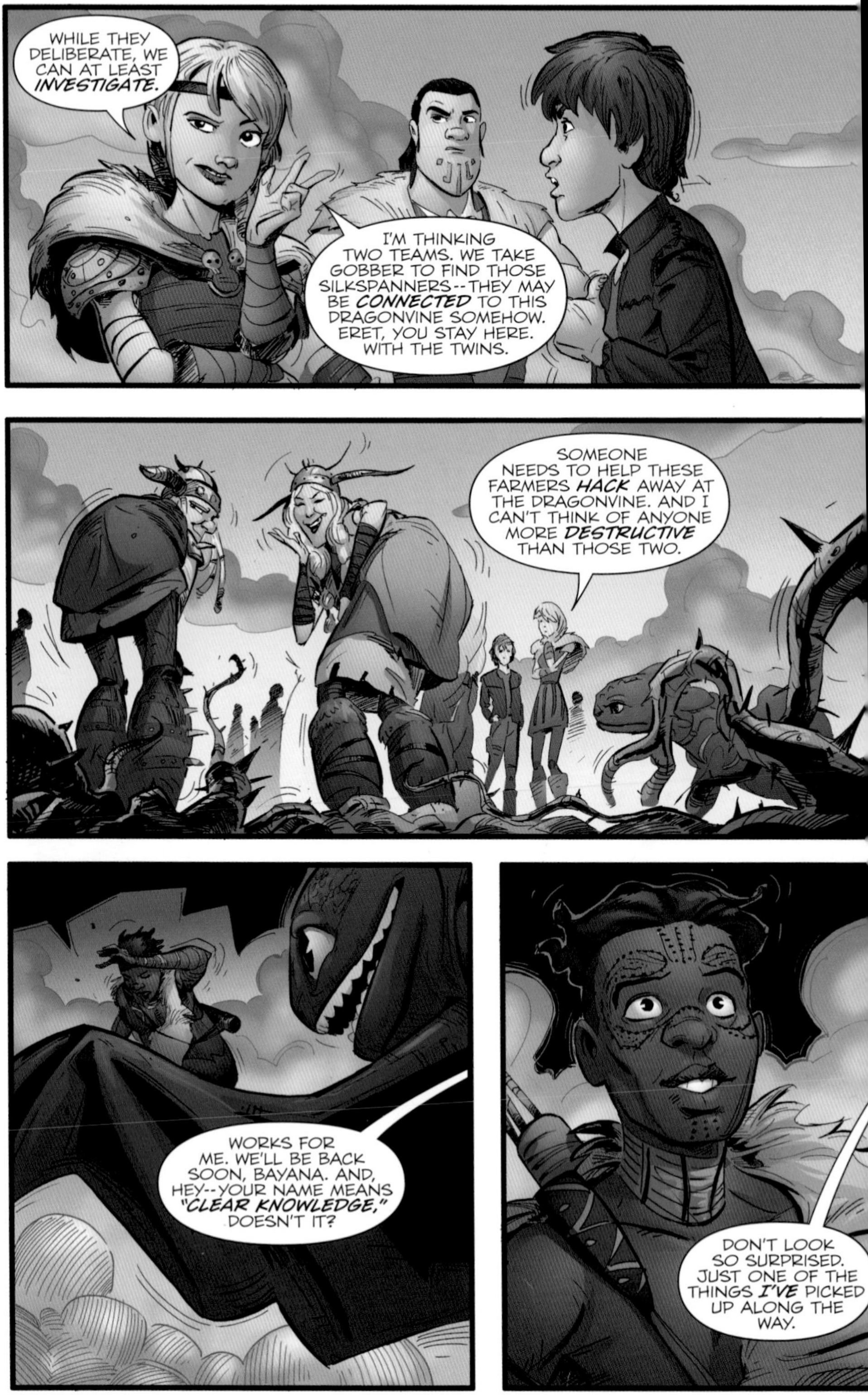
WHILE THEY DELIBERATE, WE CAN AT LEAST INVESTIGATE.
I'M THINKING TWO TEAMS. WE TAKE GOBBER TO FIND THOSE SILKSPANNERS--THEY MAY BE CONNECTED TO THIS DRAGONVINE SOMEHOW. ERET, YOU STAY HERE. WITH THE TWINS.
SOMEONE NEEDS TO HELP THESE FARMERS HACK AWAY AT THE DRAGONVINE. AND I CAN'T THINK OF ANYONE MORE DESTRUCTIVE THAN THOSE TWO.
WORKS FOR ME. WE'LL BE BACK SOON, BAYANA. AND, HEY--YOUR NAME MEANS "CLEAR KNOWLEDGE," DOESN'T IT?
DON'T LOOK SO SURPRISED. JUST ONE OF THE THINGS I'VE PICKED UP ALONG THE WAY.

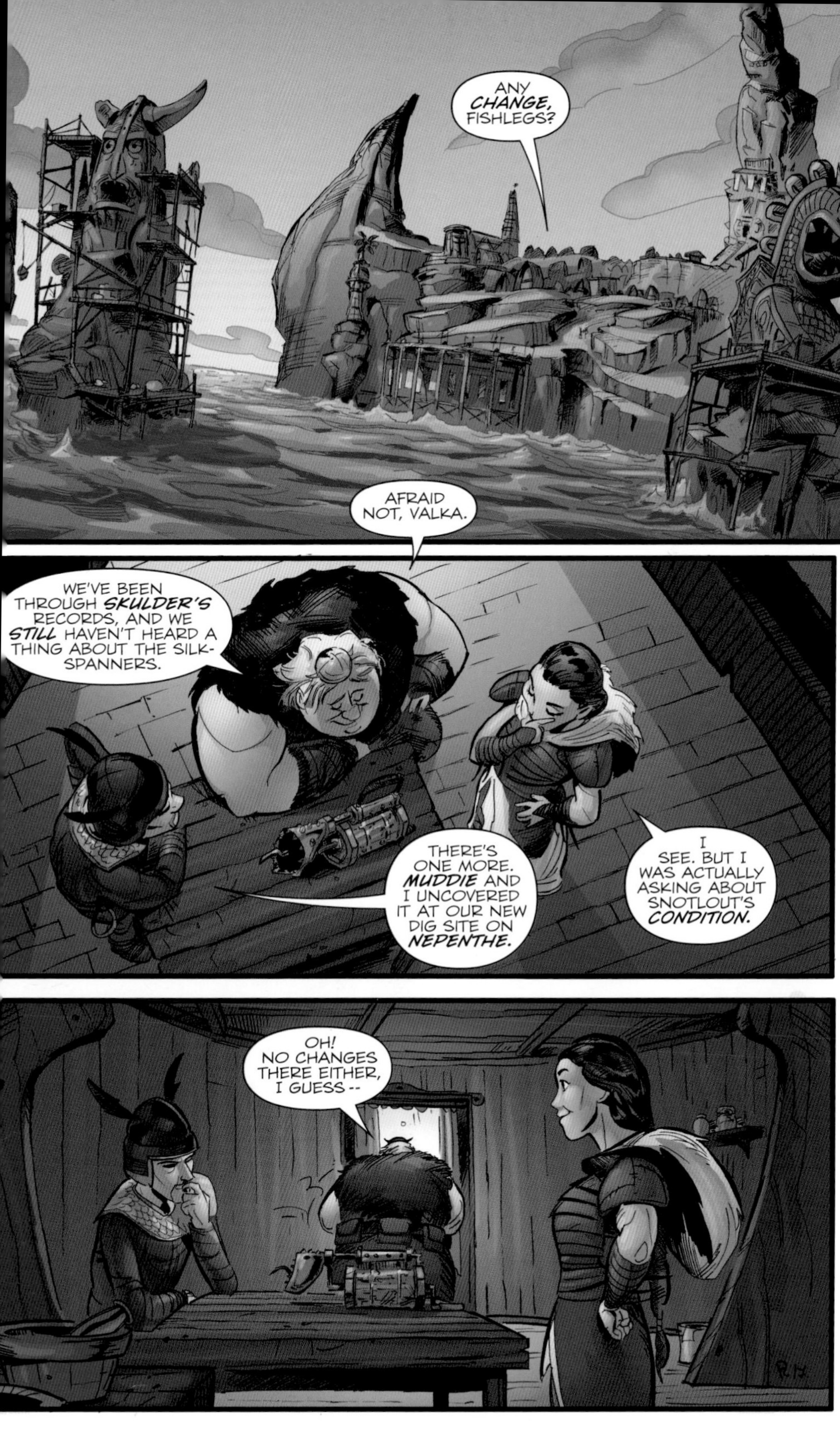
ANY CHANGE, FISHLEGS?
AFRAID NOT, VALKA.
WE'VE BEEN THROUGH SKULDER'S RECORDS, AND WE STILL HAVEN'T HEARD A THING ABOUT THE SILK-SPANNERS.
THERE'S ONE MORE. MUDDIE AND I UNCOVERED IT AT OUR NEW DIG SITE ON NEPENTHE.
I SEE. BUT I WAS ACTUALLY ASKING ABOUT SNOTLOUT'S CONDITION.
OH! NO CHANGES THERE EITHER, I GUESS --

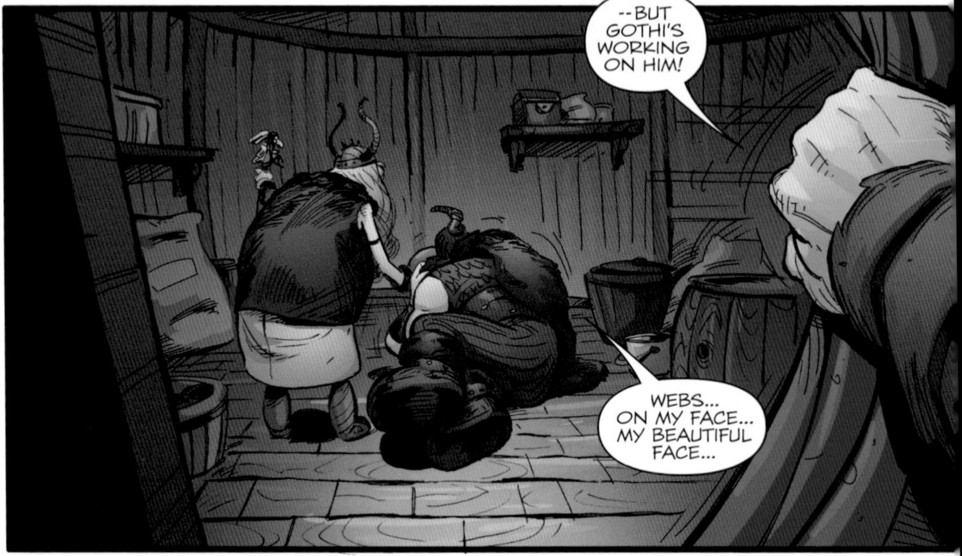
--BUT GOTHI'S WORKING ON HIM!
WEBS... ON MY FACE... MY BEAUTIFUL FACE...

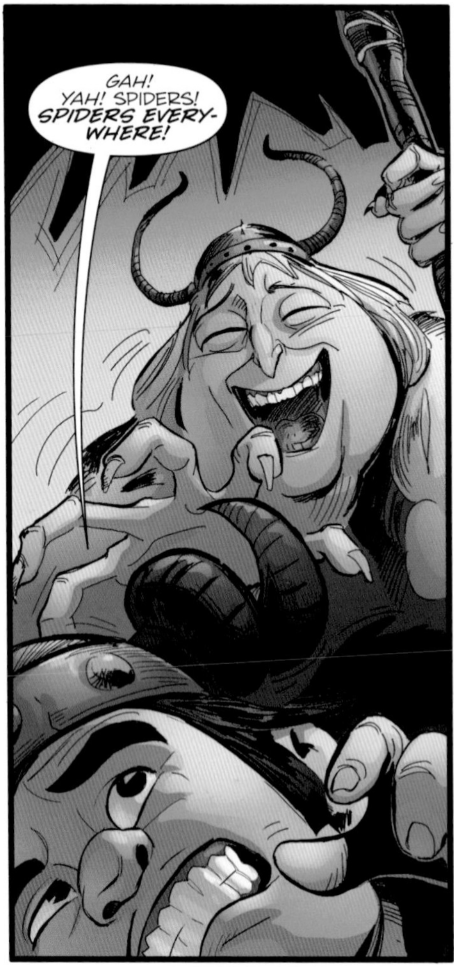
GAH! YAH! SPIDERS! **SPIDERS EVERYWHERE!**

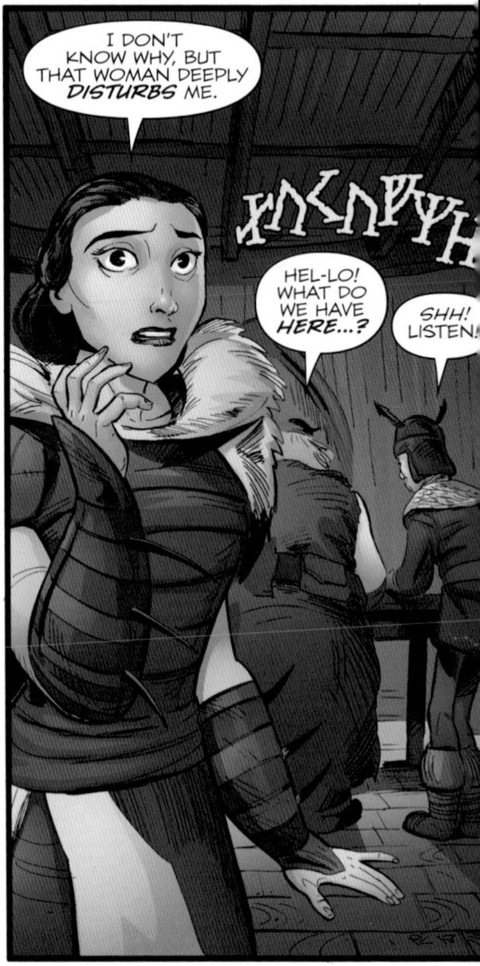
I DON'T KNOW WHY, BUT THAT WOMAN DEEPLY ***DISTURBS*** ME.
HEL-LO! WHAT DO WE HAVE ***HERE...?***
SHH! LISTEN!

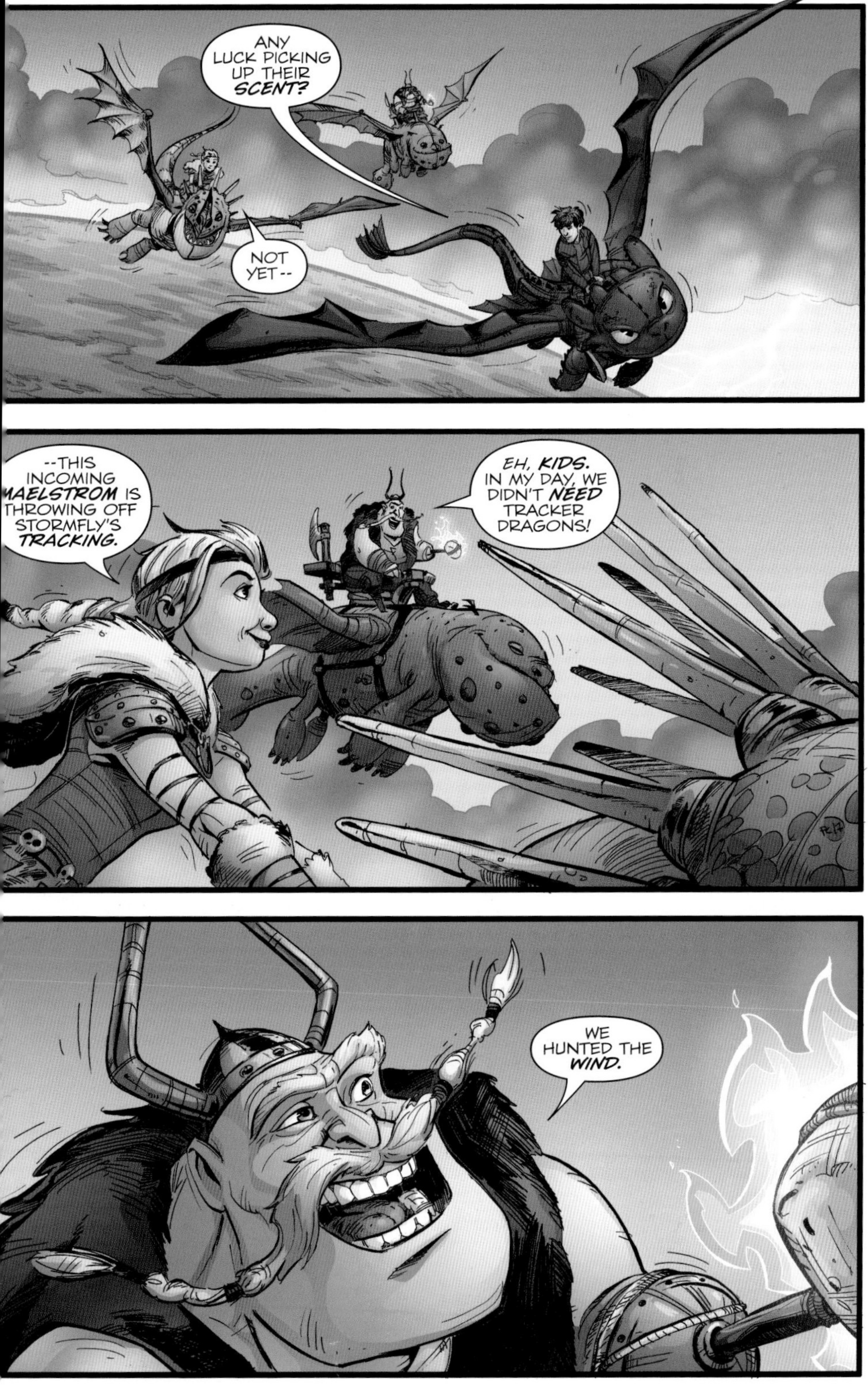
ANY LUCK PICKING UP THEIR SCENT?
NOT YET--
--THIS INCOMING MAELSTROM IS THROWING OFF STORMFLY'S TRACKING.
EH, KIDS. IN MY DAY, WE DIDN'T NEED TRACKER DRAGONS!
WE HUNTED THE WIND.

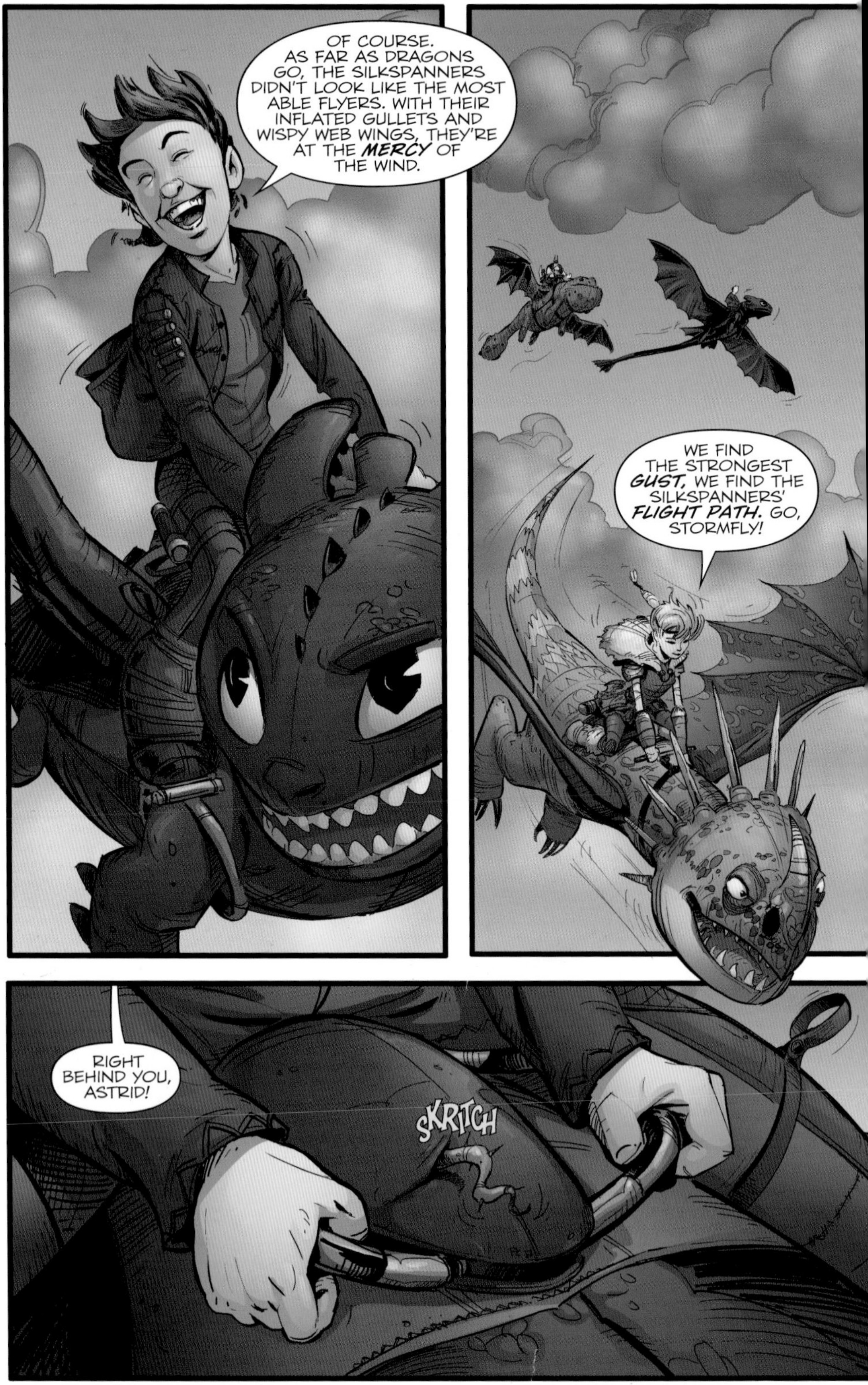
OF COURSE. AS FAR AS DRAGONS GO, THE SILKSPANNERS DIDN'T LOOK LIKE THE MOST ABLE FLYERS. WITH THEIR INFLATED GULLETS AND WISPY WEB WINGS, THEY'RE AT THE MERCY OF THE WIND.
WE FIND THE STRONGEST GUST, WE FIND THE SILKSPANNERS' FLIGHT PATH. GO, STORMFLY!
RIGHT BEHIND YOU, ASTRID!
SKRITCH

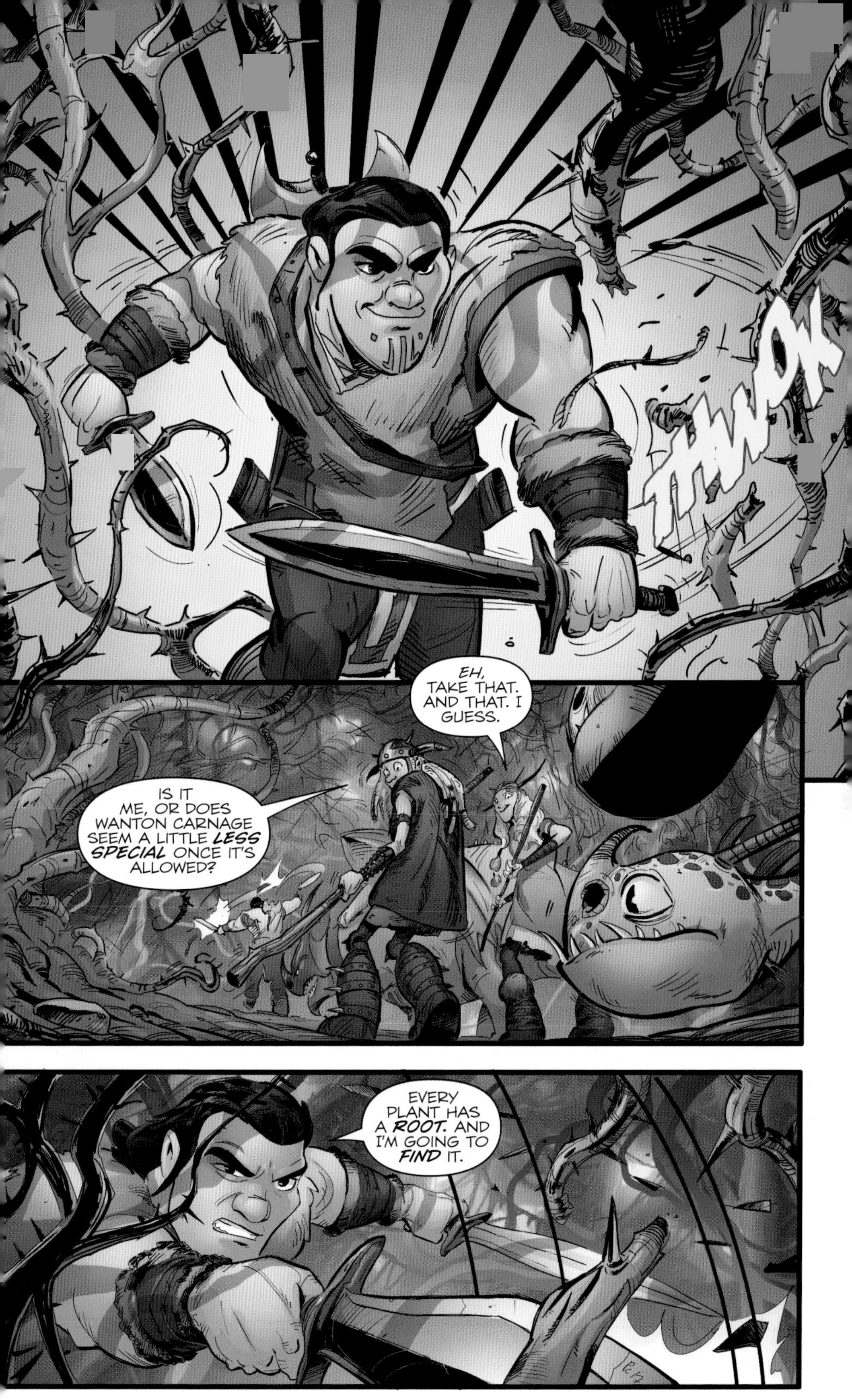
THWOK
EH, TAKE THAT. AND THAT. I GUESS.
IS IT ME, OR DOES WANTON CARNAGE SEEM A LITTLE LESS SPECIAL ONCE IT'S ALLOWED?
EVERY PLANT HAS A ROOT. AND I'M GOING TO FIND IT.

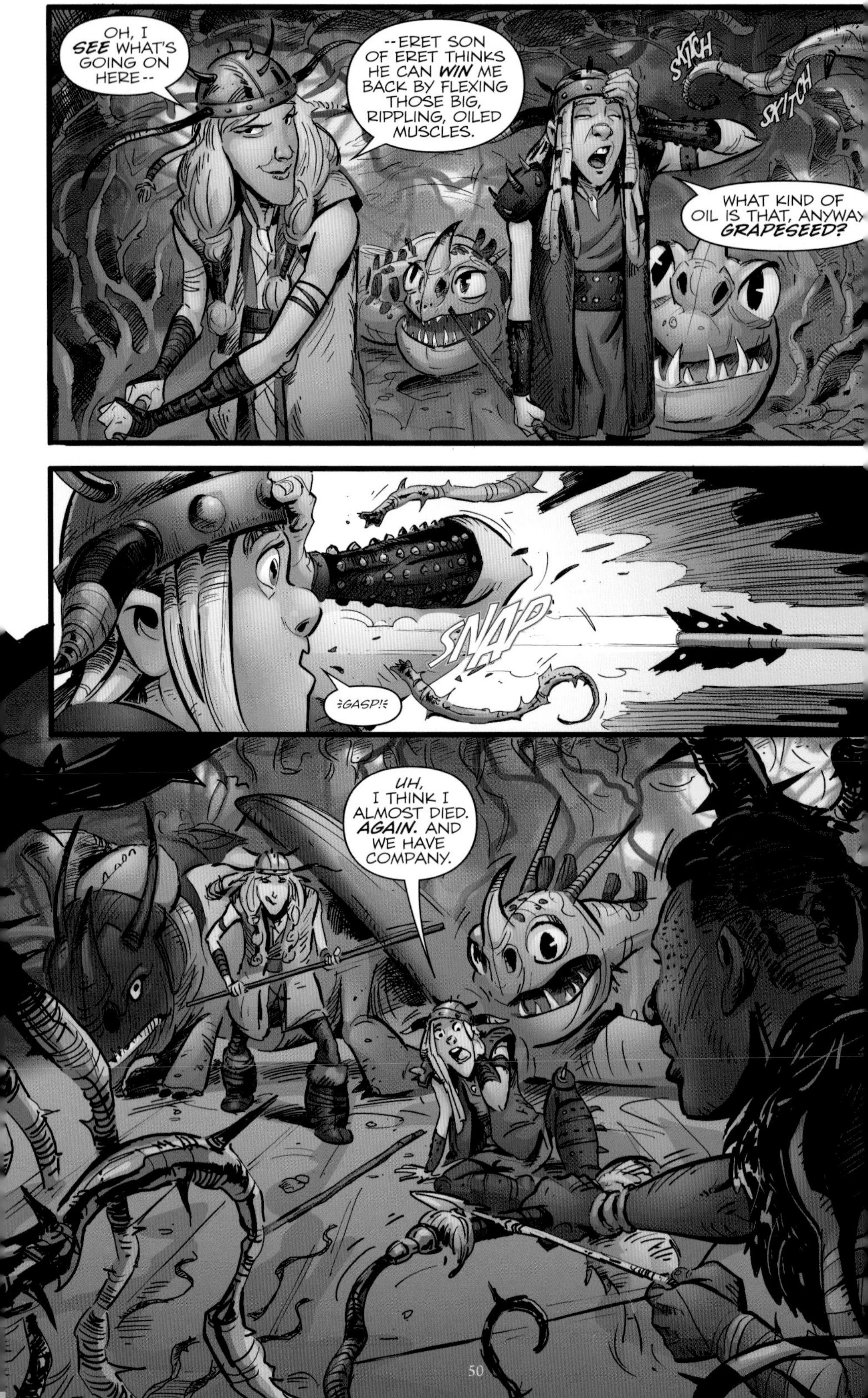
OH, I SEE WHAT'S GOING ON HERE--
--ERET SON OF ERET THINKS HE CAN WIN ME BACK BY FLEXING THOSE BIG, RIPPLING, OILED MUSCLES.
SKITCH
SKITCH
WHAT KIND OF OIL IS THAT, ANYWAY GRAPESEED?
SNAP
GASP!
UH, I THINK I ALMOST DIED. AGAIN. AND WE HAVE COMPANY.

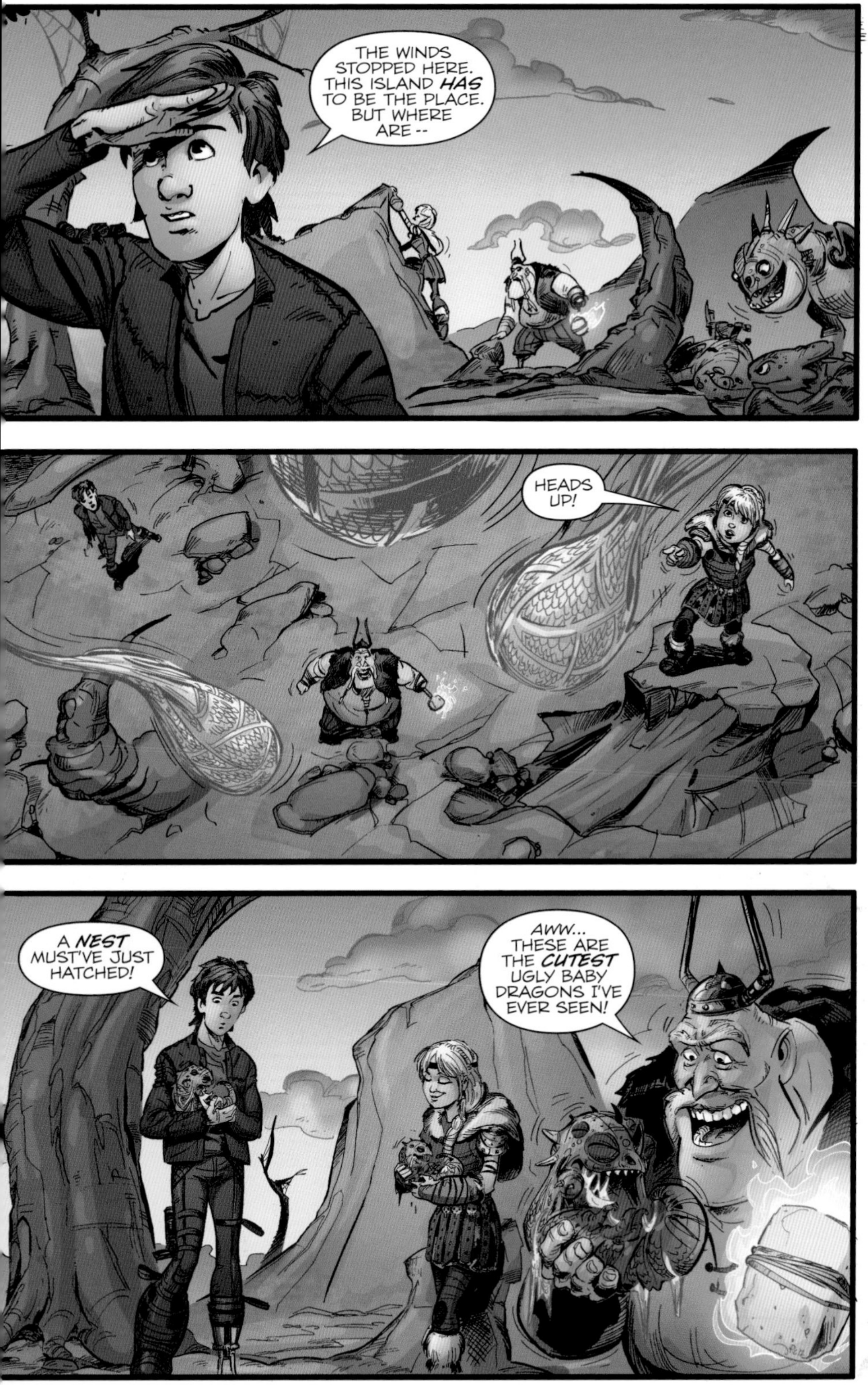
THE WINDS STOPPED HERE. THIS ISLAND *HAS* TO BE THE PLACE. BUT WHERE ARE --
HEADS UP!
A *NEST* MUST'VE JUST HATCHED!
AWW... THESE ARE THE *CUTEST* UGLY BABY DRAGONS I'VE EVER SEEN!

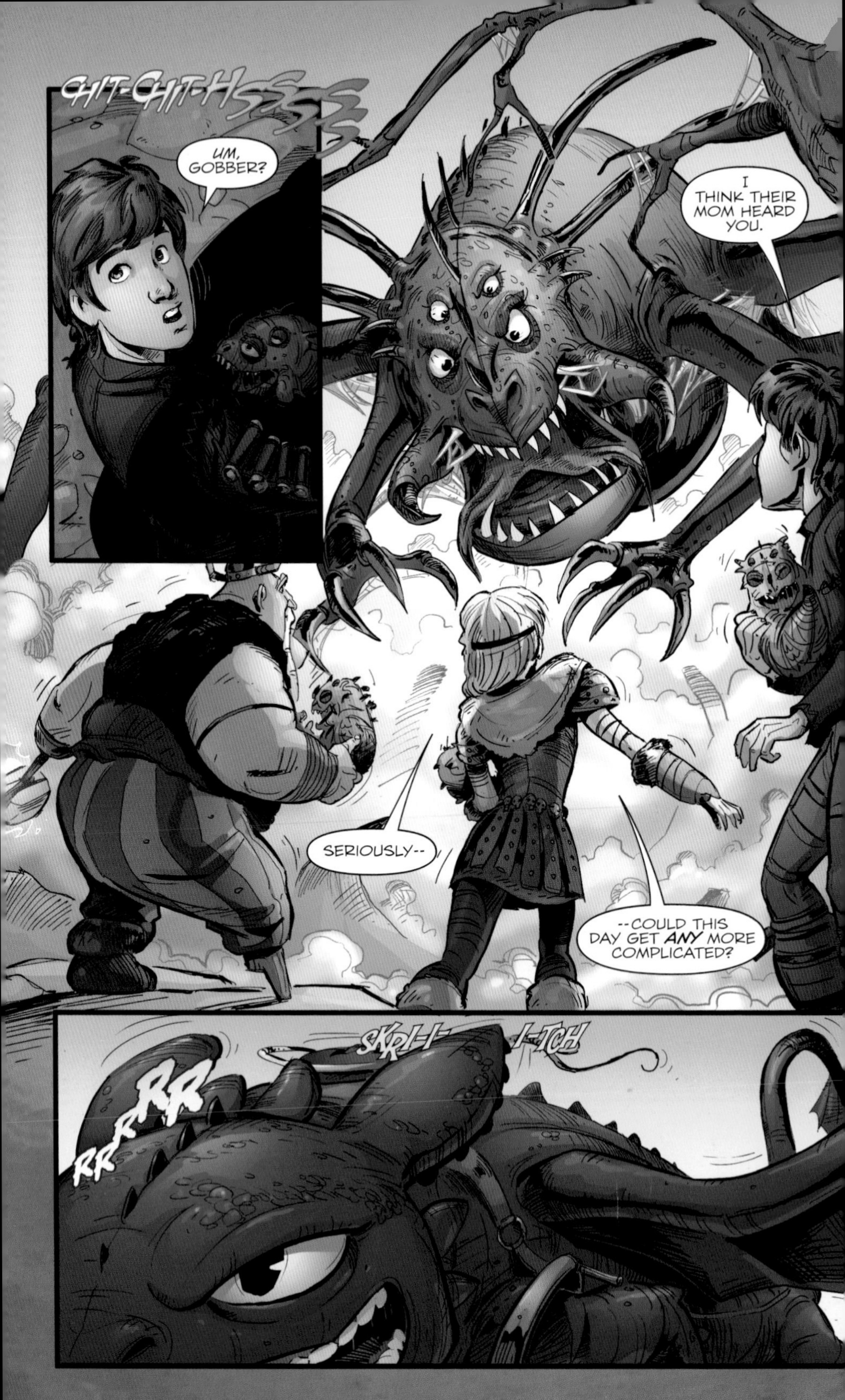
CHIT-CHIT-HSSSSSS
UM, GOBBER?
I THINK THEIR MOM HEARD YOU.
SERIOUSLY--
--COULD THIS DAY GET ANY MORE COMPLICATED?
SKRI-I-I-I-TCH
RRRRRR

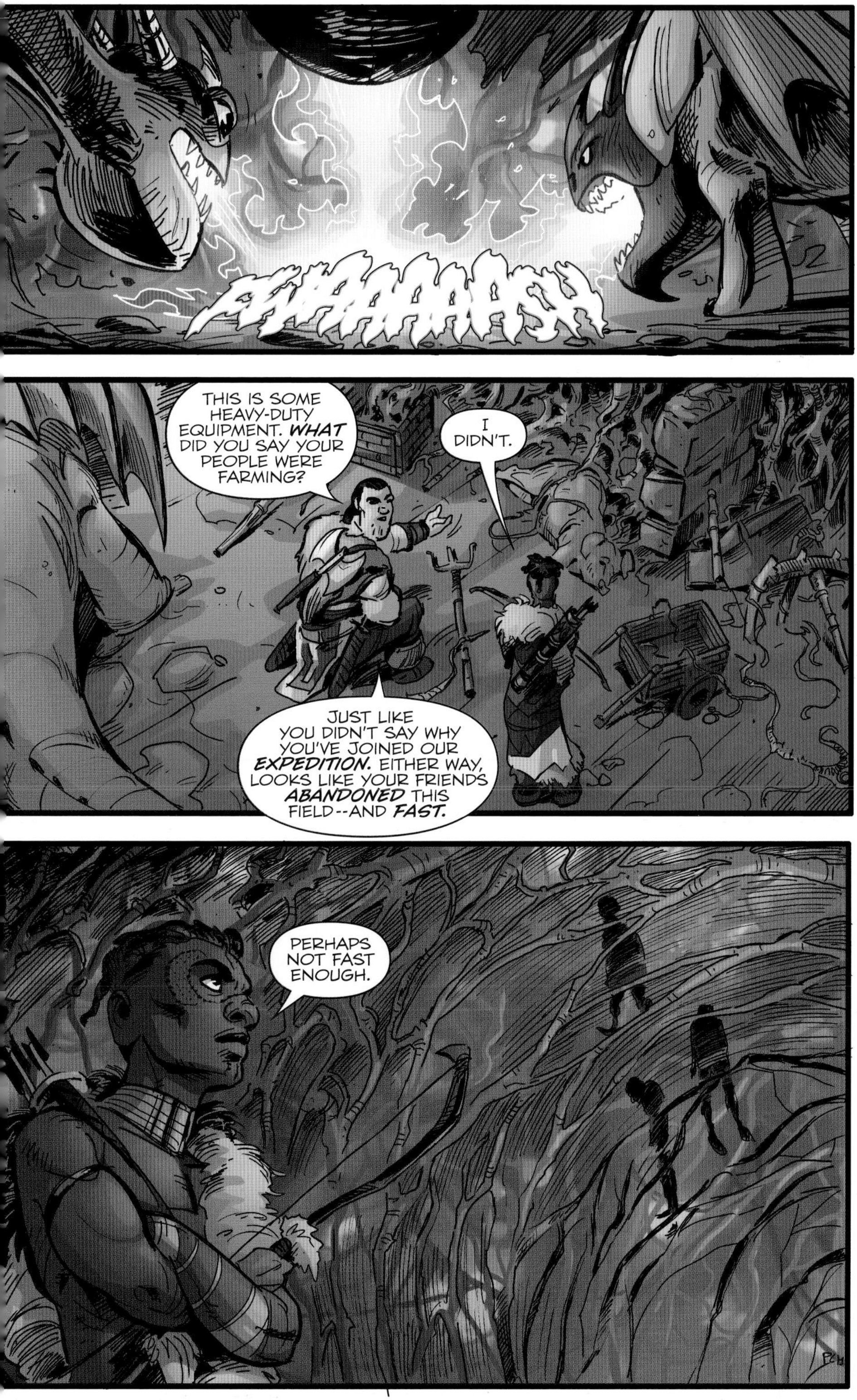
FWAAAAAASH
THIS IS SOME HEAVY-DUTY EQUIPMENT. WHAT DID YOU SAY YOUR PEOPLE WERE FARMING?
I DIDN'T.
JUST LIKE YOU DIDN'T SAY WHY YOU'VE JOINED OUR EXPEDITION. EITHER WAY, LOOKS LIKE YOUR FRIENDS ABANDONED THIS FIELD--AND FAST.
PERHAPS NOT FAST ENOUGH.

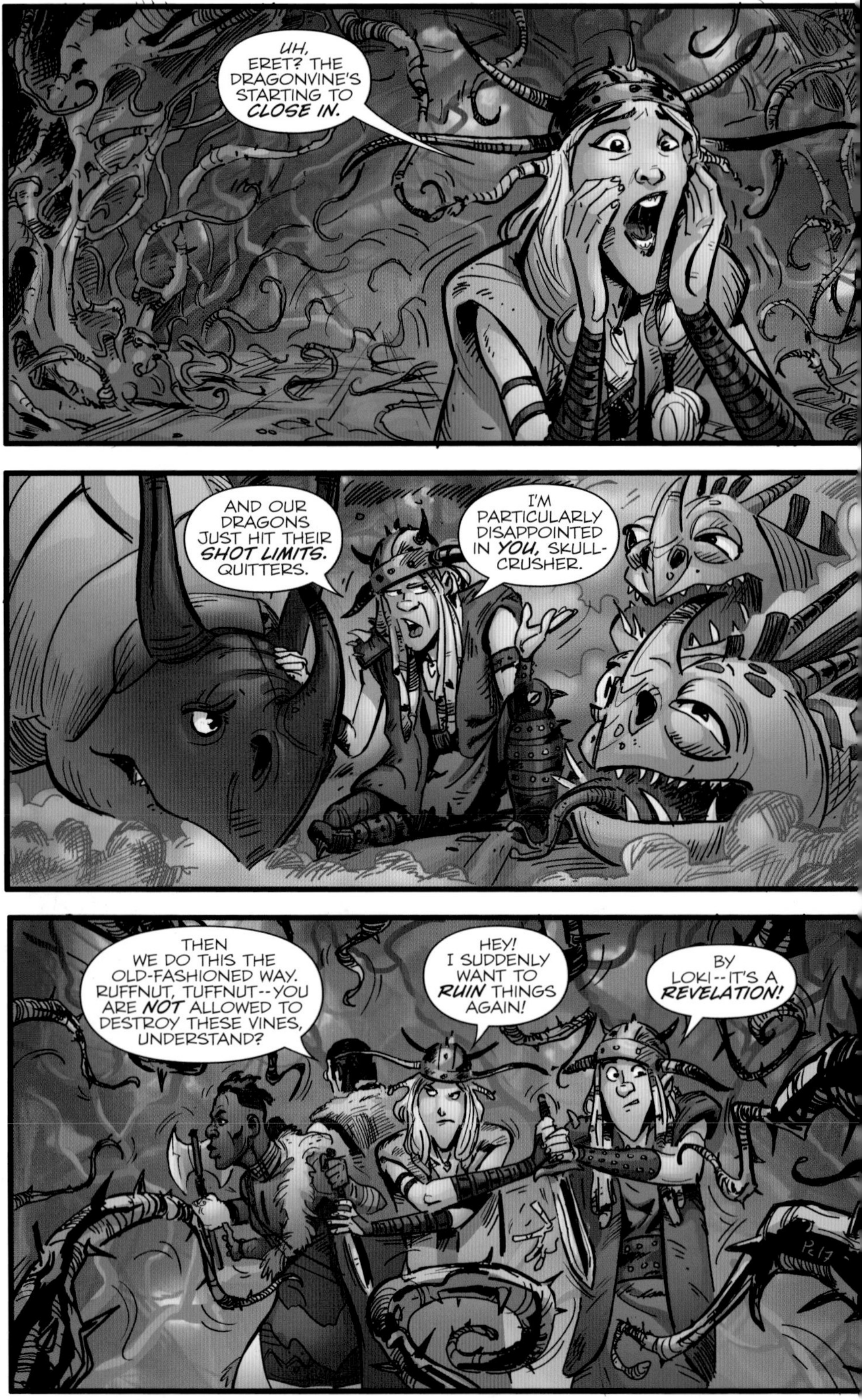
UH, ERET? THE DRAGONVINE'S STARTING TO CLOSE IN.
AND OUR DRAGONS JUST HIT THEIR SHOT LIMITS. QUITTERS.
I'M PARTICULARLY DISAPPOINTED IN YOU, SKULL-CRUSHER.
THEN WE DO THIS THE OLD-FASHIONED WAY. RUFFNUT, TUFFNUT--YOU ARE NOT ALLOWED TO DESTROY THESE VINES, UNDERSTAND?
HEY! I SUDDENLY WANT TO RUIN THINGS AGAIN!
BY LOKI--IT'S A REVELATION!

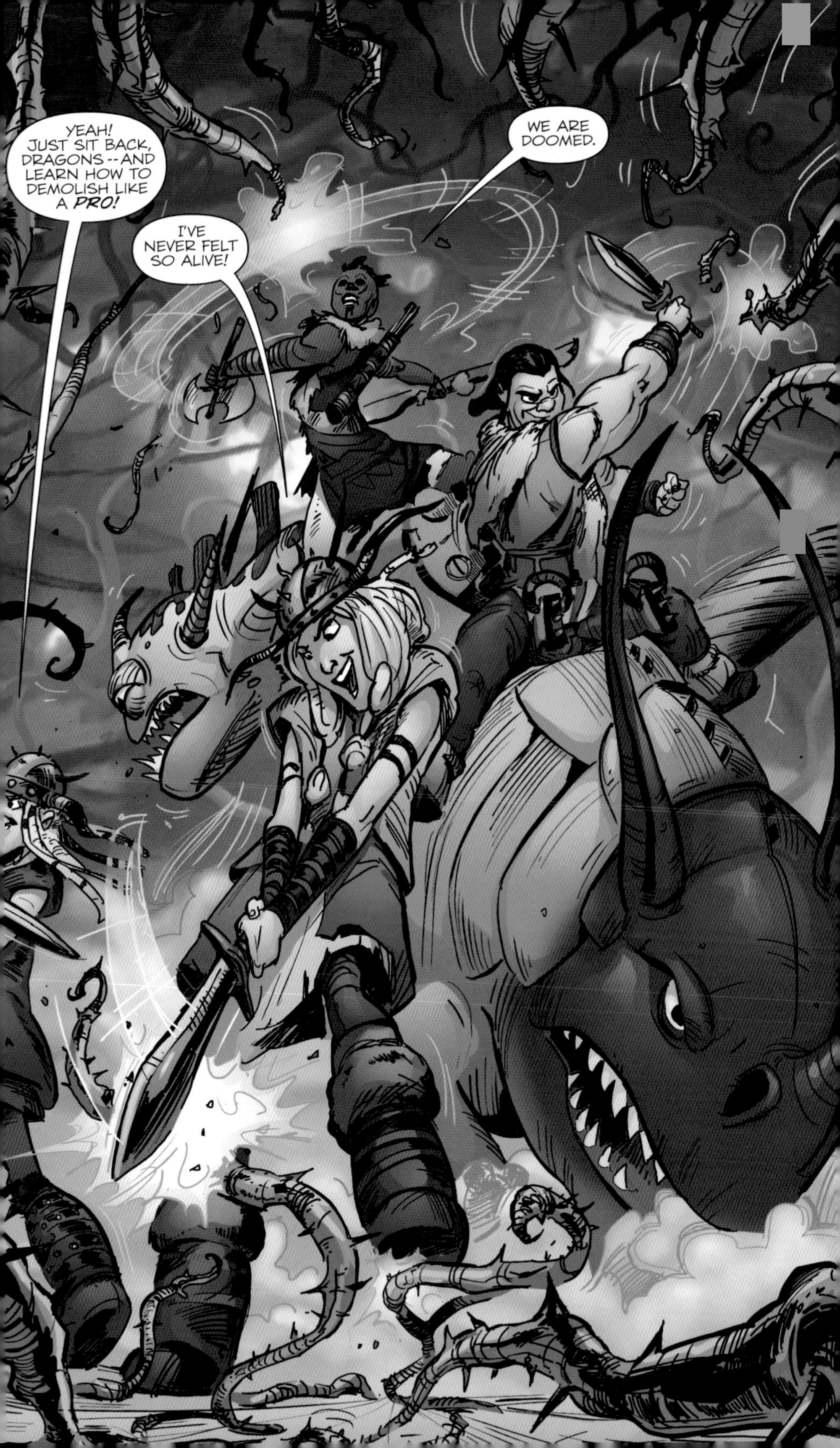
YEAH! JUST SIT BACK, DRAGONS--AND LEARN HOW TO DEMOLISH LIKE A PRO!
WE ARE DOOMED.
I'VE NEVER FELT SO ALIVE!

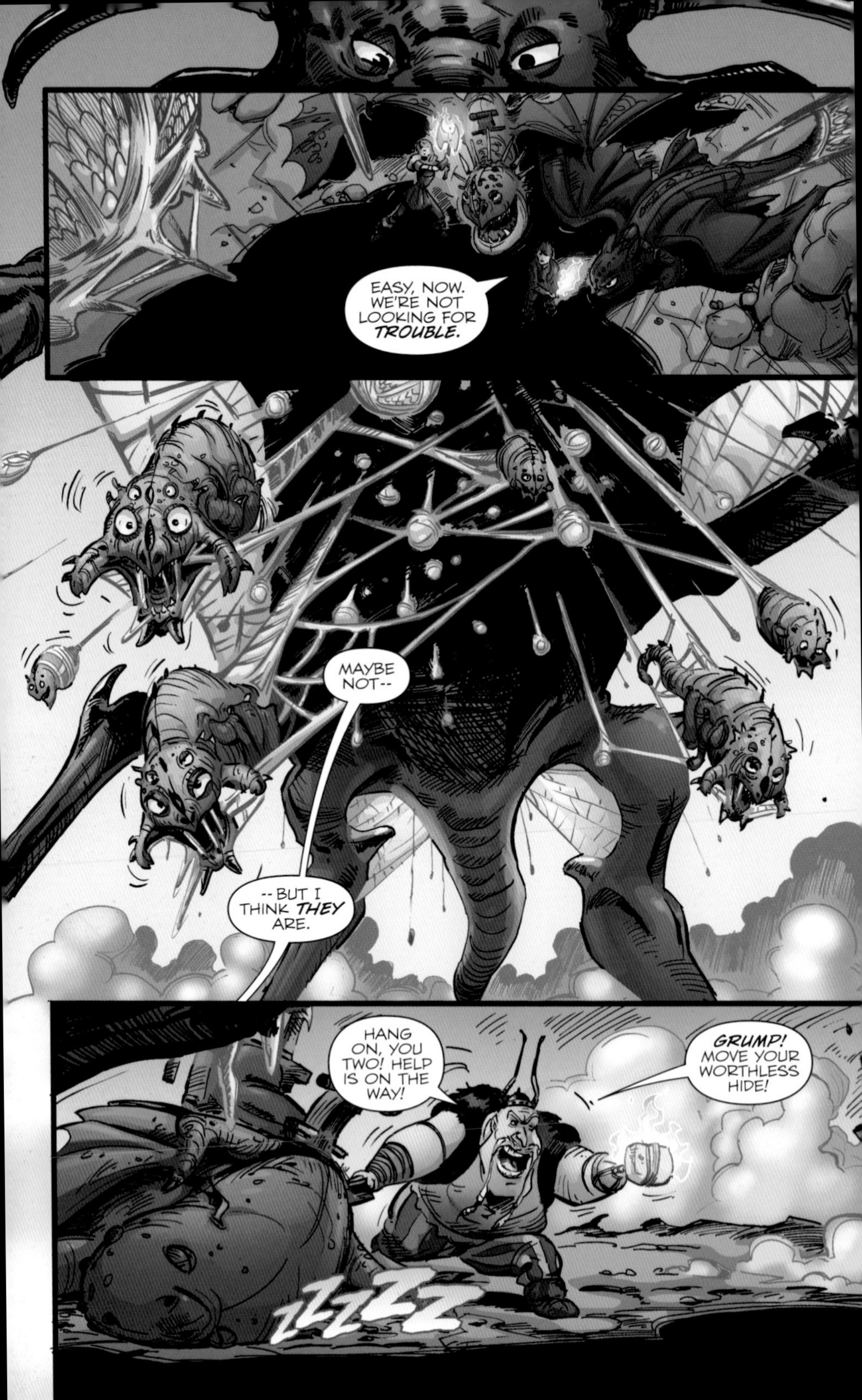
EASY, NOW. WE'RE NOT LOOKING FOR TROUBLE.
MAYBE NOT--
--BUT I THINK THEY ARE.
HANG ON, YOU TWO! HELP IS ON THE WAY!
GRUMP! MOVE YOUR WORTHLESS HIDE!
ZZZZZ

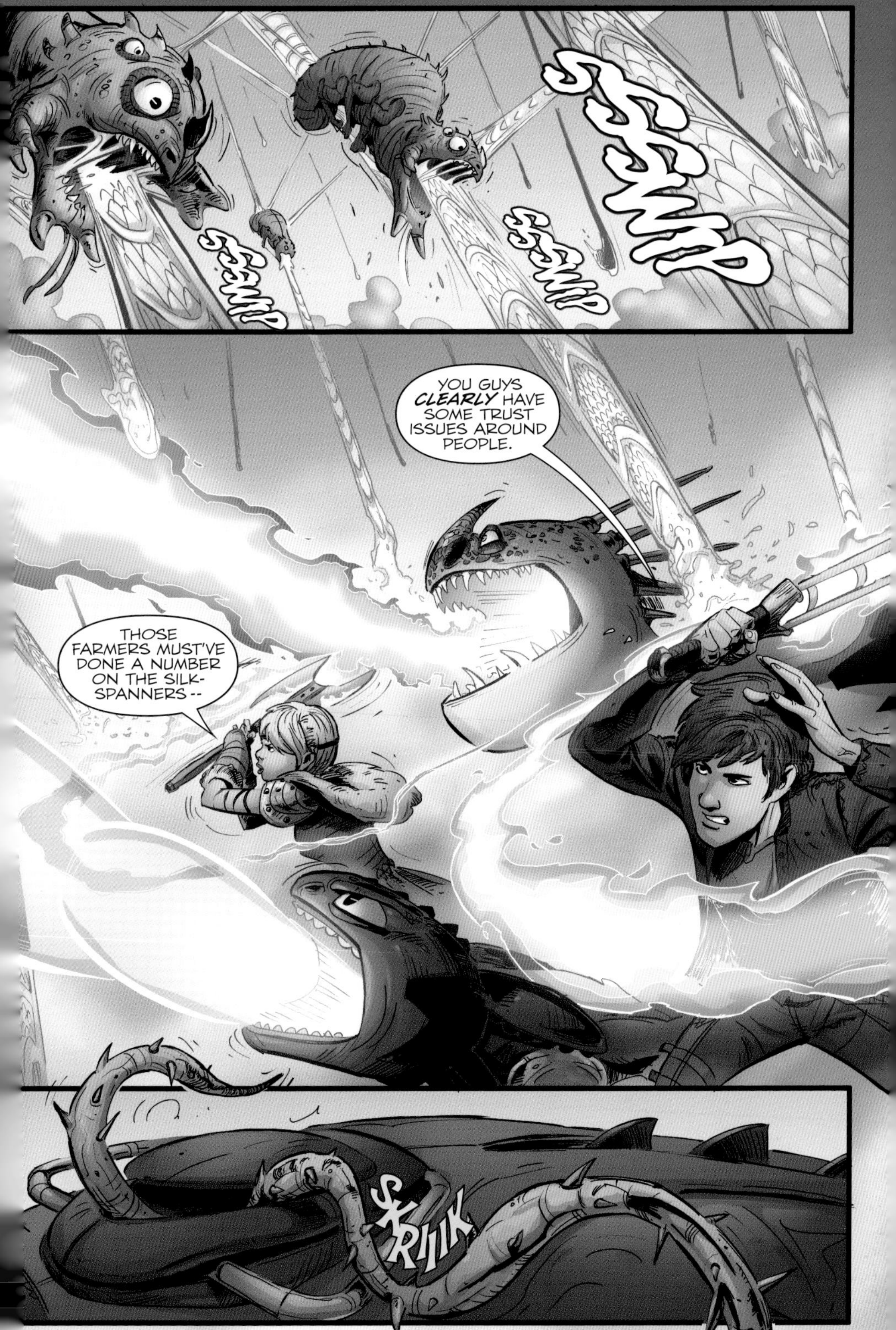
SSSWIP
SSSWIP
SSSWIP
YOU GUYS CLEARLY HAVE SOME TRUST ISSUES AROUND PEOPLE.
THOSE FARMERS MUST'VE DONE A NUMBER ON THE SILK-SPANNERS --
SKRIIIK

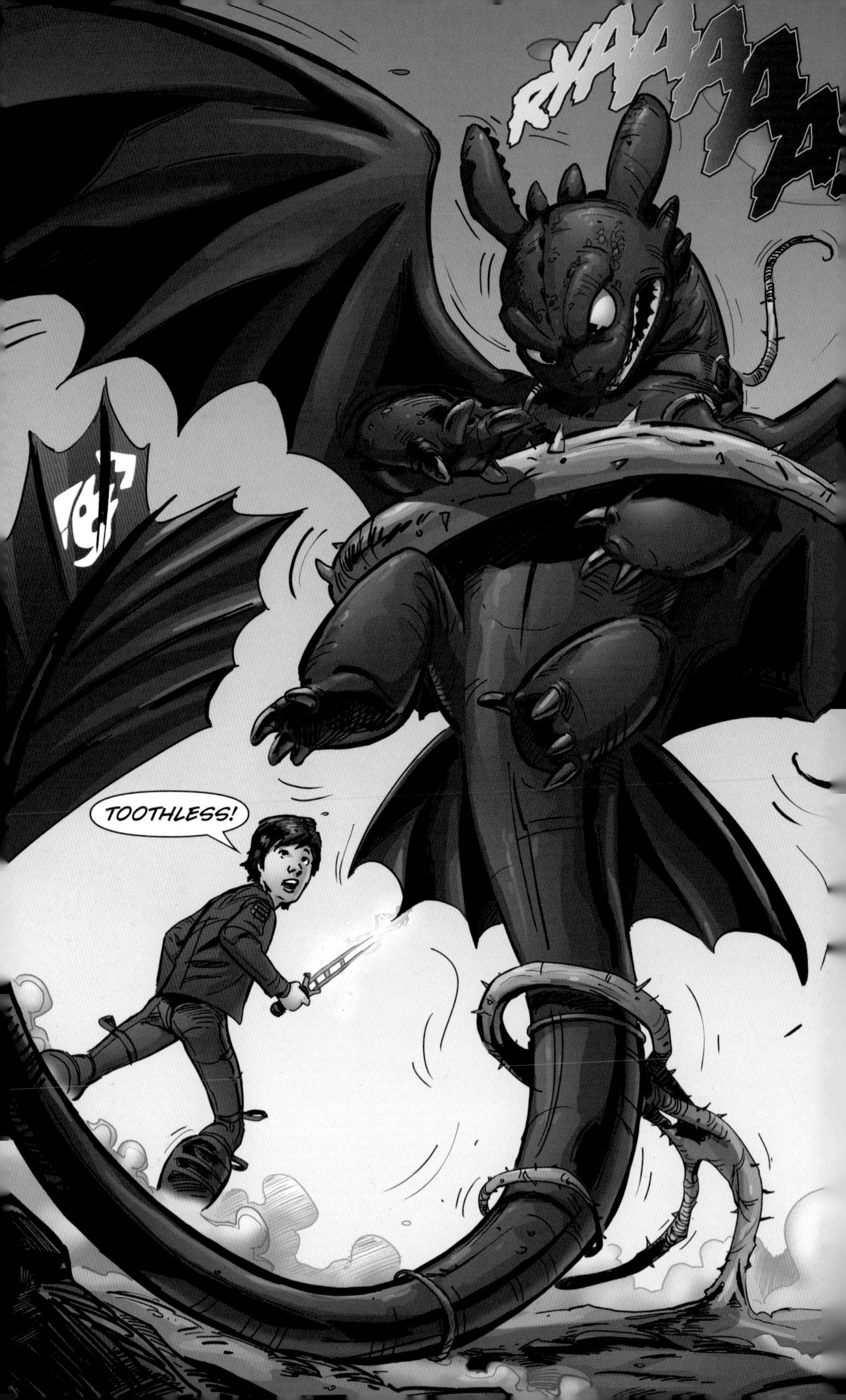
RHAAAAA!
TOOTHLESS!

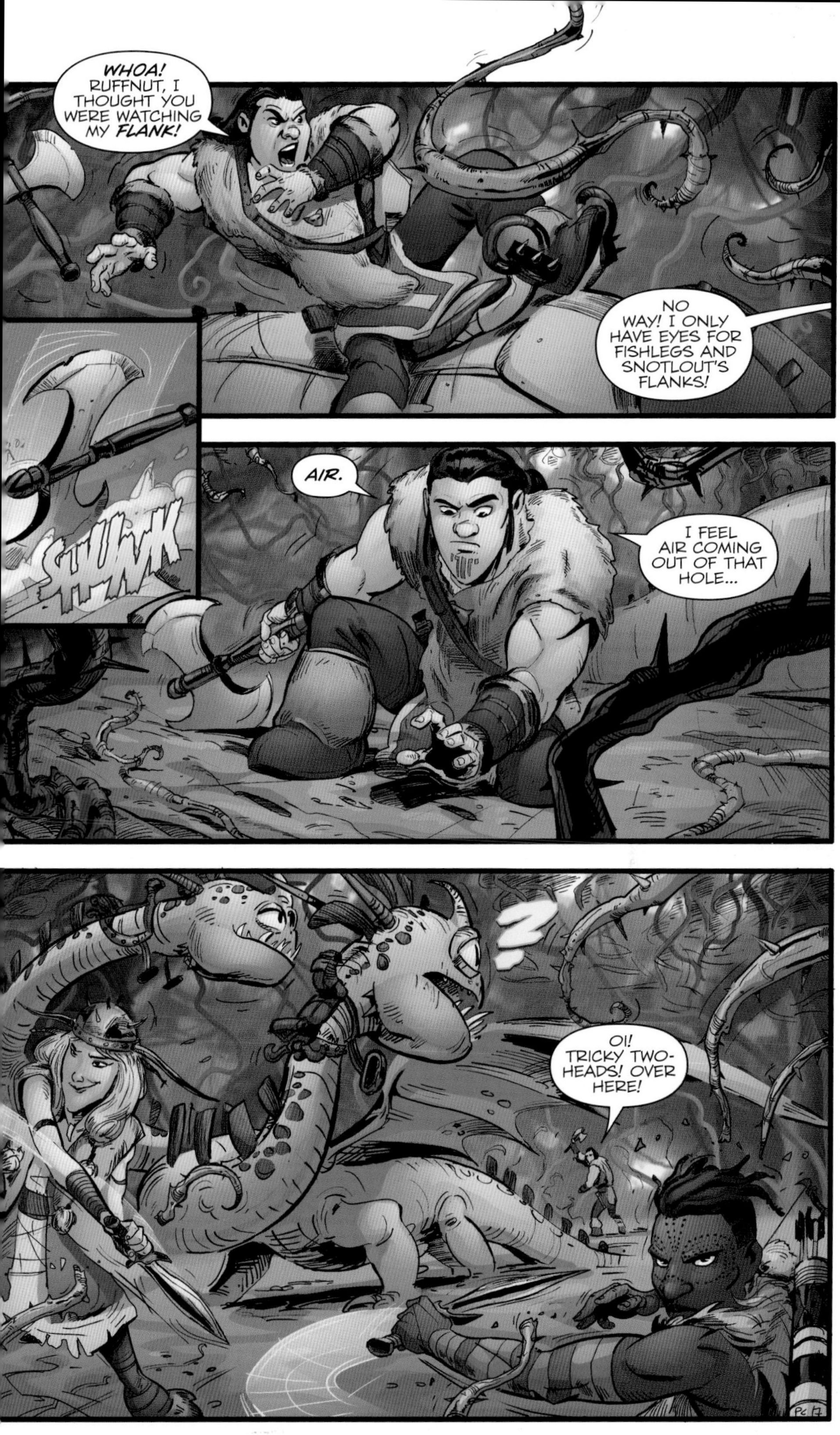
WHOA! RUFFNUT, I THOUGHT YOU WERE WATCHING MY FLANK!
NO WAY! I ONLY HAVE EYES FOR FISHLEGS AND SNOTLOUT'S FLANKS!
SHUNK
AIR.
I FEEL AIR COMING OUT OF THAT HOLE...
OI! TRICKY TWO-HEADS! OVER HERE!

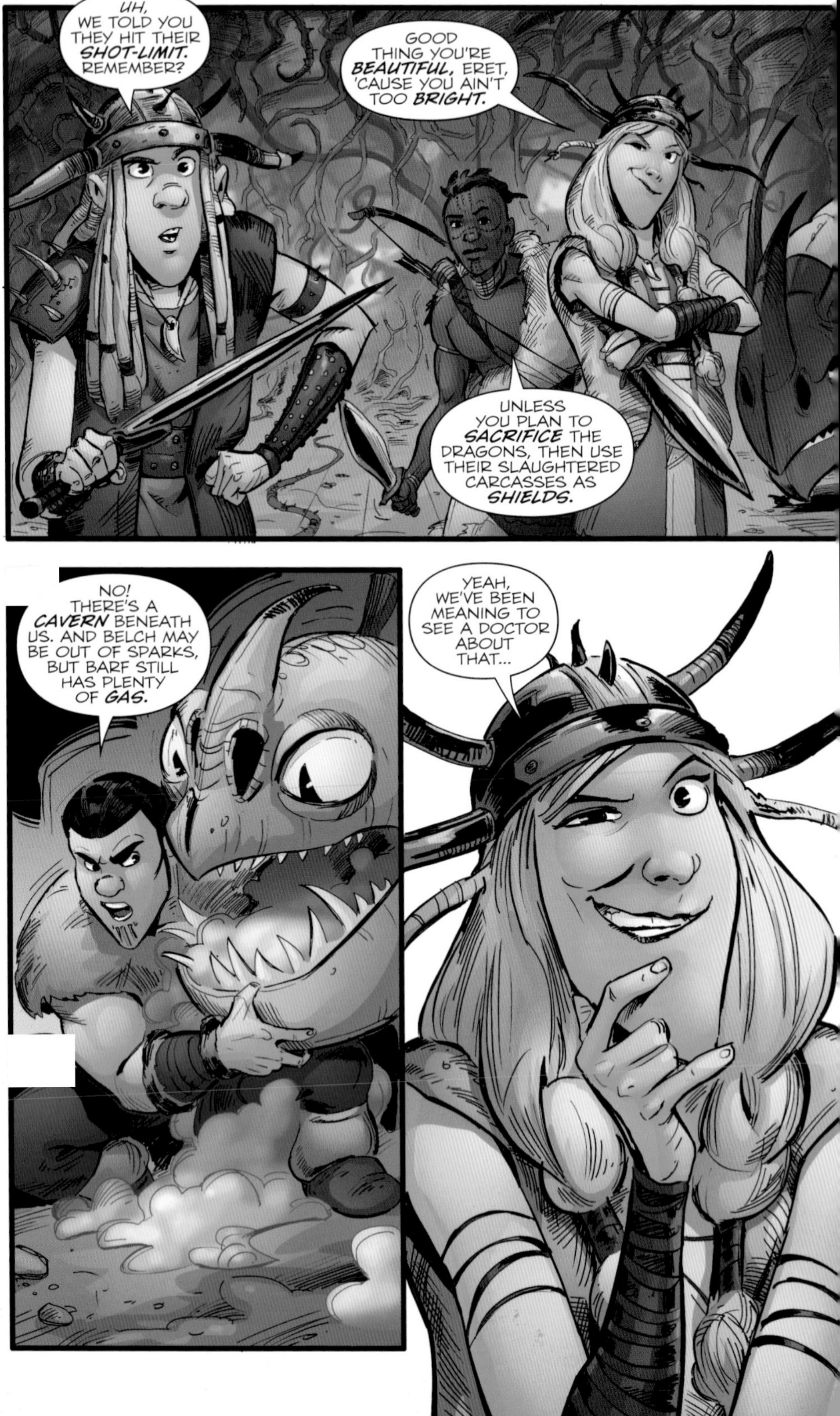
UH, WE TOLD YOU THEY HIT THEIR SHOT-LIMIT. REMEMBER?
GOOD THING YOU'RE BEAUTIFUL, ERET, 'CAUSE YOU AIN'T TOO BRIGHT.
UNLESS YOU PLAN TO SACRIFICE THE DRAGONS, THEN USE THEIR SLAUGHTERED CARCASSES AS SHIELDS.
NO! THERE'S A CAVERN BENEATH US. AND BELCH MAY BE OUT OF SPARKS, BUT BARF STILL HAS PLENTY OF GAS.
YEAH, WE'VE BEEN MEANING TO SEE A DOCTOR ABOUT THAT...

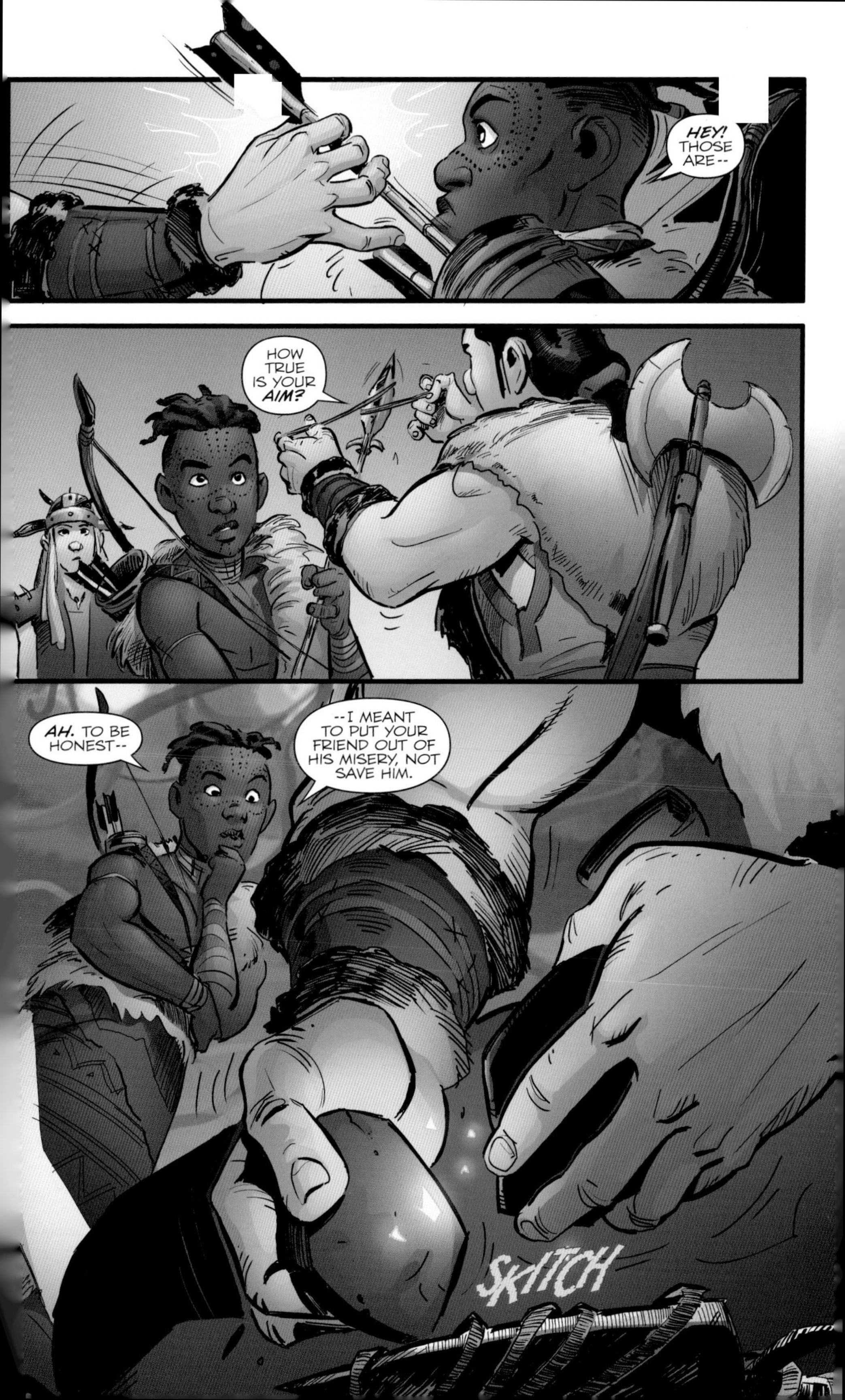
HEY! THOSE ARE--
HOW TRUE IS YOUR AIM?
AH. TO BE HONEST--
--I MEANT TO PUT YOUR FRIEND OUT OF HIS MISERY, NOT SAVE HIM.
SKITCH

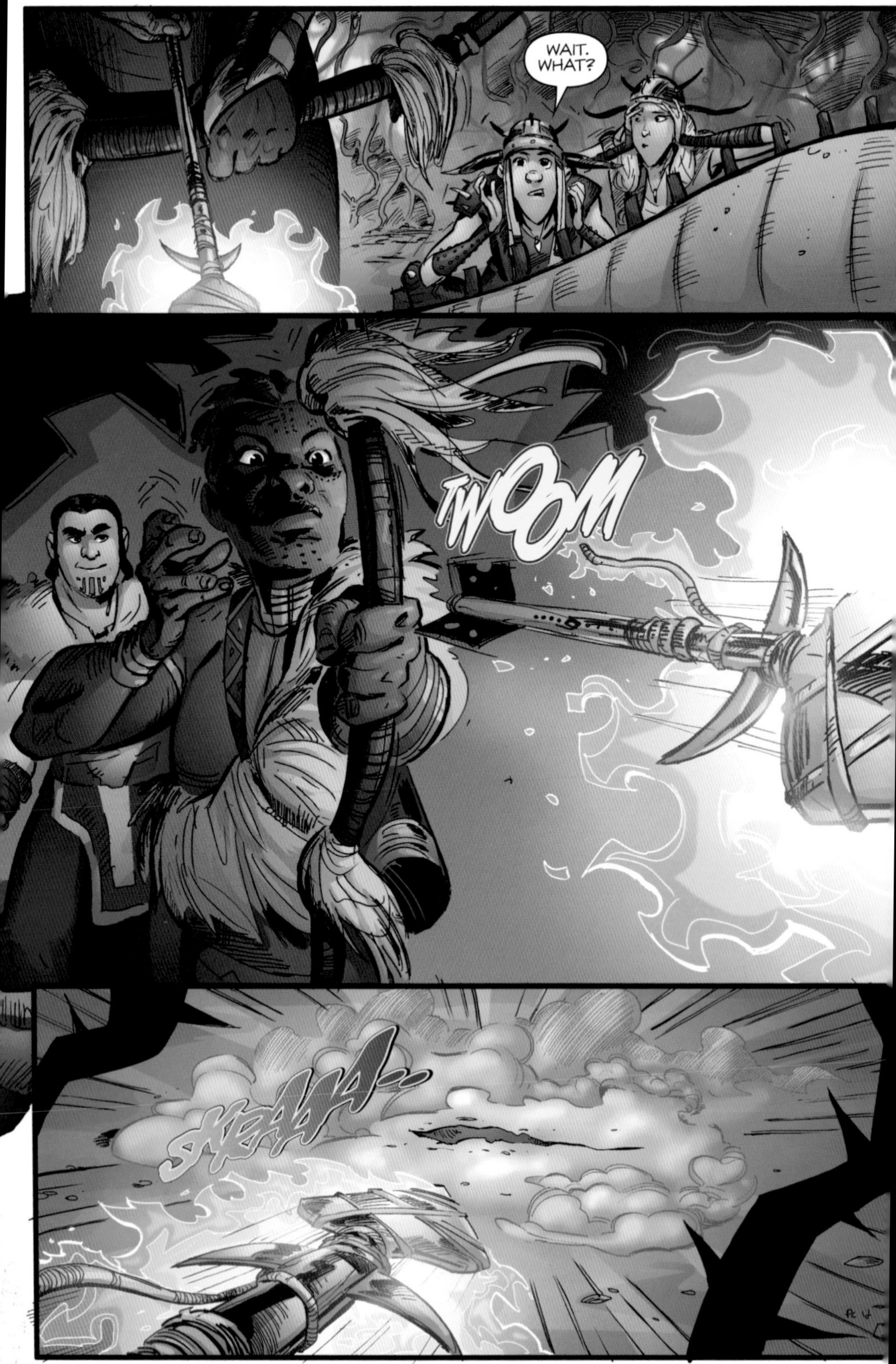
WAIT. WHAT?
TWOOM
SKRAAA--

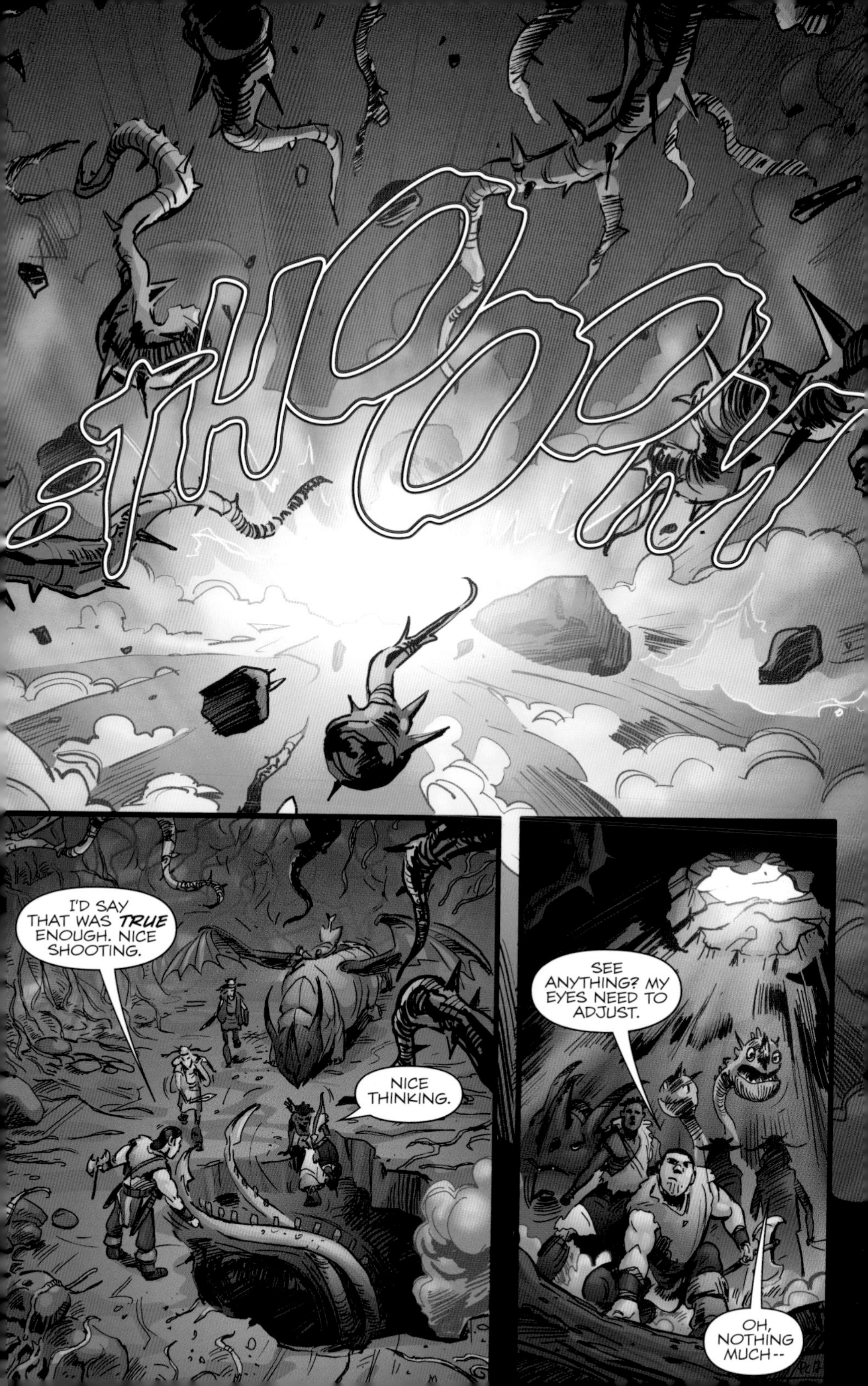
THOOM!
I'D SAY THAT WAS TRUE ENOUGH. NICE SHOOTING.
NICE THINKING.
SEE ANYTHING? MY EYES NEED TO ADJUST.
OH, NOTHING MUCH--

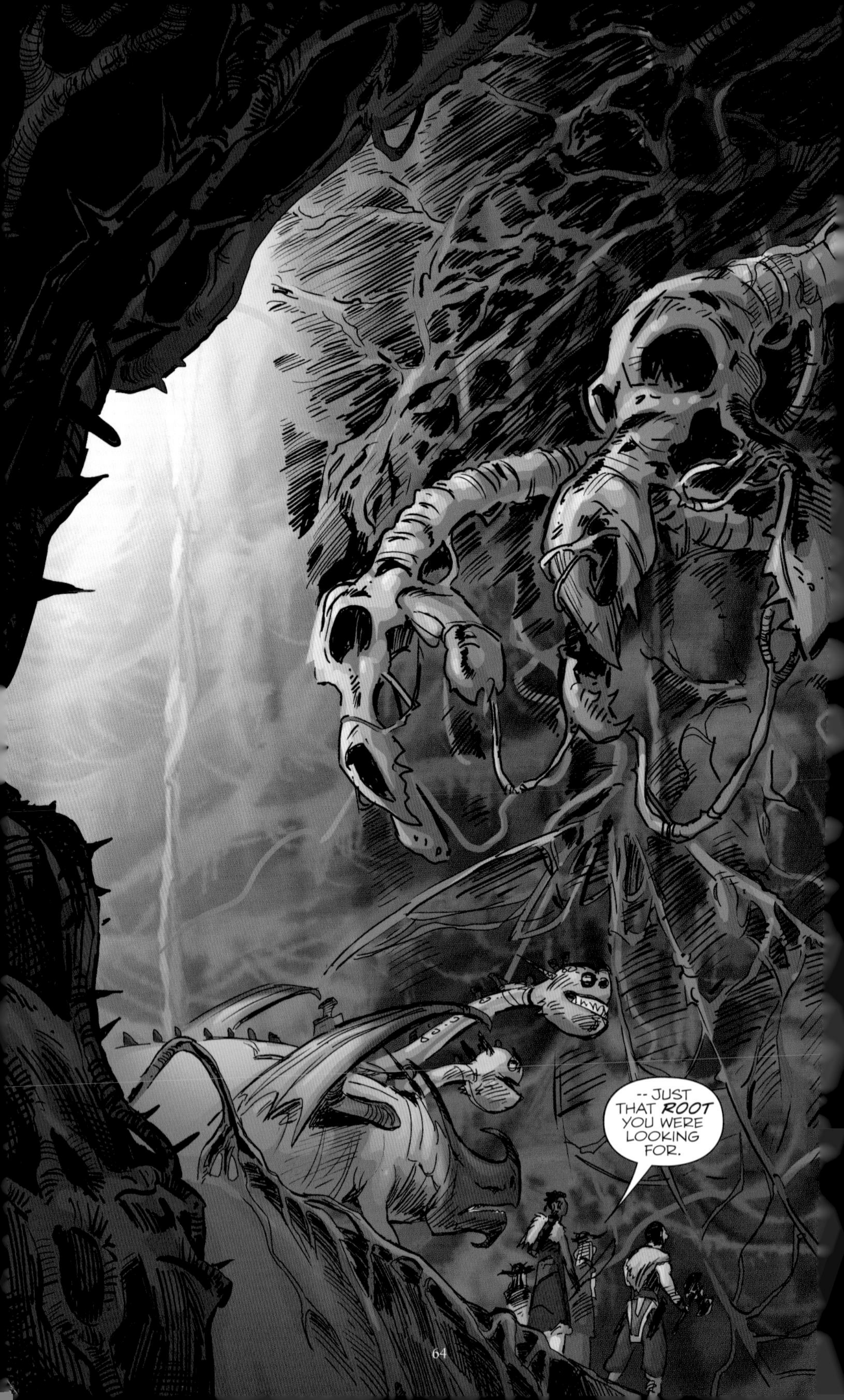
-- JUST THAT ROOT YOU WERE LOOKING FOR.

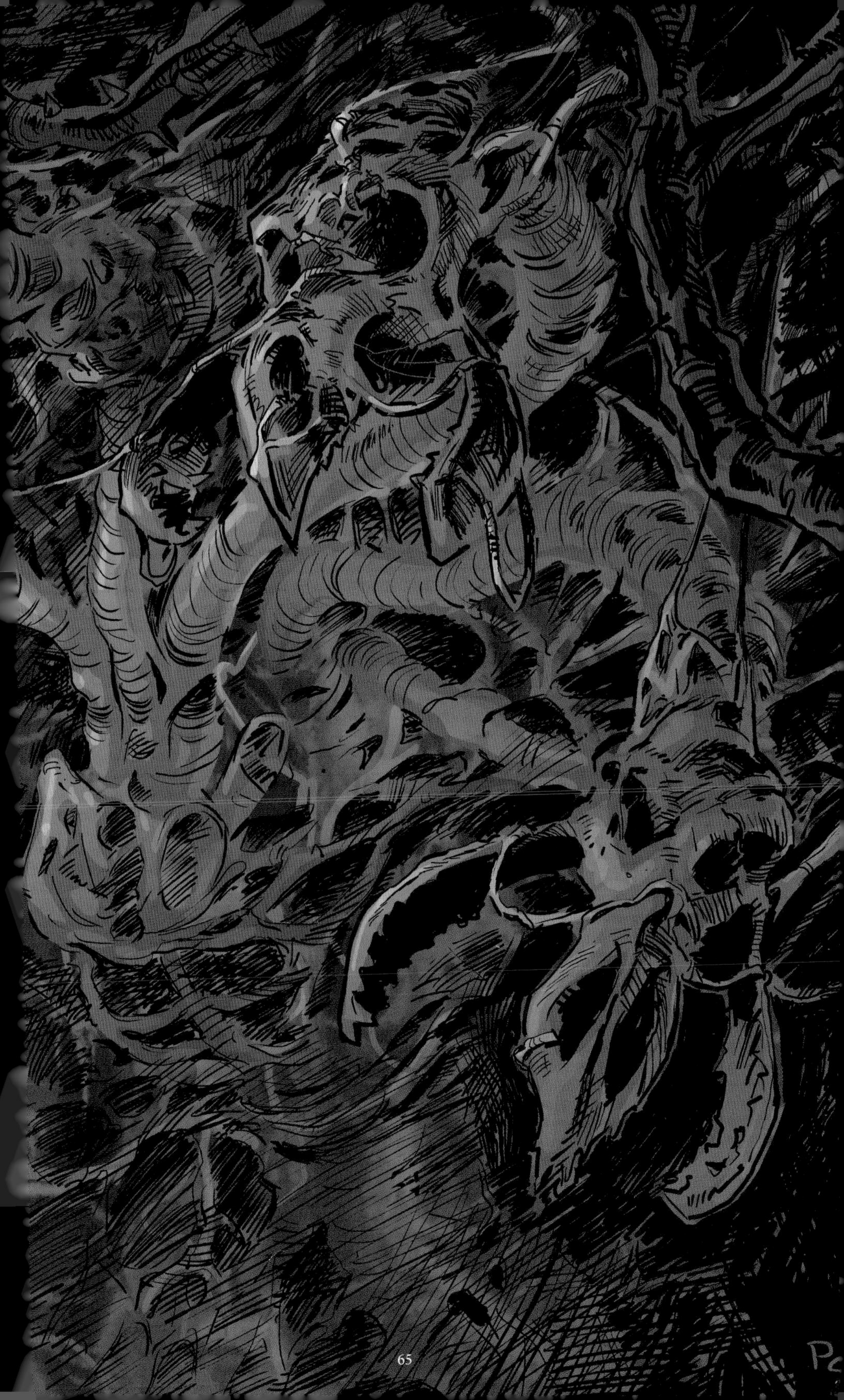

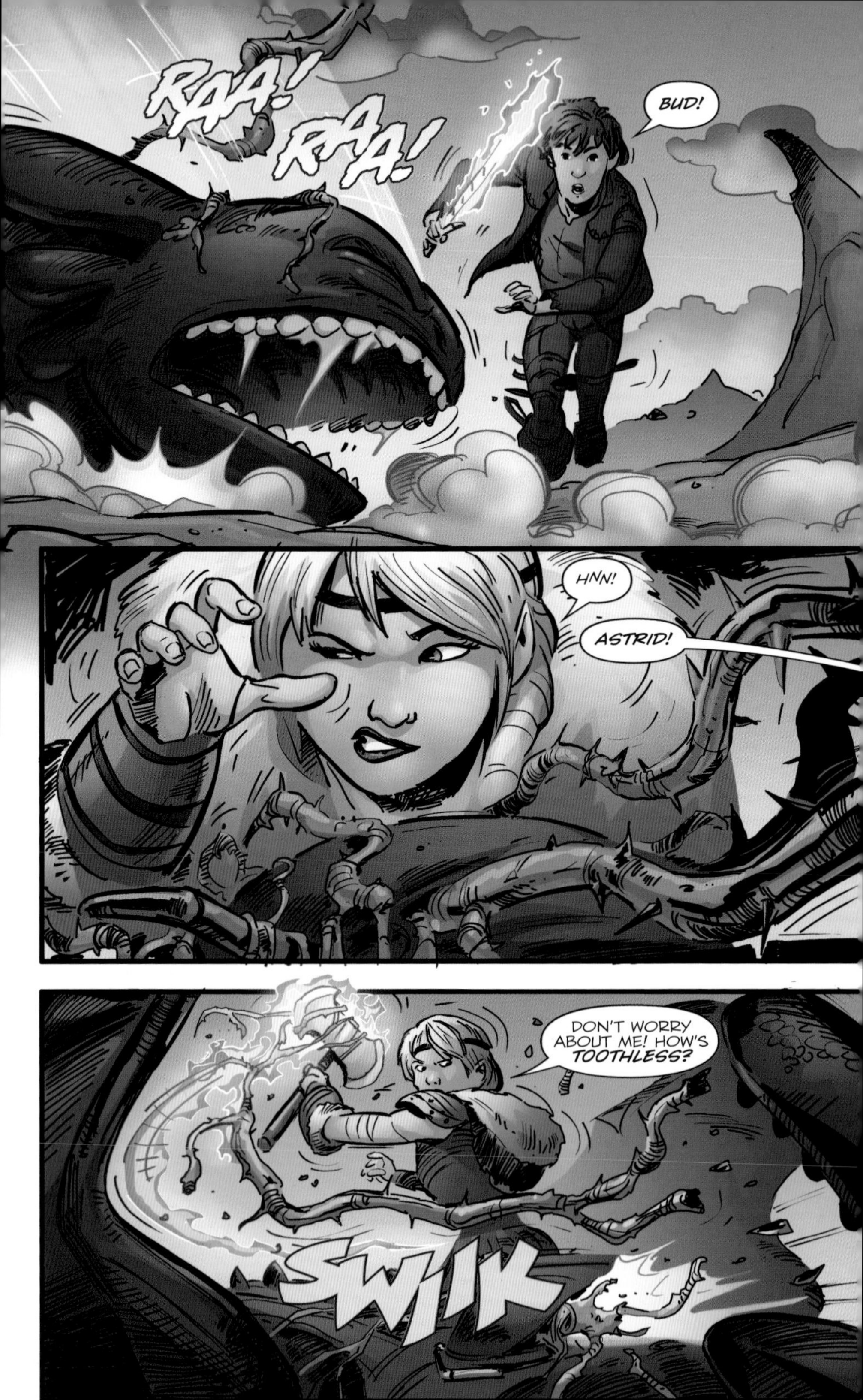
RAA! RAA!
BUD!
HNN!
ASTRID!
DON'T WORRY ABOUT ME! HOW'S TOOTHLESS?
SWIK

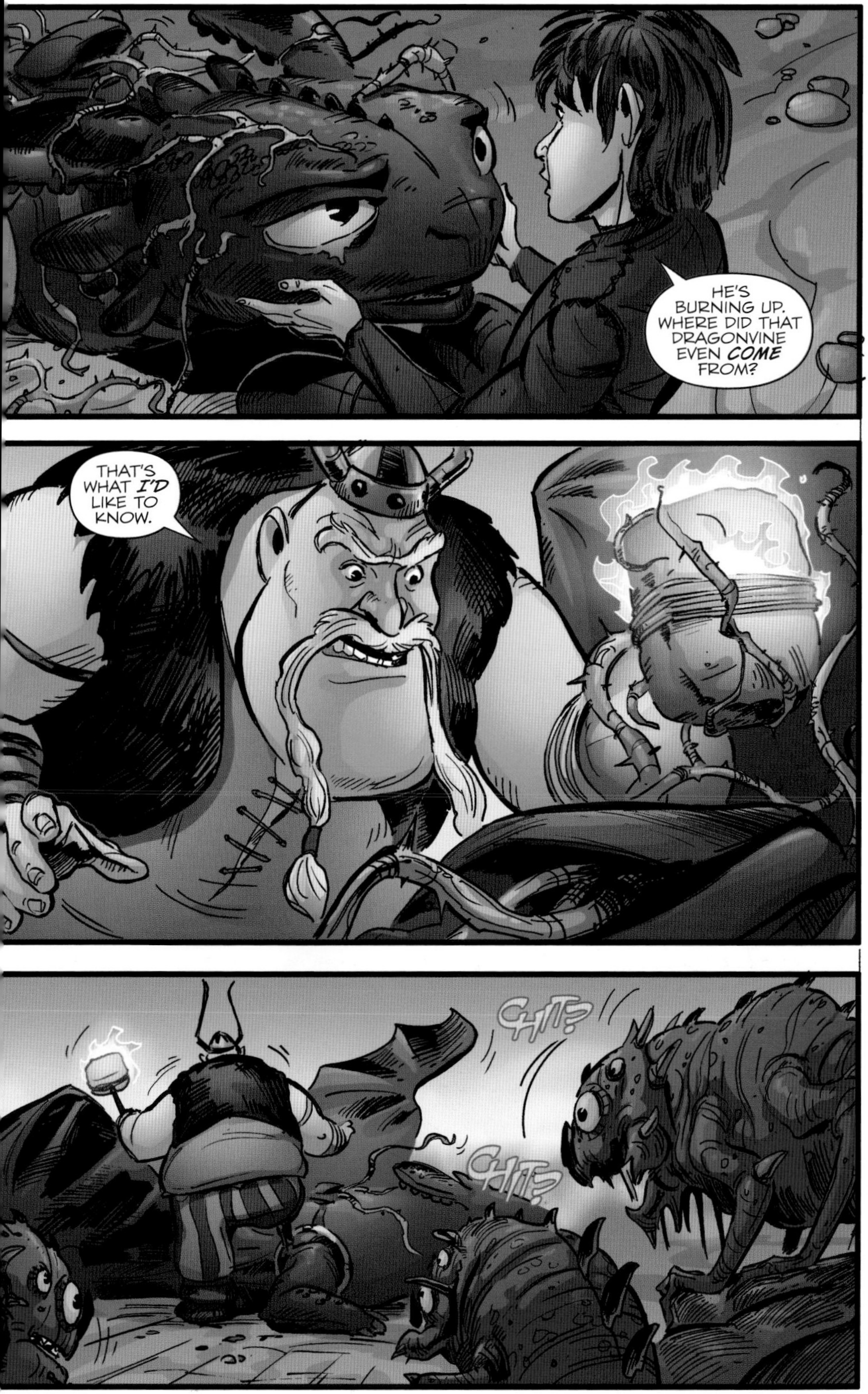
HE'S BURNING UP. WHERE DID THAT DRAGONVINE EVEN *COME* FROM?
THAT'S WHAT *I'D* LIKE TO KNOW.
CHIT?
CHIT?

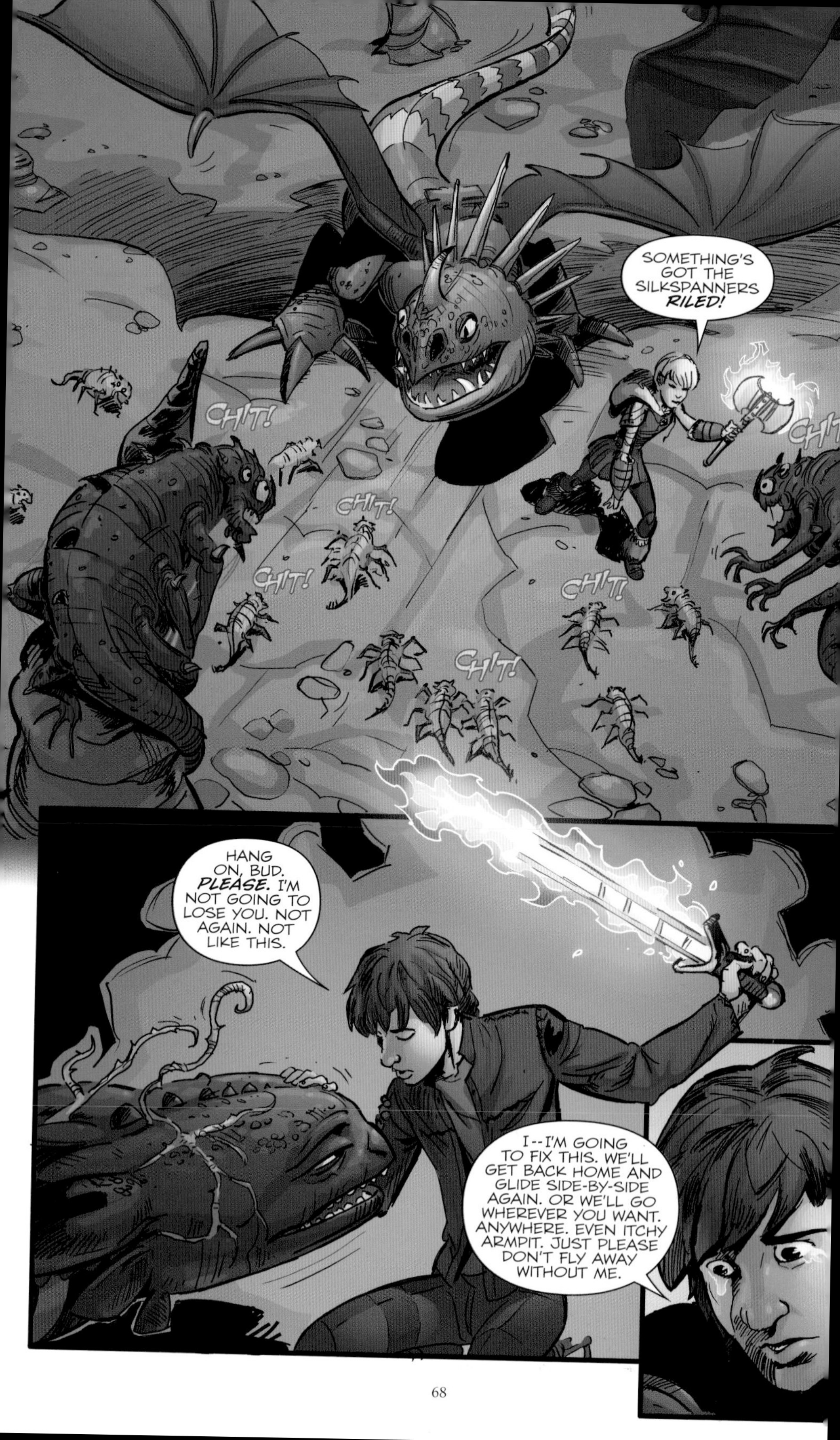
SOMETHING'S GOT THE SILKSPANNERS *RILED!*
CHIT!
CHIT!
CHIT!
CHIT!
CHIT!
CHIT!
HANG ON, BUD. *PLEASE.* I'M NOT GOING TO LOSE YOU. NOT AGAIN. NOT LIKE THIS.
I--I'M GOING TO FIX THIS. WE'LL GET BACK HOME AND GLIDE SIDE-BY-SIDE AGAIN. OR WE'LL GO WHEREVER YOU WANT. ANYWHERE. EVEN ITCHY ARMPIT. JUST PLEASE DON'T FLY AWAY WITHOUT ME.

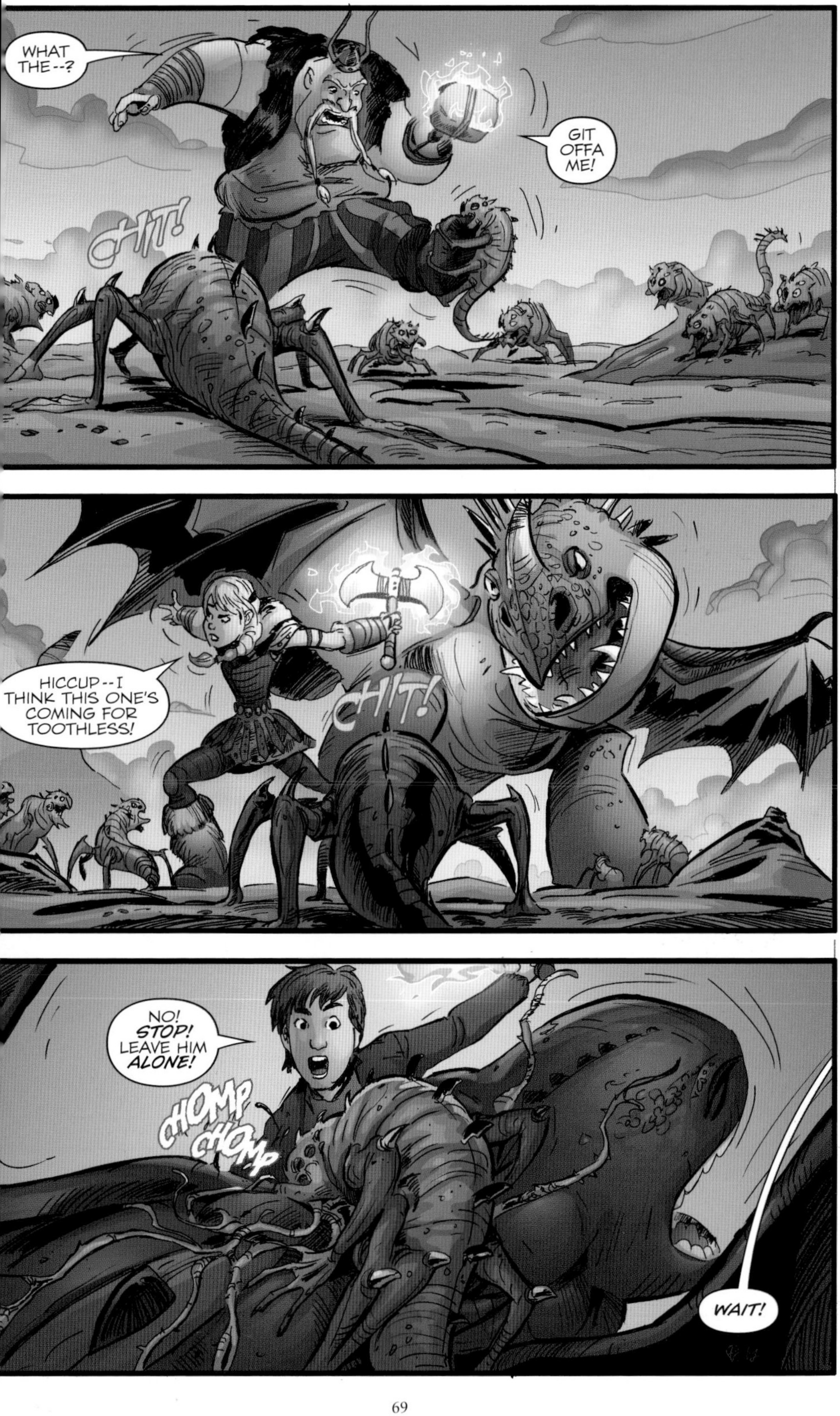
WHAT THE--?
GIT OFFA ME!
CHIT!
HICCUP--I THINK THIS ONE'S COMING FOR TOOTHLESS!
CHIT!
NO! STOP! LEAVE HIM ALONE!
CHOMP
CHOMP
WAIT!

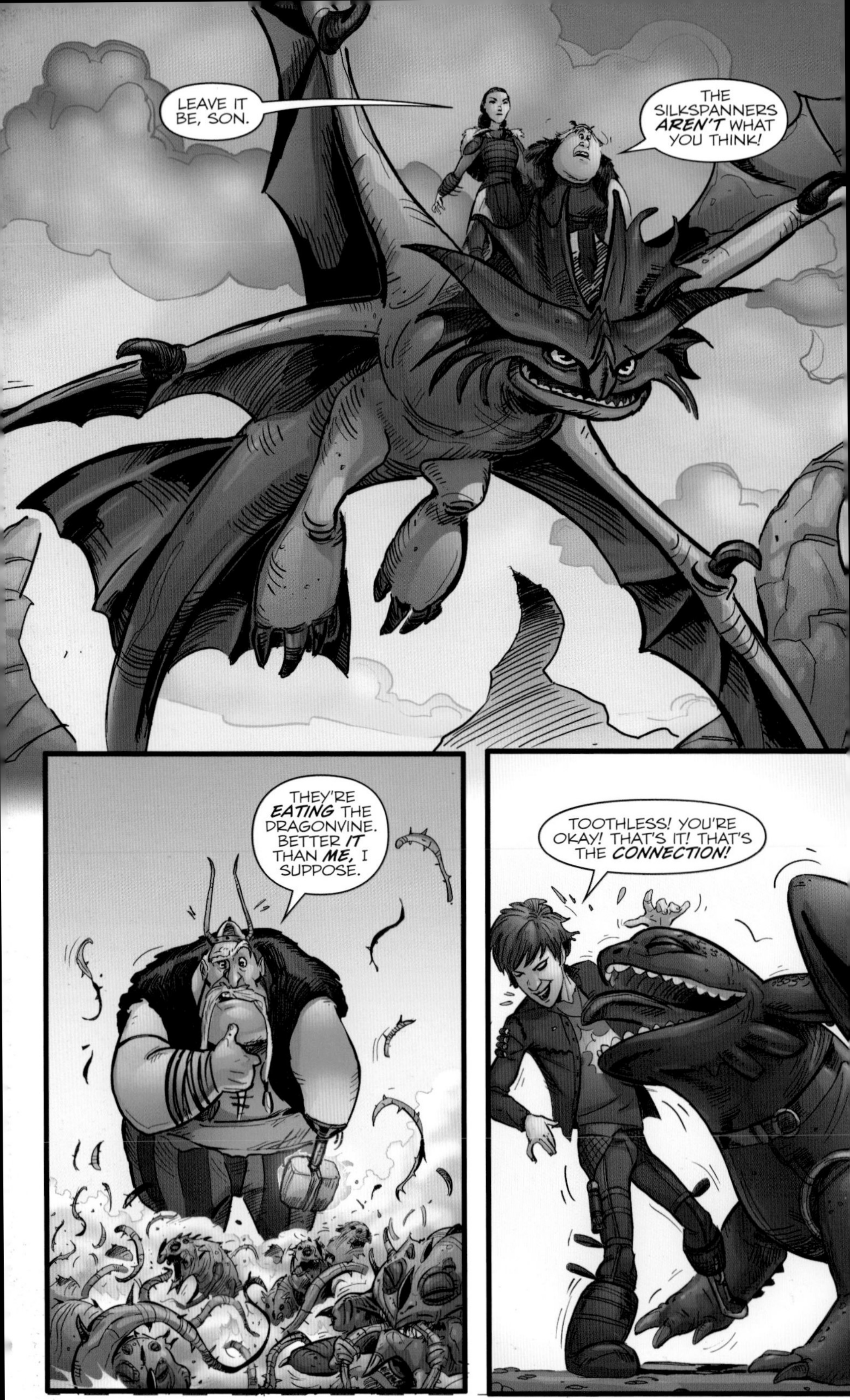
LEAVE IT BE, SON.
THE SILKSPANNERS AREN'T WHAT YOU THINK!
THEY'RE EATING THE DRAGONVINE. BETTER IT THAN ME, I SUPPOSE.
TOOTHLESS! YOU'RE OKAY! THAT'S IT! THAT'S THE CONNECTION!

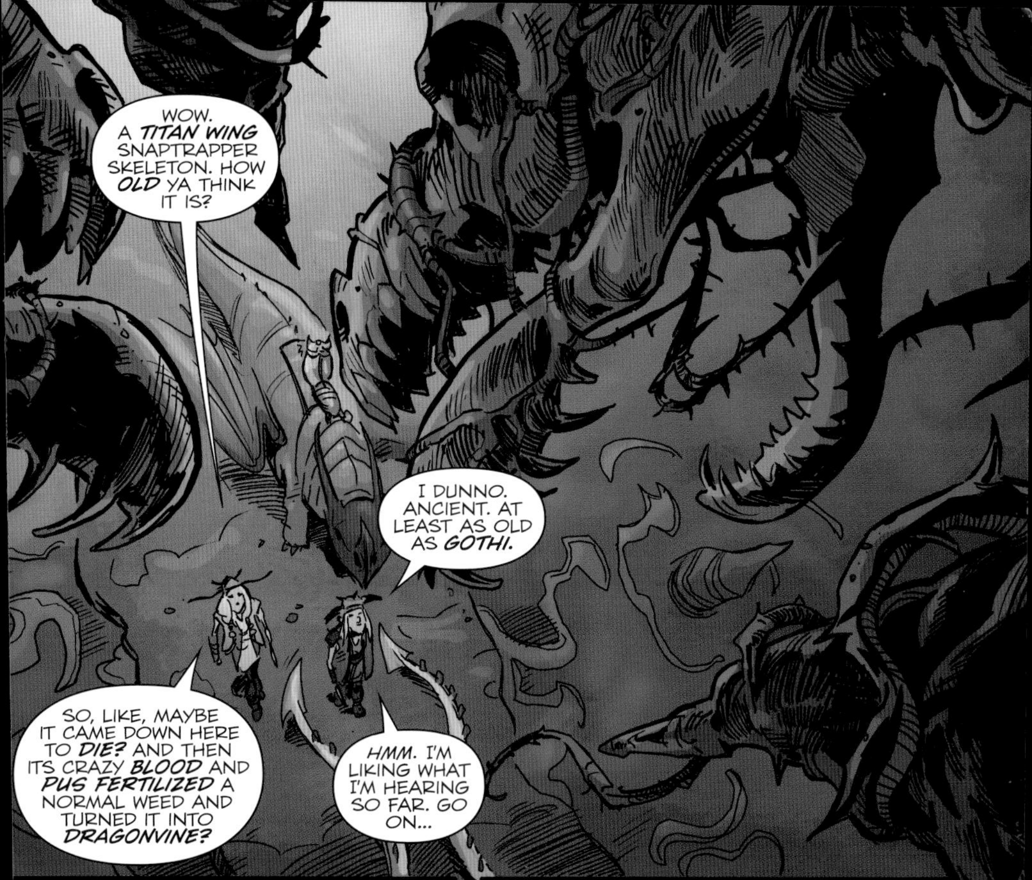
WOW. A TITAN WING SNAPTRAPPER SKELETON. HOW OLD YA THINK IT IS?
I DUNNO. ANCIENT. AT LEAST AS OLD AS GOTHI.
SO, LIKE, MAYBE IT CAME DOWN HERE TO DIE? AND THEN ITS CRAZY BLOOD AND PUS FERTILIZED A NORMAL WEED AND TURNED IT INTO DRAGONVINE?
HMM. I'M LIKING WHAT I'M HEARING SO FAR. GO ON...

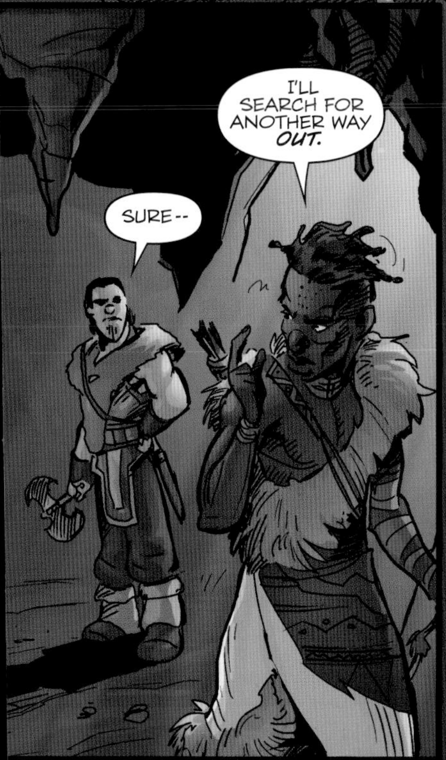
I'LL SEARCH FOR ANOTHER WAY OUT.
SURE--

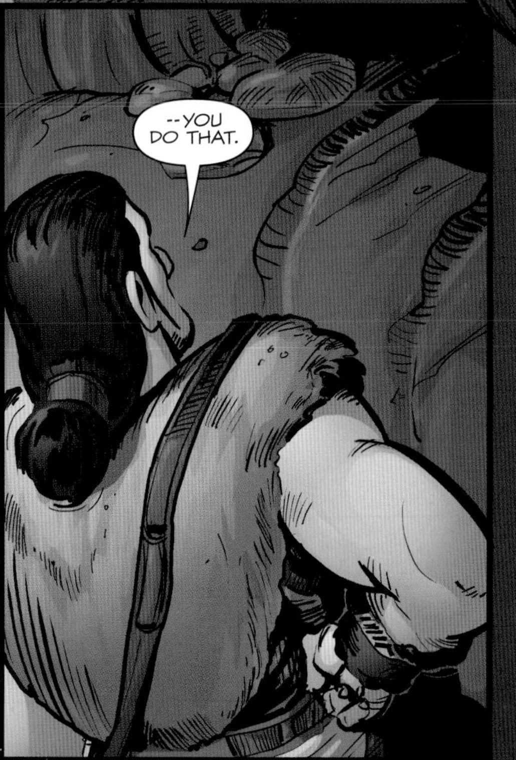
--YOU DO THAT.

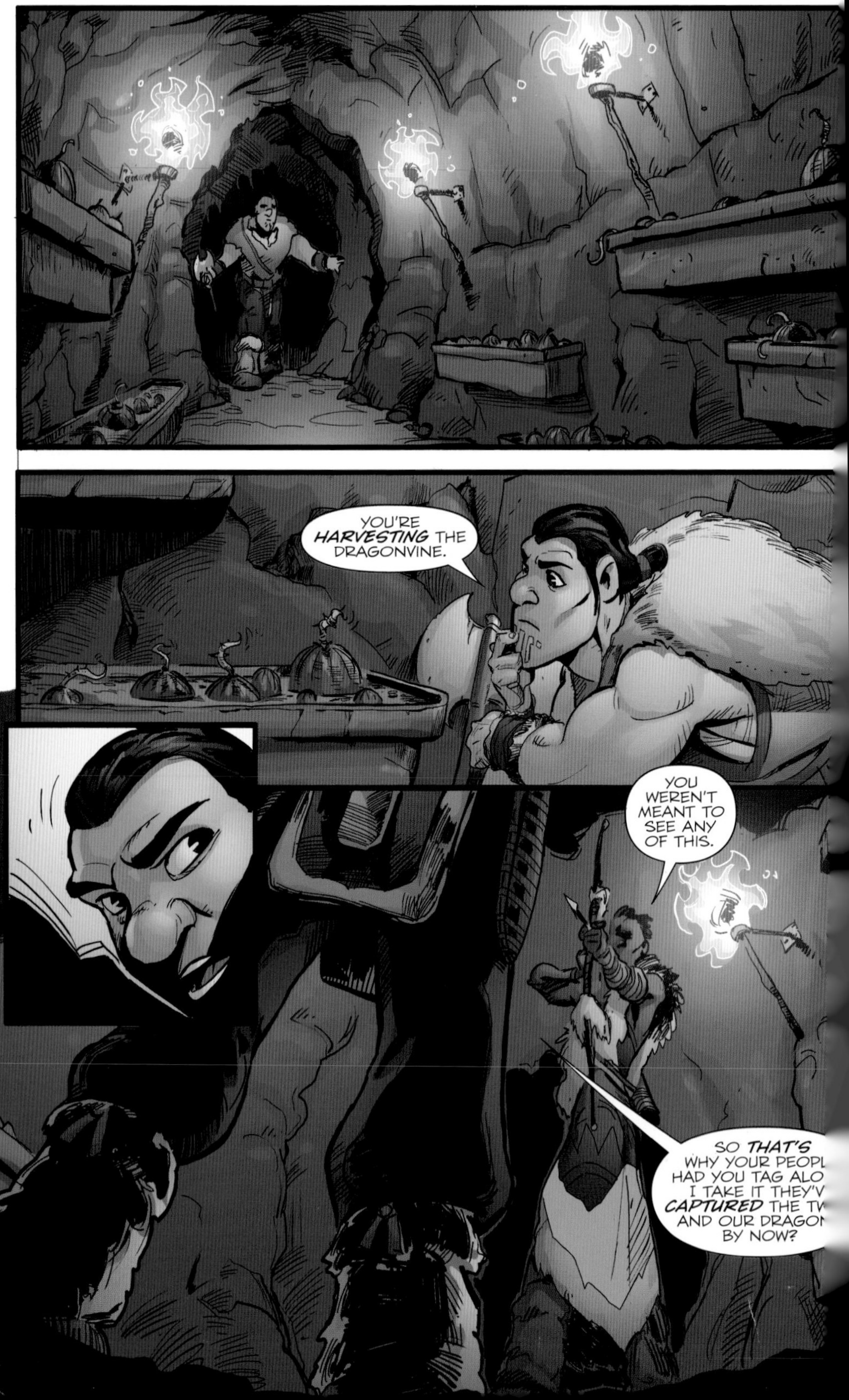

YOU'RE *HARVESTING* THE DRAGONVINE.
YOU WEREN'T MEANT TO SEE ANY OF THIS.
SO *THAT'S* WHY YOUR PEOPL HAD YOU TAG ALO I TAKE IT THEY'V *CAPTURED* THE TW AND OUR DRAGON BY NOW?

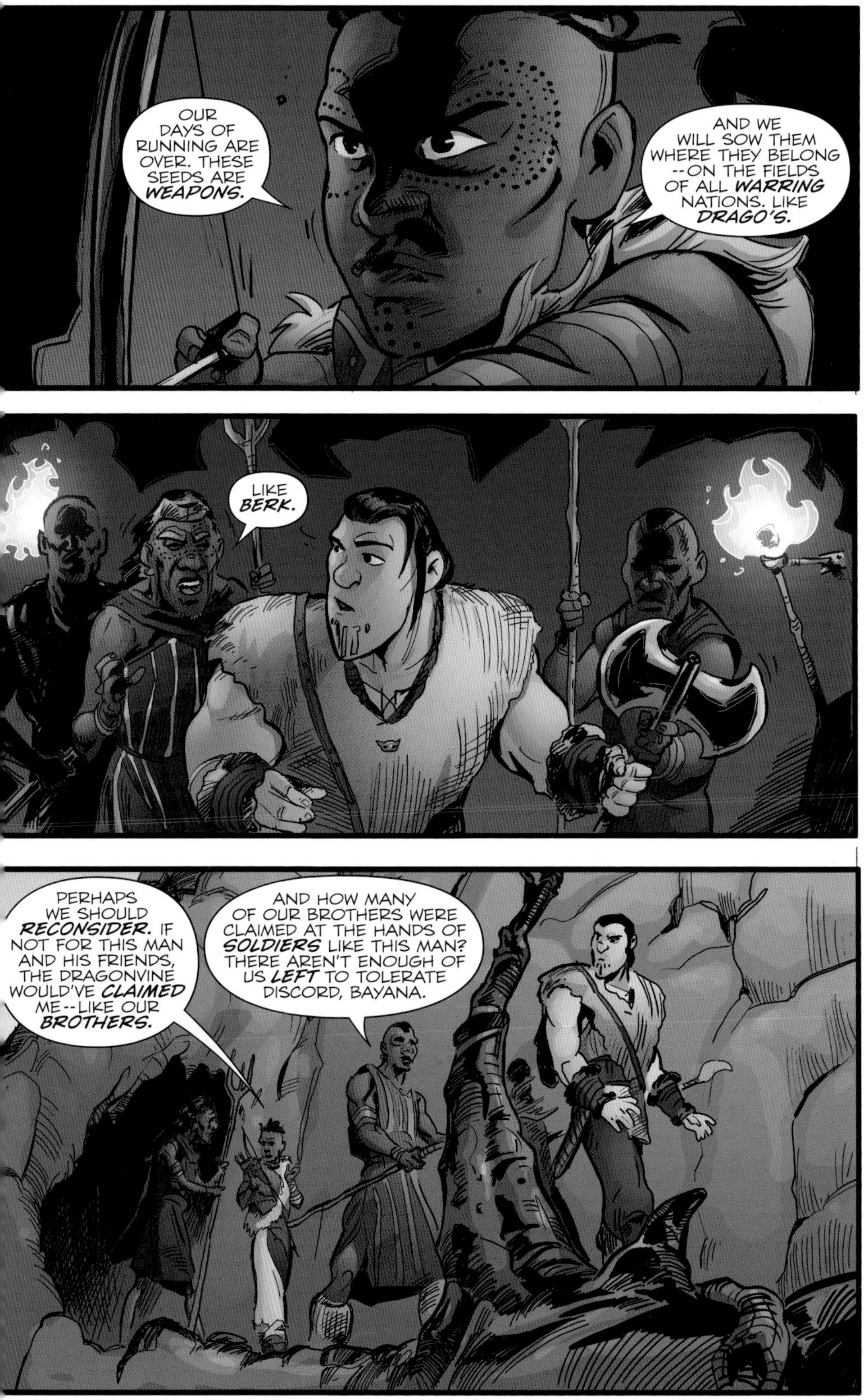
OUR DAYS OF RUNNING ARE OVER. THESE SEEDS ARE WEAPONS.
AND WE WILL SOW THEM WHERE THEY BELONG --ON THE FIELDS OF ALL WARRING NATIONS. LIKE DRAGO'S.
LIKE BERK.
PERHAPS WE SHOULD RECONSIDER. IF NOT FOR THIS MAN AND HIS FRIENDS, THE DRAGONVINE WOULD'VE CLAIMED ME--LIKE OUR BROTHERS.
AND HOW MANY OF OUR BROTHERS WERE CLAIMED AT THE HANDS OF SOLDIERS LIKE THIS MAN? THERE AREN'T ENOUGH OF US LEFT TO TOLERATE DISCORD, BAYANA.

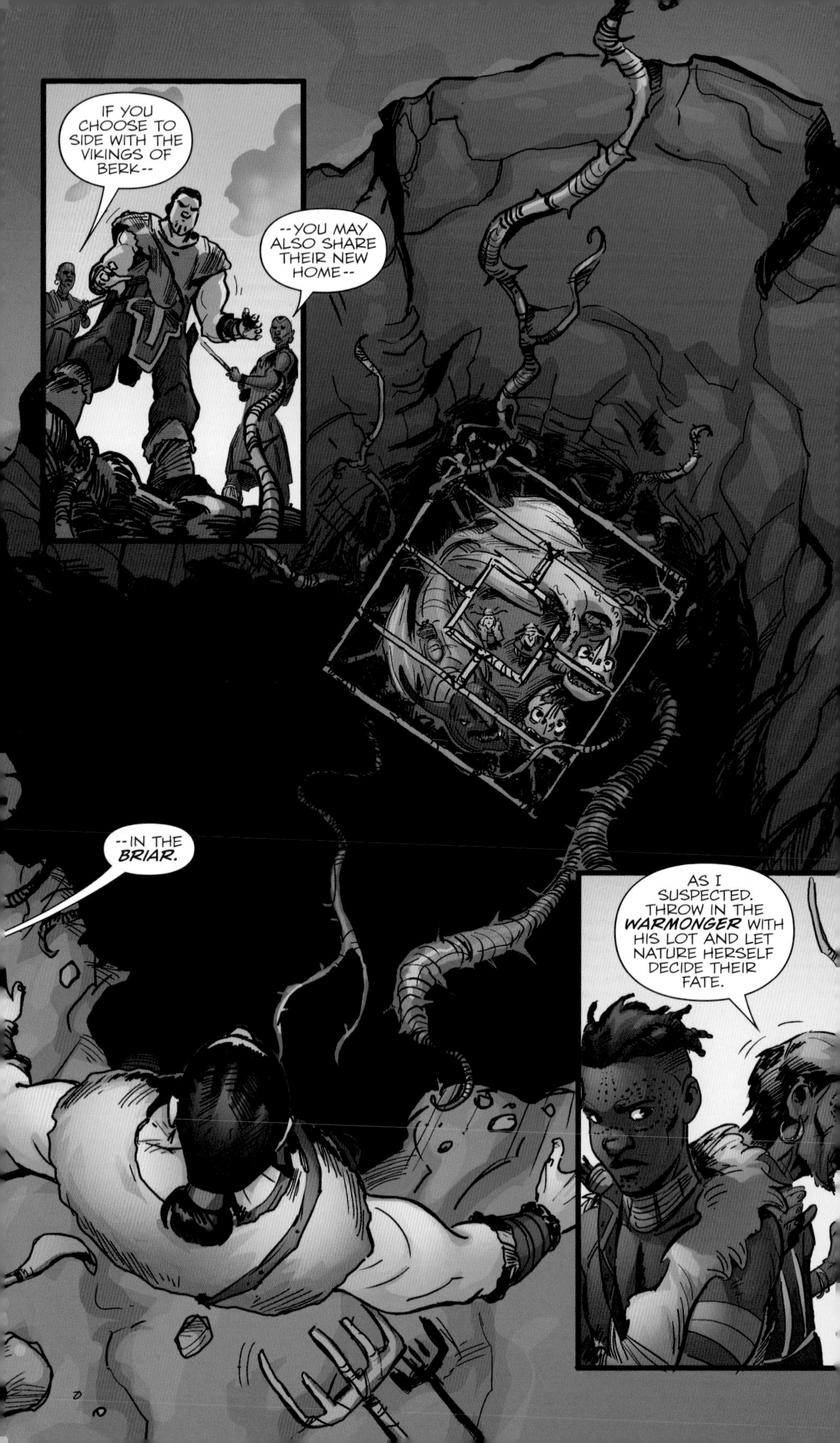
IF YOU CHOOSE TO SIDE WITH THE VIKINGS OF BERK--
--YOU MAY ALSO SHARE THEIR NEW HOME--
--IN THE *BRIAR.*
AS I SUSPECTED. THROW IN THE *WARMONGER* WITH HIS LOT AND LET NATURE HERSELF DECIDE THEIR FATE.

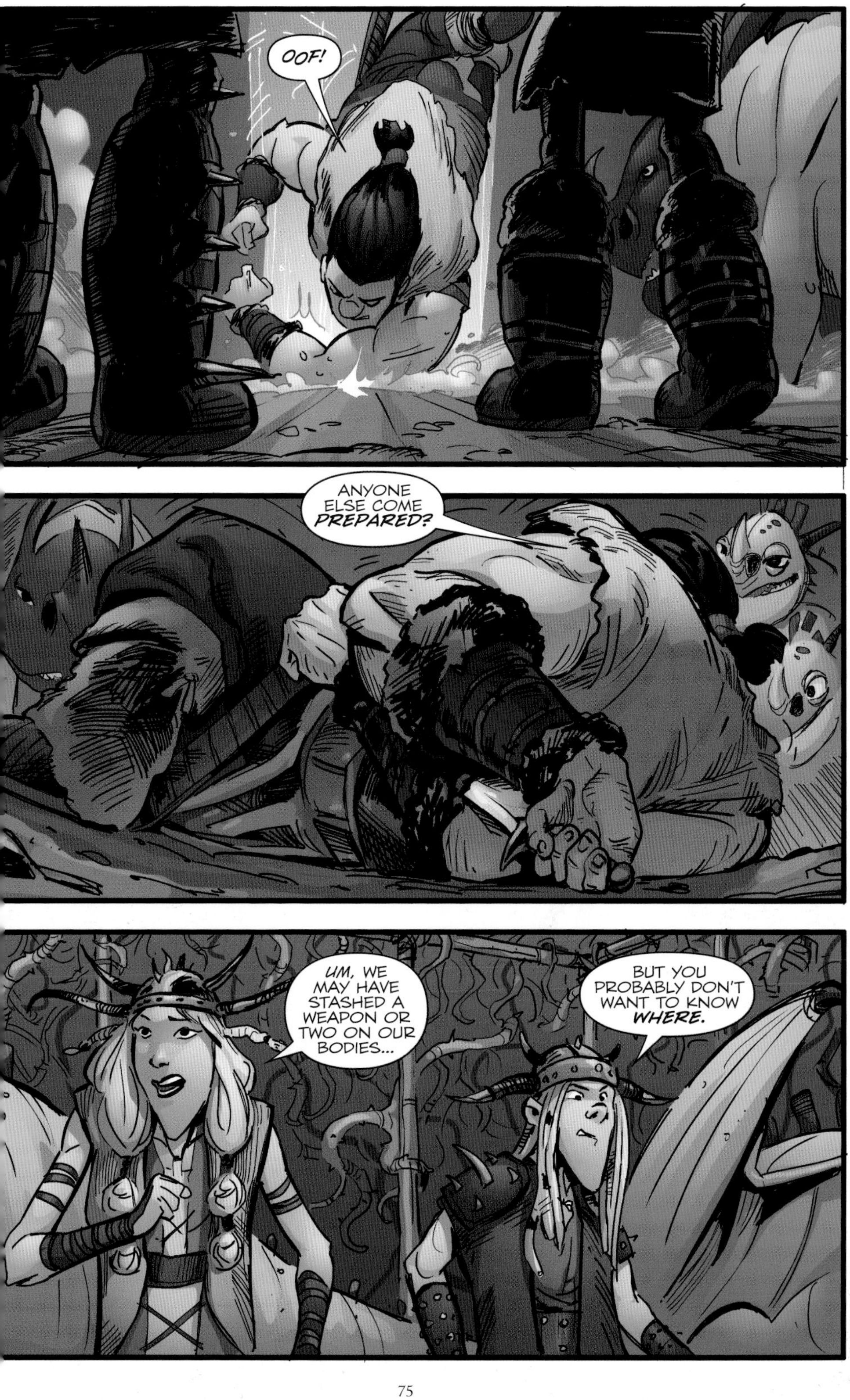
OOF!
ANYONE ELSE COME *PREPARED?*
UM, WE MAY HAVE STASHED A WEAPON OR TWO ON OUR BODIES...
BUT YOU PROBABLY DON'T WANT TO KNOW ***WHERE.***

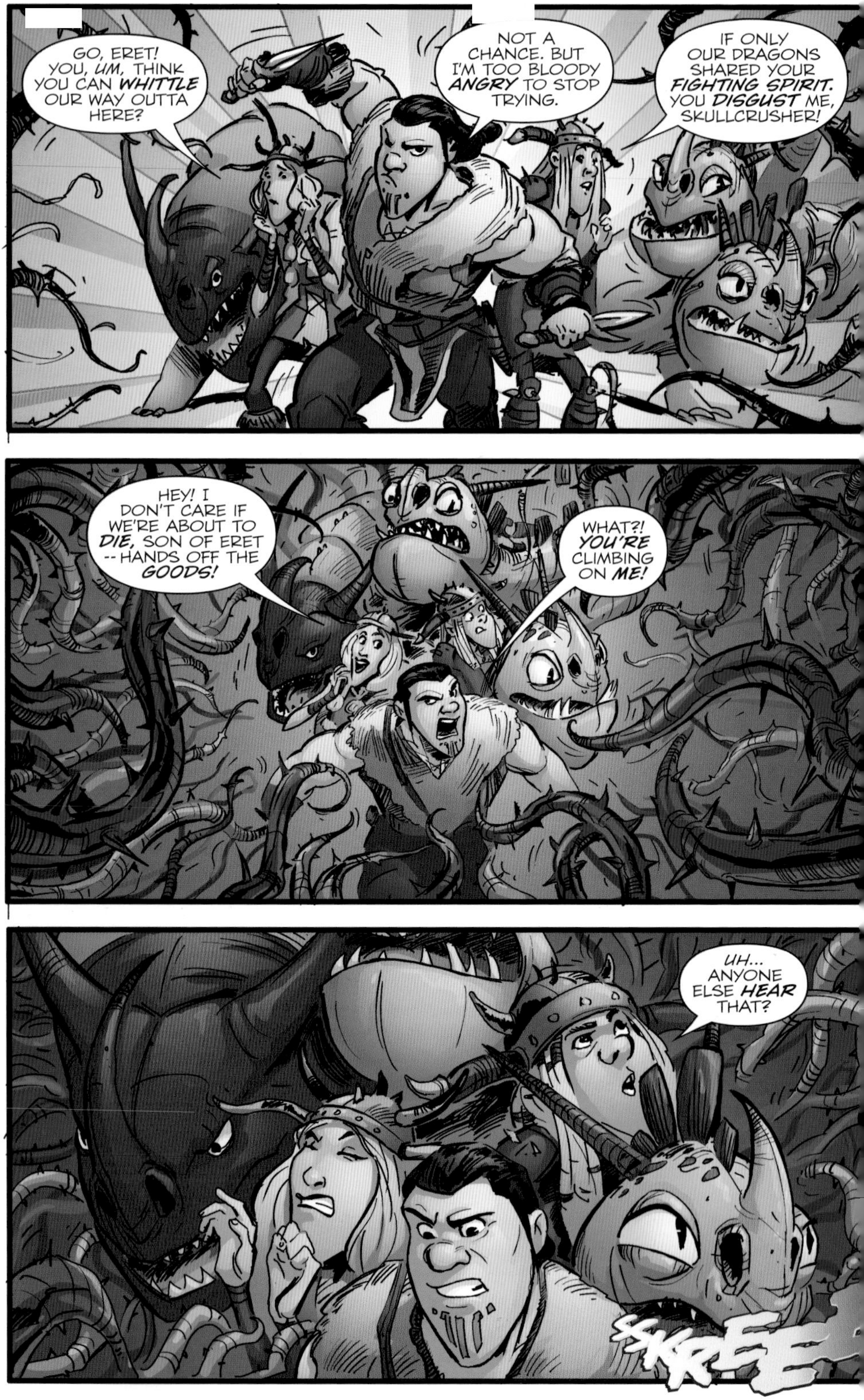
GO, ERET! YOU, *UM,* THINK YOU CAN ***WHITTLE*** OUR WAY OUTTA HERE?
NOT A CHANCE. BUT I'M TOO BLOODY ***ANGRY*** TO STOP TRYING.
IF ONLY OUR DRAGONS SHARED YOUR ***FIGHTING SPIRIT.*** YOU ***DISGUST*** ME, SKULLCRUSHER!
HEY! I DON'T CARE IF WE'RE ABOUT TO ***DIE,*** SON OF ERET --HANDS OFF THE ***GOODS!***
WHAT?! ***YOU'RE*** CLIMBING ON ***ME!***
UH... ANYONE ELSE ***HEAR*** THAT?
SSKREE

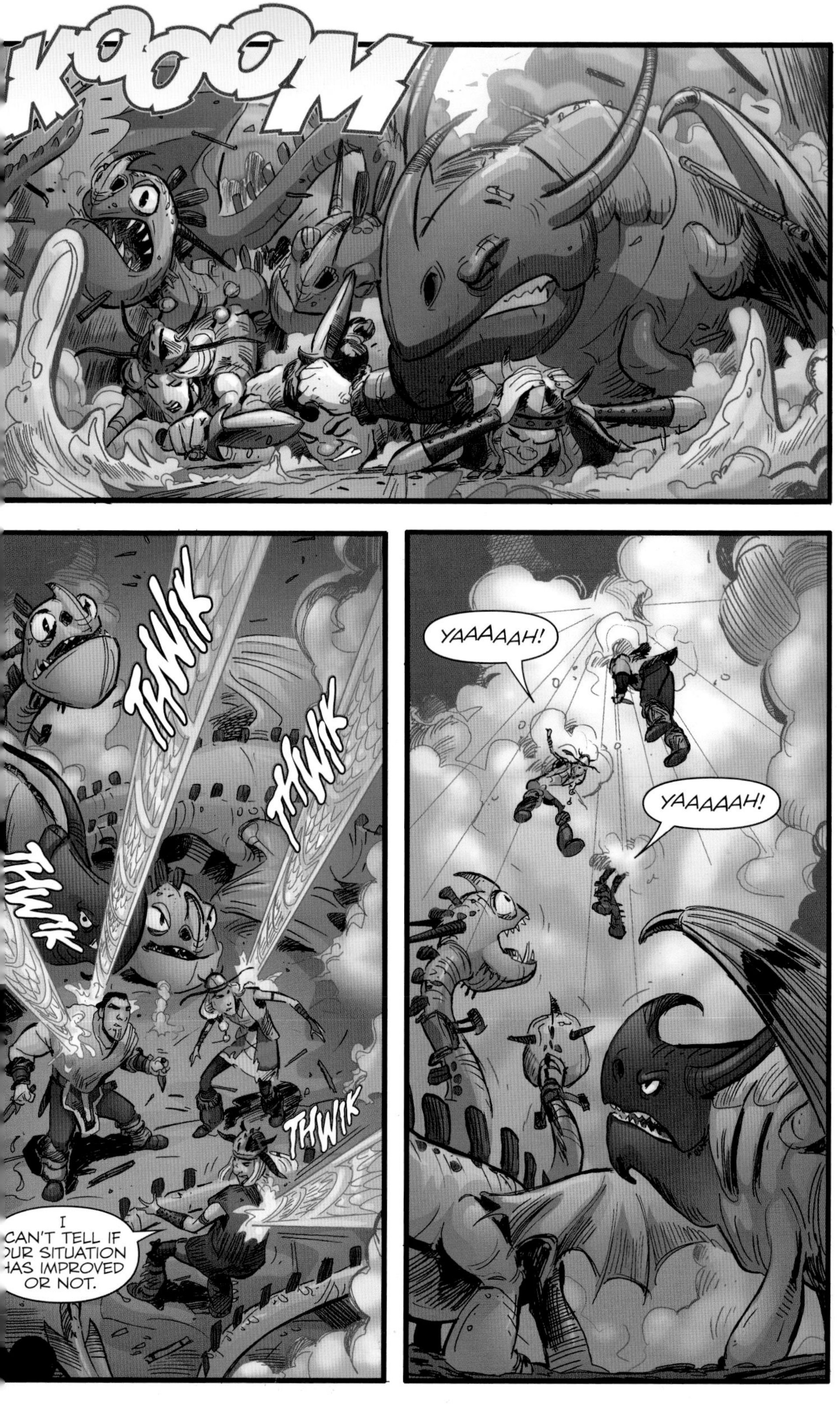
KOOOM
THWIK
THWIK
THWIK
THWIK
I CAN'T TELL IF OUR SITUATION HAS IMPROVED OR NOT.
YAAAAAH!
YAAAAAH!

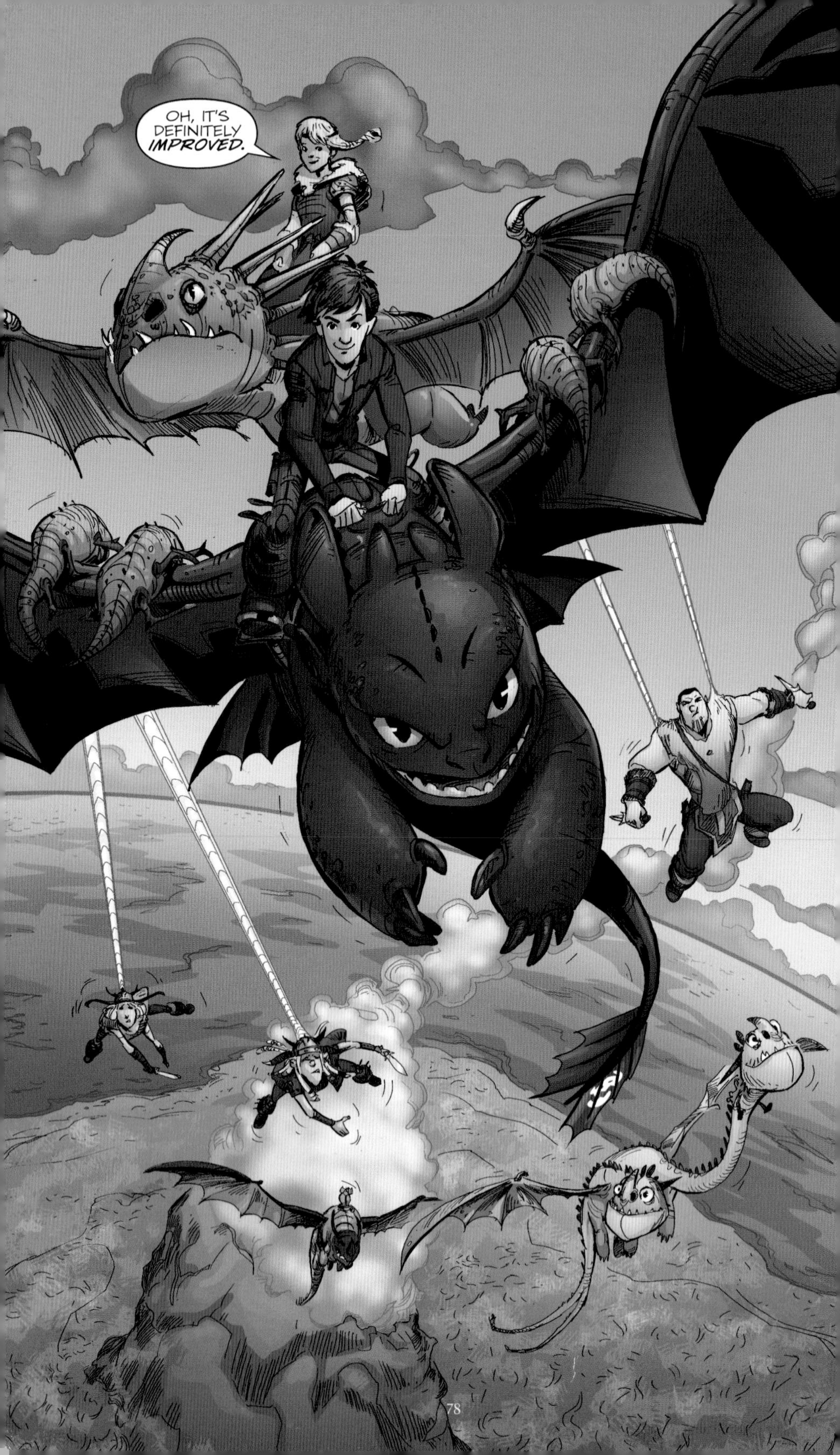
OH, IT'S DEFINITELY IMPROVED.

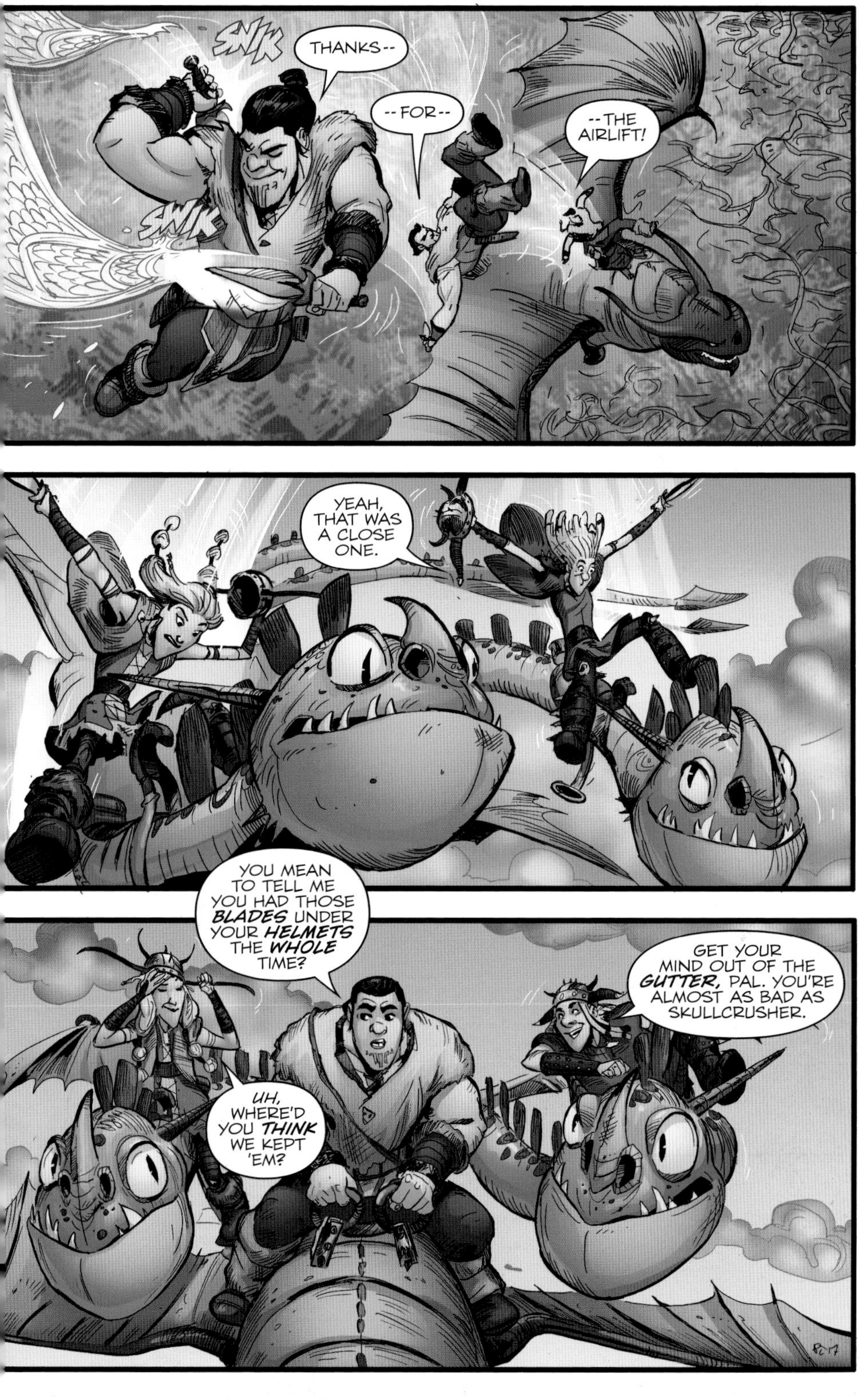
SNIK
THANKS--
--FOR--
--THE AIRLIFT!
SNIK
YEAH, THAT WAS A CLOSE ONE.
YOU MEAN TO TELL ME YOU HAD THOSE BLADES UNDER YOUR HELMETS THE WHOLE TIME?
GET YOUR MIND OUT OF THE GUTTER, PAL. YOU'RE ALMOST AS BAD AS SKULLCRUSHER.
UH, WHERE'D YOU THINK WE KEPT 'EM?

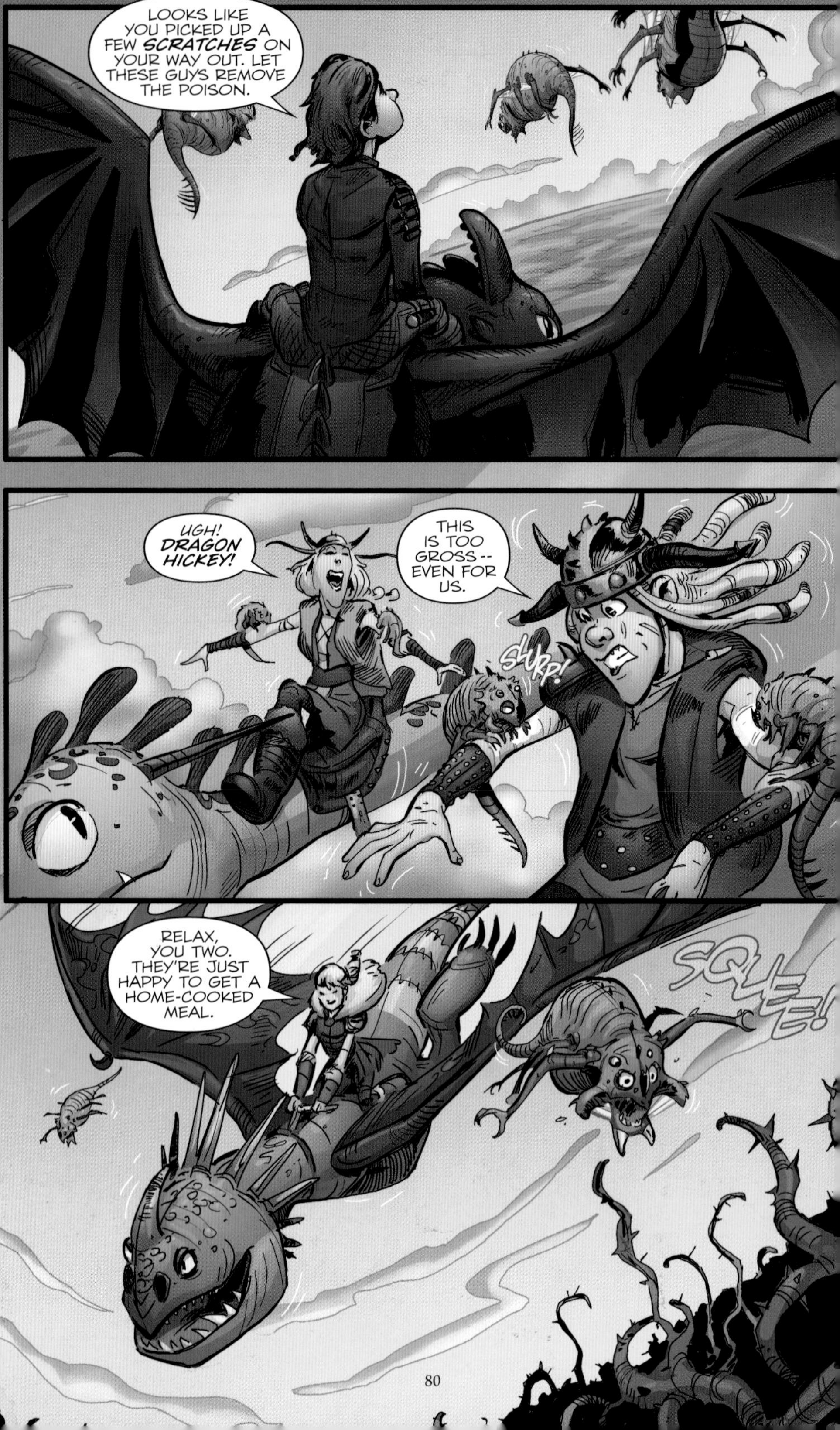
LOOKS LIKE YOU PICKED UP A FEW SCRATCHES ON YOUR WAY OUT. LET THESE GUYS REMOVE THE POISON.
UGH! DRAGON HICKEY!
THIS IS TOO GROSS -- EVEN FOR US.
SLURP!
RELAX, YOU TWO. THEY'RE JUST HAPPY TO GET A HOME-COOKED MEAL.
SQUEEE!!

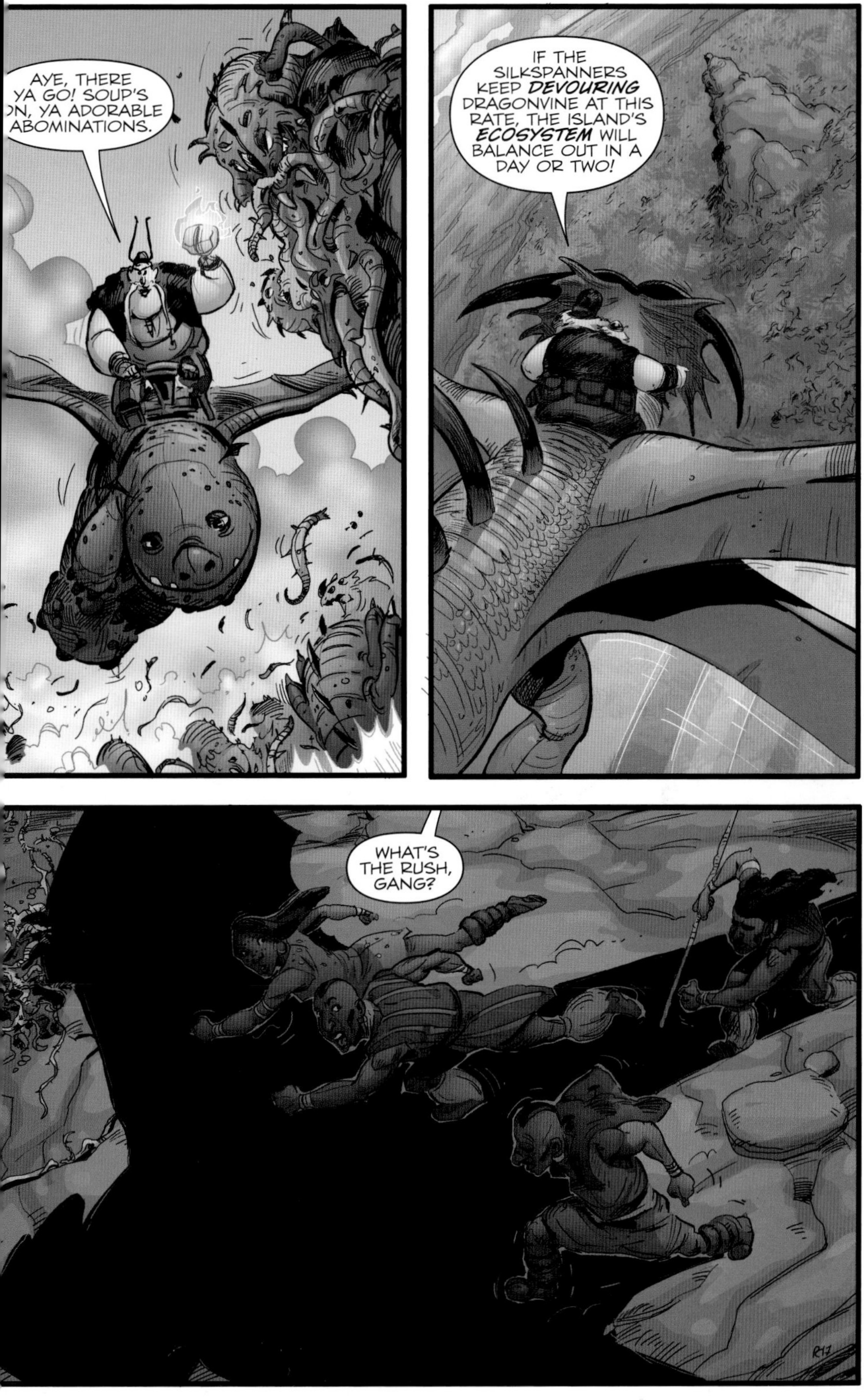
AYE, THERE YA GO! SOUP'S ON, YA ADORABLE ABOMINATIONS.
IF THE SILKSPANNERS KEEP DEVOURING DRAGONVINE AT THIS RATE, THE ISLAND'S ECOSYSTEM WILL BALANCE OUT IN A DAY OR TWO!
WHAT'S THE RUSH, GANG?

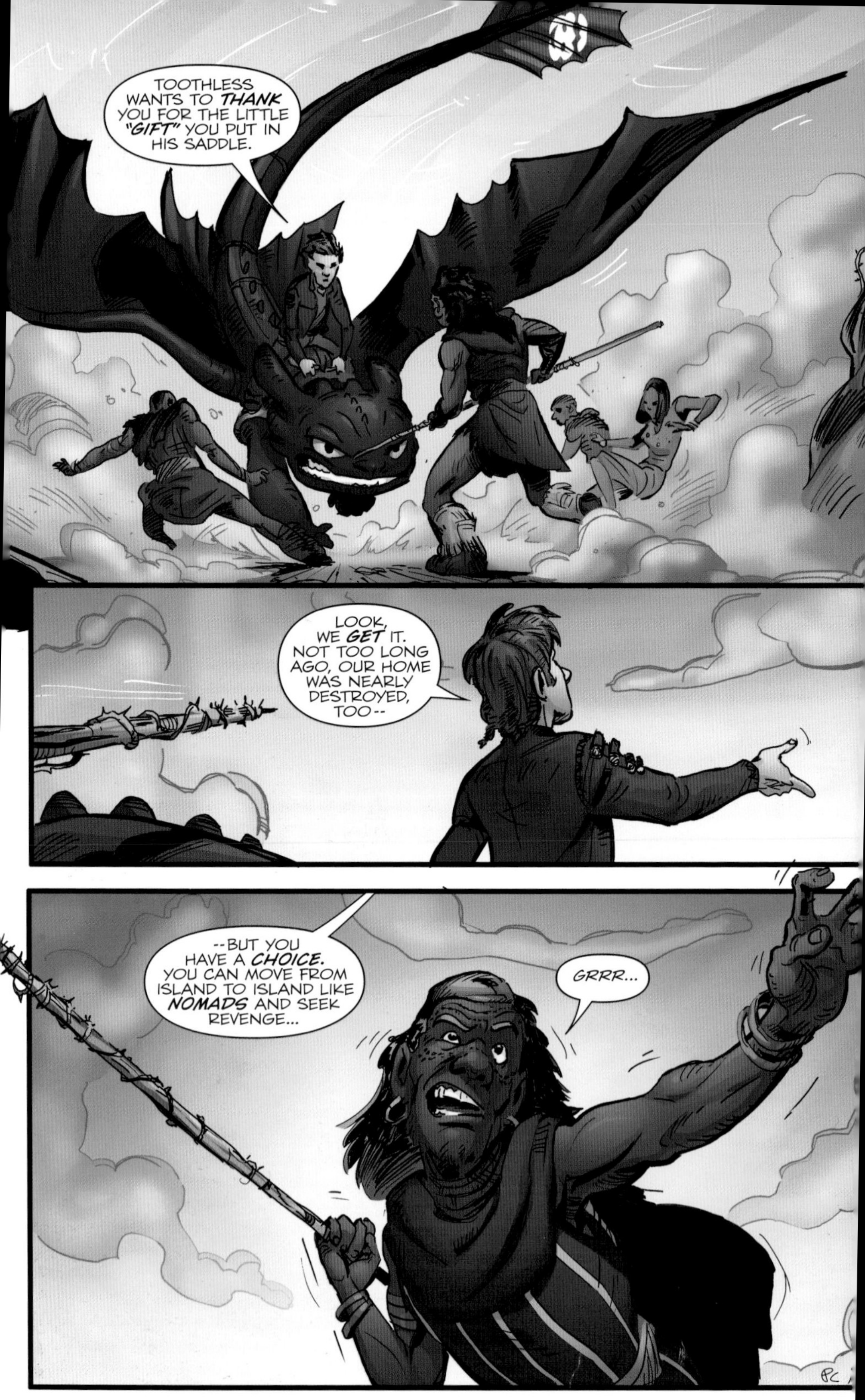
TOOTHLESS WANTS TO THANK YOU FOR THE LITTLE "GIFT" YOU PUT IN HIS SADDLE.
LOOK, WE GET IT. NOT TOO LONG AGO, OUR HOME WAS NEARLY DESTROYED, TOO--
--BUT YOU HAVE A CHOICE. YOU CAN MOVE FROM ISLAND TO ISLAND LIKE NOMADS AND SEEK REVENGE...
GRRR...

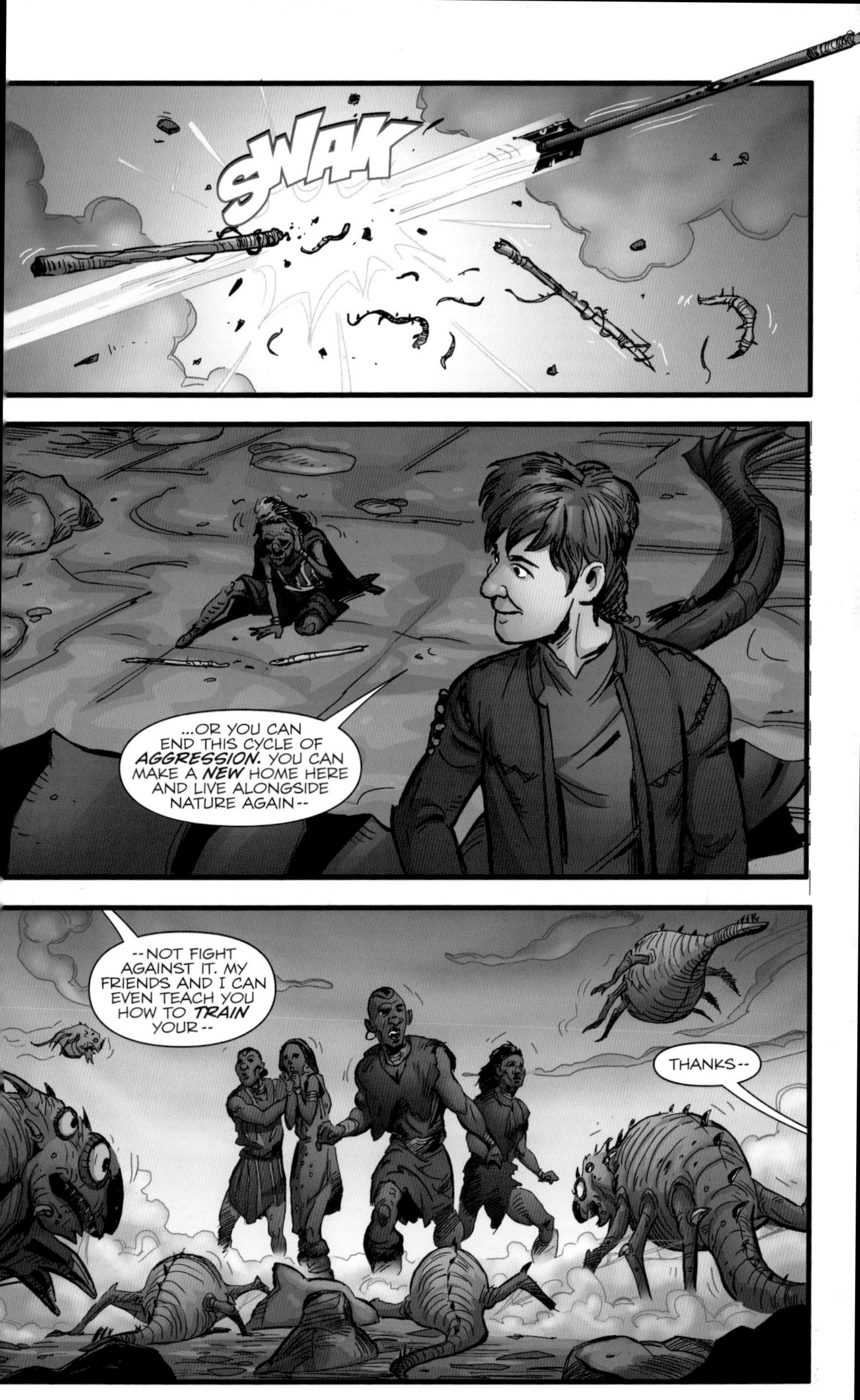
SWAK
...OR YOU CAN END THIS CYCLE OF AGGRESSION. YOU CAN MAKE A NEW HOME HERE AND LIVE ALONGSIDE NATURE AGAIN--
--NOT FIGHT AGAINST IT. MY FRIENDS AND I CAN EVEN TEACH YOU HOW TO TRAIN YOUR--
THANKS--

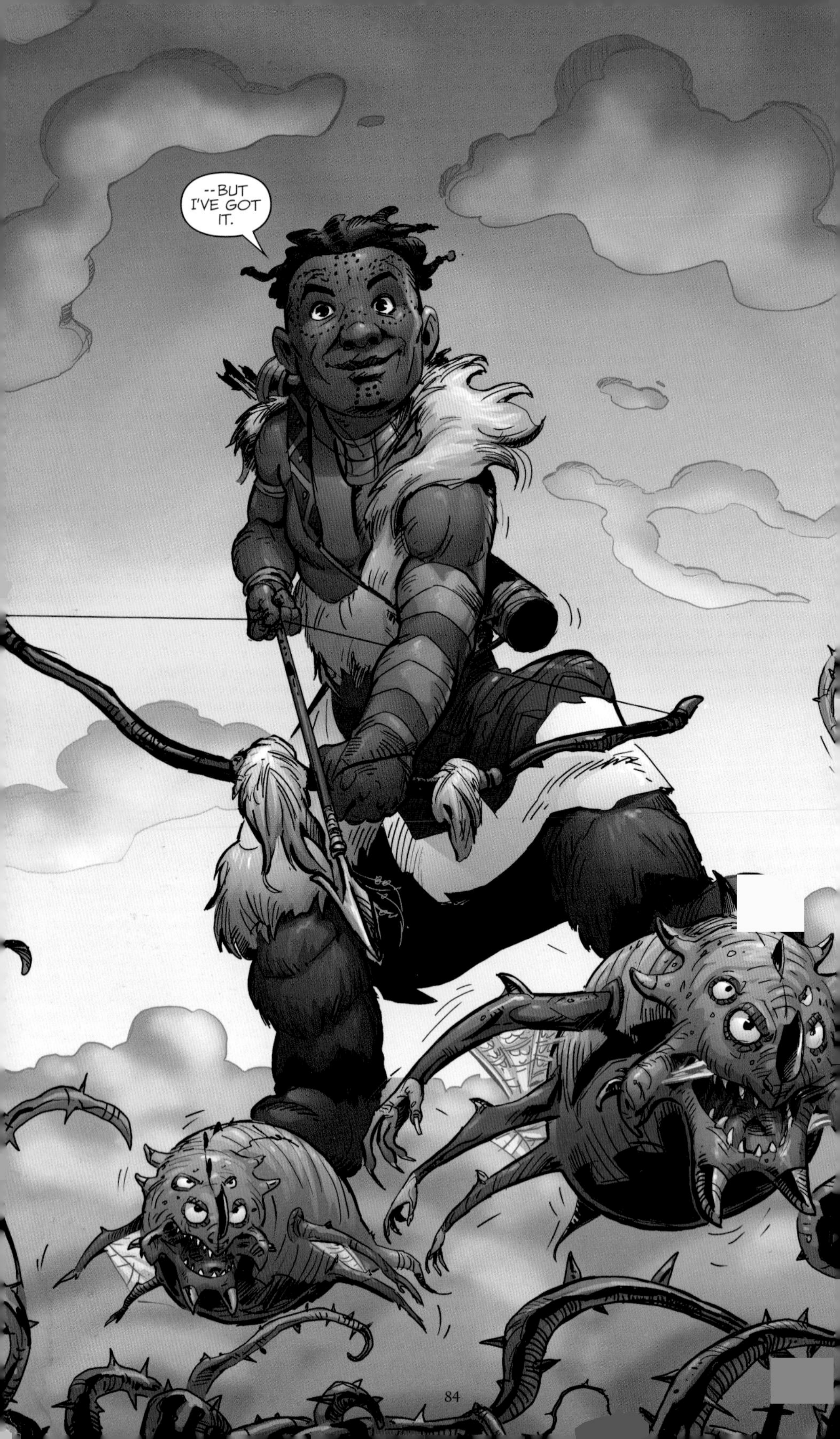
--BUT I'VE GOT IT.

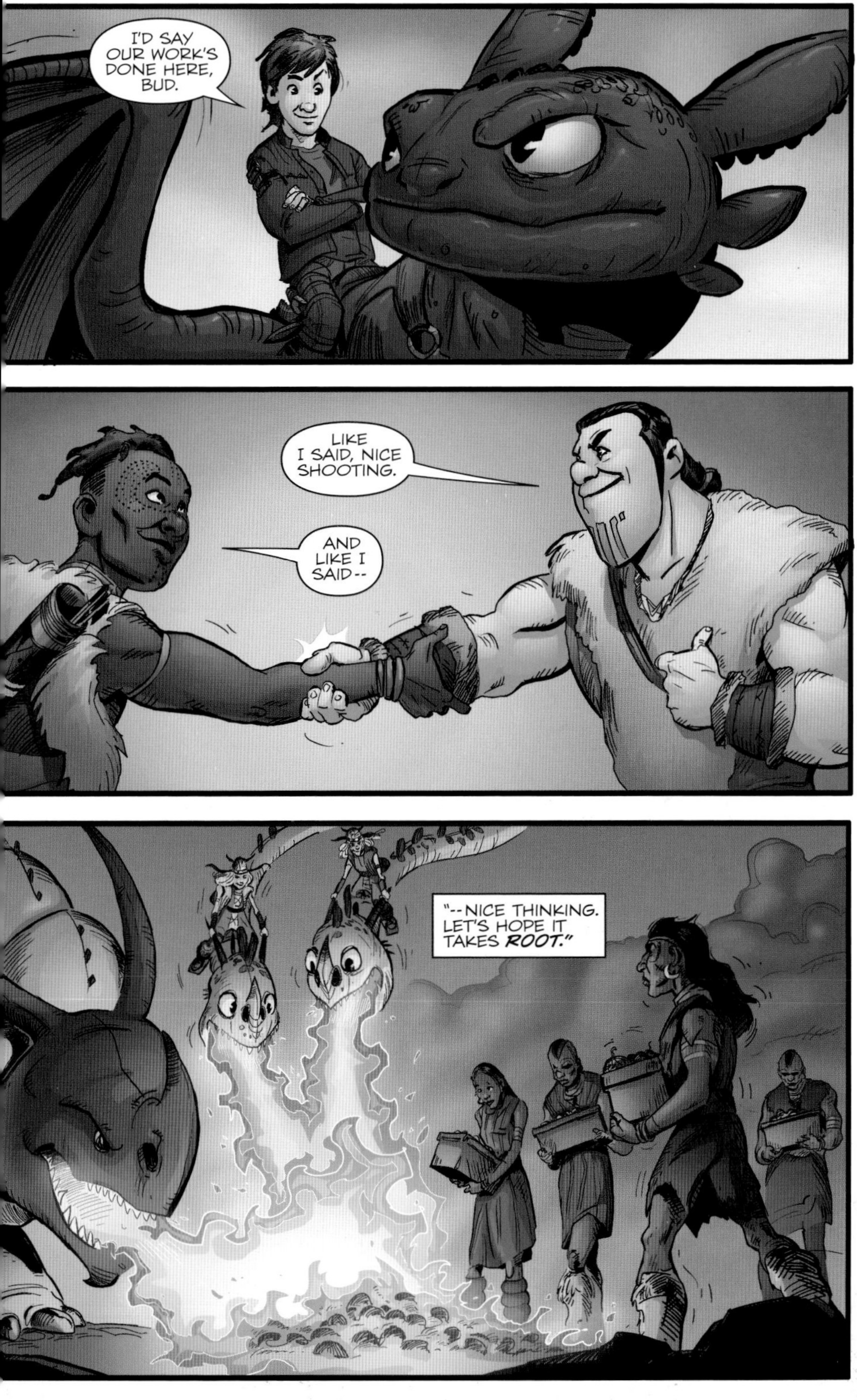
I'D SAY OUR WORK'S DONE HERE, BUD.
LIKE I SAID, NICE SHOOTING.
AND LIKE I SAID--
"--NICE THINKING. LET'S HOPE IT TAKES **ROOT**."

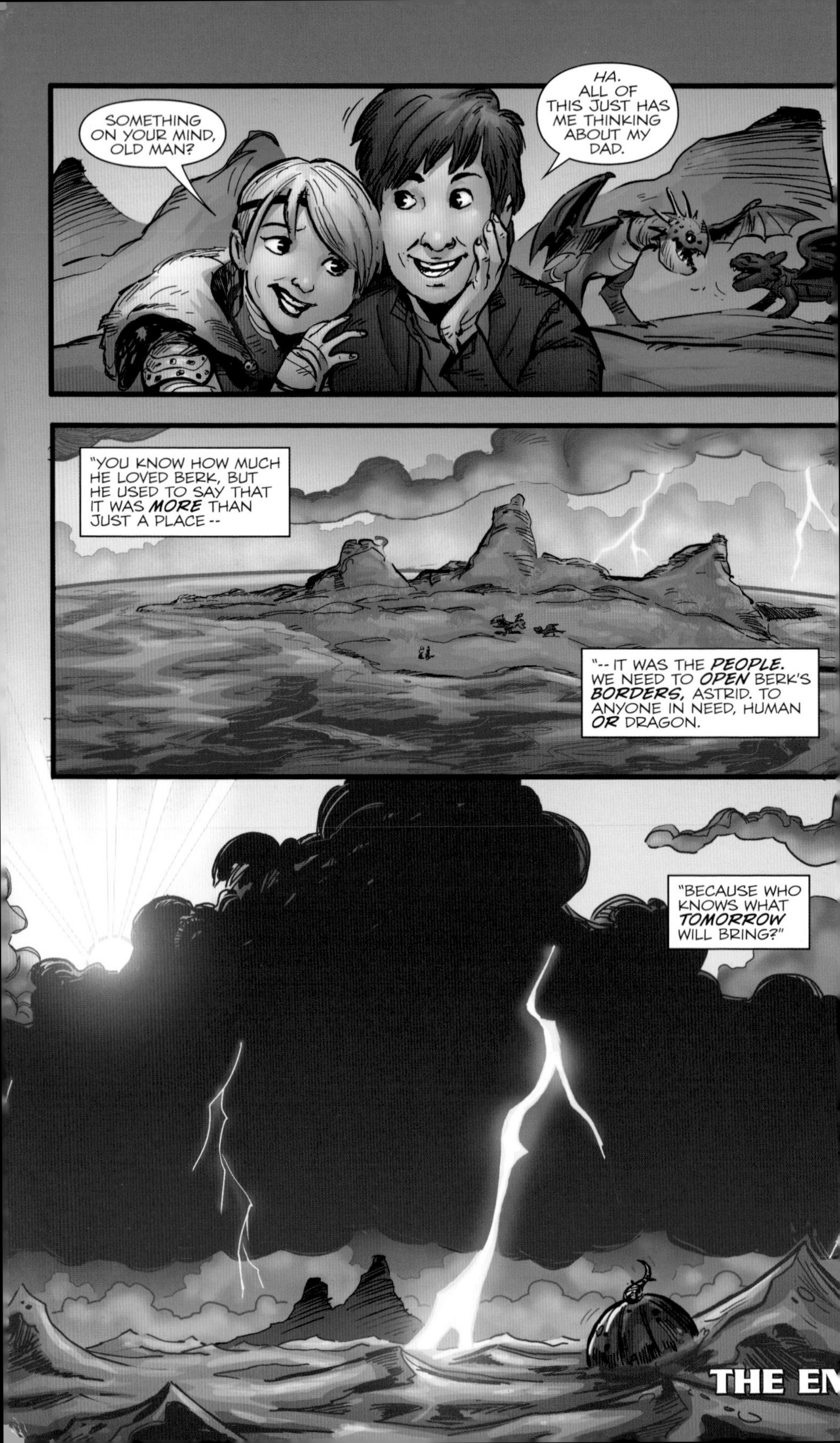
SOMETHING ON YOUR MIND, OLD MAN?
HA. ALL OF THIS JUST HAS ME THINKING ABOUT MY DAD.
"YOU KNOW HOW MUCH HE LOVED BERK, BUT HE USED TO SAY THAT IT WAS MORE THAN JUST A PLACE --
"-- IT WAS THE PEOPLE. WE NEED TO OPEN BERK'S BORDERS, ASTRID. TO ANYONE IN NEED, HUMAN OR DRAGON.
"BECAUSE WHO KNOWS WHAT TOMORROW WILL BRING?"
THE EN

ALENA
Kim W. Andersson

Since arriving at a snobbish boarding school, Alena's been harassed every day by the lacrosse team. But Alena's best friend Josephine is not going to accept that anymore. If Alena does not fight back, then she will take matters into her own hands. There's just one problem . . . Josephine has been dead for a year.

$17.99 | ISBN 978-1-50670-215-5

ASTRID: CULT OF THE VOLCANIC MOON
Kim W. Andersson

Formerly the Galactic Coalition's top recruit, the now-disgraced Astrid is offered a special mission from her old commander. She'll prove herself worthy of another chance at becoming a Galactic Peacekeeper . . . if she can survive.

$19.99 | ISBN 978-1-61655-690-7

BANDETTE
Paul Tobin, Colleen Coover

A costumed teen burglar by the *nome d'arte* of Bandette and her group of street urchins find equal fun in both skirting and aiding the law, in this enchanting, Eisner-nominated series!

$14.99 each
Volume 1: Presto! | ISBN 978-1-61655-279-4
Volume 2: Stealers, Keepers! | ISBN 978-1-61655-668-6
Volume 3: The House of the Green Mask | ISBN 978-1-50670-219-3

BOUNTY
Kurtis Wiebe, Mindy Lee

The Gadflies were the most wanted criminals in the galaxy. Now, with a bounty to match their reputation, the Gadflies are forced to abandon banditry for a career as bounty hunters . . . 'cause if you can't beat 'em, join 'em—then rob 'em blind!

$14.99 | ISBN 978-1-50670-044-1

HEART IN A BOX
Kelly Thompson, Meredith McClaren

In a moment of post-heartbreak weakness, Emma wishes her heart away and a mysterious stranger obliges. But emptiness is even worse than grief, and Emma sets out to collect the pieces of her heart and face the cost of recapturing it.

$14.99 | ISBN 978-1-61655-694-5

HENCHGIRL
Kristen Gudsnuk

Mary Posa hates her job. She works long hours for little pay, no insurance, and worst of all, no respect. Her coworkers are jerks, and her boss doesn't appreciate her. He's also a supervillain. Cursed with a conscience, Mary would give anything to be something other than a henchgirl.

$17.99 | ISBN 978-1-50670-144-8

DARKHORSE.COM AVAILABLE AT YOUR LOCAL COMICS SHOP OR BOOKSTORE • TO FIND A COMICS SHOP IN YOUR AREA, VISIT COMICSHOPLOCATOR.COM
For more information or to order direct: • On the web: DarkHorse.com • Email: mailorder@darkhorse.com • Phone: 1-800-862-0052 Mon.–Fri. 9 AM to 5 PM Pacific Time.

Alena™, Astrid™ © Kim W. Andersson, by agreement with Grand Agency. Bandette™ © Paul Tobin and Colleen Coover. Bounty™ © Kurtis Wiebe and Mindy Lee. Heart in a Box™ © 1979 Semi-Finalist, Inc., and Meredith McClaren. Henchgirl™ © Kristen Gudsnuk. Dark Horse Books® and the Dark Horse logo are registered trademarks of Dark Horse Comics, Inc. All rights reserved. (BL 6041 P1)

DARK HORSE COMICS